Bruce B

Murder at Shake Holes

A detective novel

LUCiUS

Text copyright 2019 Bruce Beckham

All rights reserved. Bruce Beckham asserts his right always to be identified as the author of this work. No part may be copied or transmitted without written permission from the publisher.

This is a work of fiction. Names, characters, places and incidents either are the product of the author's imagination or are used fictitiously. Any resemblance to actual persons, living or dead, events and locales is entirely coincidental.

Kindle edition first published by Lucius 2019

Paperback edition first published by Lucius 2019

For more details and Rights enquiries contact:
Lucius-ebooks@live.com

Cover design by Moira Kay Nicol

EDITOR'S NOTE

Murder at Shake Holes is a stand-alone crime mystery, the thirteenth in the series 'Detective Inspector Skelgill Investigates'. It is set primarily in and around the English Lake District – a National Park of 885 square miles that lies in the rugged northern county of Cumbria.

BY THE SAME AUTHOR

Murder in Adland

Murder in School

Murder on the Edge

Murder on the Lake

Murder by Magic

Murder in the Mind

Murder at the Wake

Murder in the Woods

Murder at the Flood

Murder at Dead Crags

Murder Mystery Weekend

Murder on the Run

Murder at Shake Holes

Murder at the Meet

Murder on the Moor

Murder Unseen

(Above: Detective Inspector Skelgill Investigates)

Murder, Mystery Collection

The Dune

The Sexopaths

Glossary

Some of the British dialect words, slang and local usage appearing in *'Murder at Shake Holes'* are as follows:

Adam an' Eve – believe
Aboot – about
Ah – I
Arrows – darts
Ars – I am
Bait – packed lunch/sandwiches
Baltic – freezing cold
Beck – mountain stream
Blag – persuade by guile
Blighty – Britain
Bob – shilling
Bonce – head
Buckshee – free
Cannae – cannot
Cooking lager – standard quality lager
Cushat – wood pigeon
Dae – do
Deek – look/look at
Derby – belly (= Derby Kelly)
Didnae – did not
Dinnae – don't
Donnat – idiot
Fae – for
Foily – smelly
Frae – from
Goolies – testicles
Gregory – cheque (= Gregory Peck)
Half-inch – steal (= pinch)
Heid – head
Her indoors – wife
High heid yin – boss
How's-your-father – sexual intercourse

Hunners – hundreds
Irn-Bru – a Scots brand of soda, reputedly made from girders
Jimmy – urinate (Jimmy Riddle = piddle)
Jimmy hat – tartan cap with fake ginger hair
Karsey – toilet
Keg palace – pub that does not serve real ale
Kegs – underwear
Ken – know; you know
Lass/lassie – girl, young woman
Marra – mate (friend)
Mind – remember
Mithering – bothering
Nobbut – only
Oche – line from behind which darts are thrown (pronounced *'ockey'*)
Owt – anything
Pissed – drunk (inebriated)
Polis – police
Reet – right
Scooby – clue (= Scooby Doo)
Scratting – scratching
Shake hole – collapsed shaft/sinkhole in limestone
Spring-heeled Jack – a mythical urban figure capable of leaping over buildings
Sommat – something
Tae – to
Tea leaf – thief
The Smoke – London
Twat – to hit
Us – me
Wasnae – was not
Wean – infant
Went – gone (Scots)
Yer – your
Yin – one, person
Youse – you (plural)

List of characters

The detectives:
DI Skelgill, 37 – Cumbrian
DS Jones, 26 – Cumbrian
DS Leyton, 37 – Londoner

And, in order of appearance:
Ruairidh McLeod, 59 – Scots; train guard & steward
Richard Bond, 42 – naturalised British citizen; venture capitalist, former soldier
Egor Volkov, 28 – Russian; employee of Richard Bond
François Mouton, 29 – French; employee of Richard Bond
Wiktoria Adamska, 32 – Russian; fashion designer, former supermodel
Jenny Hackett, 44 – English; journalist
Ivanna Karenina, 39 – Russian; TV producer
Sir Ewart Cameron-Kinloch, 63 – Scots; TV presenter, former Cabinet Minister
Bill Faulkner, 39 – American; banker & tourist
Mikal Mital, 71 – naturalised American citizen; academic
Laura Wilson, 34 – Cumbrian; train driver
Mr Harris – details unknown; passenger
Samanta, 25 – Lithuanian; housekeeper
Joost Merlyn, 46 – South African; hotel landlord
Lucinda Hobhouse, 38 – English; equestrian

1. LONDON EUSTON

Wednesday, approaching midnight

'Looks like we've made it, Guv – there she blows.'

The trio of Skelgill, Leyton and Jones – Skelgill flanked by his sergeants – cut a slightly incongruous jib as they lurch at something between a fast walk and the beginnings of a jog across the polished concourse of what is, by London standards, a relatively deserted Euston Station. Of course, there is nothing unusual about three people hurrying for a train – it is a daily occurrence (if not de rigueur) in all of the capital's many rail termini – nor even particularly that they are clad in formal attire – at this time of the evening, approaching midnight (and especially this time of year, the last Wednesday before Christmas) thousands of revellers are on the great city's neon-bathed streets seeking transport home, the majority, it must be said, unsuitably dressed and swaying on kerbs hailing in vain cabs that are already hired. No, if there is any inconsistency, it is something just hinted at by a small matter of detail: where DS Leyton and DS Jones tow wheeled trolley bags, black like their outfits and in keeping with their general smart appearance, Skelgill has on his shoulder a worn and faded army issue khaki rucksack. But his counter: why struggle with a daft trolley when you can have both hands free to repel would-be muggers? And no need to worry about it being snatched when your back is turned. Of course, for someone in the know there is a much greater discordancy – indeed a virtual oxymoron – that of Skelgill in a dinner jacket and dicky bow. It is along such lines that he is evidently thinking.

'Can't wait to get this penguin suit off.'

'Know what you mean, Guv – these flippin' shoes are giving me corns.'

DS Jones cannot suppress a laugh – for if anyone should complain it is her, keeping pace with her male colleagues despite four-inch heels and a cocktail mini-dress that required her to be assisted for the purposes of modesty into and out of the taxi that has brought them from a Park Lane hotel, an awards banquet, to their present location.

'The Chief didn't seem to be in any hurry to get away, Guv.'

Skelgill makes scoffing sound.

'I reckon the bigwigs have all got penthouse suites for the night, Leyton.'

DS Leyton utters what may be a grumble of agreement – but DS Jones knows otherwise.

'Actually, Guv – I was standing with her at the drinks reception – she was telling the Commissioner that she's staying with her sister in Twickenham – to keep costs down.'

Skelgill harrumphs.

'She was making up for it in Bloody Marys.'

DS Leyton turns to his female colleague.

'You still in touch with that feller of yours, girl? Could have saved yourself a night on the train with us.'

DS Jones looks suddenly rather bashful.

'Oh, you know – it's hard not to be in touch, with social media these days.' She brightens. 'But here I am.'

Any further discussion that may prolong the moment of awkwardness is now truncated – for they reach their designated platform and are intercepted by a man in rail uniform.

'Tickets please, ladies.'

The guard is dour and unsmiling, and there is nothing about his demeanour to indicate that his words might be an attempt at humour, perhaps a reference to the way they are all dressed. Skelgill estimates him to be in his late fifties; balding, he is of a slightly shabby appearance, shoes scuffed and seams shiny, which is hardly the impression the rail company would wish to portray. Short and rather squat, he has a harsh Scots accent – which is perhaps to be expected, since the train terminates somewhere in the Highlands. DS Leyton, custodian of their travel documents, produces the necessary paperwork, a crumpled computer printout in lieu of the more standard credit-card-sized tickets. The official pores over the item; his eyes appear unmoving though his lips tremble as if he might be silently reciting some ode to procrastination, waiting for the momentum of the little

8

group of passengers to dissipate; and indeed they do sink slowly back upon their heels, defeated by bureaucracy.

'Who's the lucky yin?'

'What's that, mate?'

Without raising his head the man regards them from beneath unkempt ginger eyebrows. He hands the document back to DS Leyton.

'Three passengers, two cabins. Nine and ten – sleeping car, first door.'

Without waiting for a reaction he appears to lose interest in their presence – for another group of travellers approaches in haste, three men in smart business suits, and he shifts to intercept them. Skelgill and company realise they are at liberty to move on.

'Tickets please, ladies.'

'You are incorrigible, Ruairidh, my man – is *Glenmorangie* replenished?'

The question is loudly brayed with an English public school accent.

'I've told you before, sir, it's *mor*angie.' He pronounces the word to rhyme with 'orangey', with the stress on the first syllable.

'A Scotch by any other name, my good chap.'

'Ye drank us dry on yer last trip doon, sir.'

Skelgill, eavesdropping, notices the guard's concession to status, calling the man 'sir' – and as he glances back he sees the foremost of the three men, the elder, a tall, well-built, tanned figure in his forties, slip a fold of banknotes into the railway employee's hand.

The sleeping carriage is immediately adjacent to the guard's van and Skelgill's colleagues are already lifting their cases aboard. DS Leyton's voice reaches him.

'You take number ten, girl – at least you'll only have us snoring on one side of you.'

As he passes her compartment and catches her eye Skelgill raises his eyebrows in a curious gesture, perhaps an advance apology along such lines.

'Mine's a *Jennings* if you beat us to the bar.'

9

DS Jones flashes him a smile as she heaves her bag onto the upper bunk. Skelgill proceeds to the next cabin to find DS Leyton scratching his dark tousled head.

'Cor blimey, Guvnor – you can't swing a cat in here. You want the top or the bottom?'

'I'm not fussed, Leyton – I used to kip in a chest of drawers – worked me way up.'

'Maybe I should have the bottom, Guv – seeing as you're in the mountain rescue.'

Skelgill scowls as though he disapproves of his sergeant's logic – but it would have been his choice, and he swings his rucksack onto the narrow berth. DS Leyton is examining the fixtures and fittings, and discovers a tiny washbasin concealed beneath a hinged shelf. He glances around pensively.

'I suppose there's a proper karsey somewhere.'

Skelgill is still frowning.

'What do you mean *proper* karsey?'

DS Leyton looks surprised that his superior does not immediately go along with his reasoning.

'Must be tempting – middle of the night, Guv – have a Jimmy in the sink instead of traipsing down the train trying to find it.'

For a man who spends much of his spare time inhabiting wild country lacking any form of ablution facilities, Skelgill seems unreasonably prim.

'Don't get any bright ideas, Leyton.'

But his sergeant continues musingly.

'Not so easy for a lady, of course.'

'Leyton! Can we talk about something else?'

DS Leyton is shocked by the severity of his superior's retort.

'Righto, Guv.' However, he is not entirely subdued. 'Bit of a queer thing – don't you reckon – these shared cabins?'

'In what way?'

'Well – unless you pay for the whole caboodle – like Admin have done for DS Jones – you never know who you're gonna bunk up with. You could get a right old weirdo. Pervert – strangler – anything.'

'Leyton – how much have you had to drink?'

'Only the same as you, Guv – but you know me, I'm not a big drinker. And I'm out of practice – the nippers are needing driven everywhere these days – all the flippin' clubs they're in, sleepovers and whatnot. Can't even have a beer watching the footie.'

Skelgill is frowning, as if irked by the suggestion that he might be a 'big drinker' by his subordinate's estimation. However, he relents.

'Aye, well – it were flowing free tonight, hard to avoid – even if you're no fan of wine.'

'Reckon I could get used to it, Guv. Though, I must say, it all tastes the same to me. I wouldn't know a Claret from a Bordeaux.'

Skelgill is about to respond – but a raised voice, female and shrill, reaches them from beyond their cabin – indeed it has an echoing quality that sounds like it emanates from outwith the carriage itself. Skelgill, who as yet has only removed his shoes, pads out onto the corridor to see that DS Jones – herself barefooted but still wearing her cocktail dress – has also had cause to investigate, and is standing at the open door, leaning out and looking onto the platform.

'I repeat – I must travel on this train!'

'Madam, *Ah* repeat – all cabins are taken.'

Ruairidh, the guard, is standing his ground, his feet planted apart. A woman confronts him. She looks in her early thirties. She is tall and strikingly dressed in an unfastened horizontally striped fur coat over a short leopard-pattern dress, crazily patterned stockings, and platform shoes that mirror the dress and cause her to tower above the man. Her hair is immaculate, a long straight blonde coiffure so perfect that it looks almost artificial. To Skelgill's eye she is of foreign extraction, perhaps Slavic – a broad face with prominent cheekbones and pale eyes that narrow as they rise. Her make up, too, proclaims a fashion statement that seems from beyond these shores. Her accent, however, is perfectly British, and lacks any regional brogue. She appears determined to get her way.

11

'I have an open first-class ticket – it is the most expensive fare. I expect to travel to Edinburgh.'

'Then ye'll have tae wait until the morning, Madam. The first train leaves at 6:12. Arrives 11:09. Ye'll need tae go tae King's Cross.'

The woman literally stamps her foot.

'I need to go on *this* train.' She flails an arm that has pale gold bangles jangling and sends a designer handbag flapping in the air – then she gestures first at leopard-skin luggage that matches her dress and then more generally in frustration around her. 'What else do you expect me to do at this time of night, you halfwit?'

To Skelgill's consternation DS Jones steps down onto the platform and approaches the pair. He moves up, observing from the open carriage door. Perhaps she senses that tempers might flare beyond control, and has decided to mediate. That said, the Scotsman grins with a certain masochistic satisfaction, as though the insult has merely served to bolster his contrariness. The woman inhales as if she intends to continue with her tirade, but the sight of DS Jones – Cinderella-like, barefoot in her evening gown and no less striking in her own way than the diva herself – serves to give her pause for thought. It is DS Jones who speaks.

'I'm travelling with two male colleagues. My organisation had to book a cabin for sole occupancy for me – so there is a vacant berth. I'm leaving the train at Carlisle – if you're going on to Edinburgh you'll have it to yourself when you wake. I'll just be sleeping in jeans and t-shirt so that I can grab my stuff and go – so you should hardly be disturbed.'

'Ah dinnae ken aboot that –'

But the objection that Ruairidh wrestles to formulate does not come quickly enough, and the woman snatches the projecting handles of her matching wheeled suitcases – one enormous, the other tiny, like a Great Dane and a Chihuahua – and pushes past him. She aims directly at DS Jones, hands her control of the oversized valise, links their free arms and hustles her at pace towards the train.

'Show me – before that tiresome jobsworth thinks of something else.'

Skelgill is obliged to step back – indeed he retreats like a hermit crab into his cabin – exchanging a brief glance (of alarm in his case) with DS Jones, who seems more amused than perturbed by the situation. He notices the woman has not thanked DS Jones – more that she has treated her as she might a personal assistant. However, as they enter the cabin he hears her voice, suddenly gracious in its tone.

'That is a beautiful dress – it fits you so well – is it *Versace?*'

But now the door closes – and behind him DS Leyton speaks.

'What's all the palaver, Guv?'

Skelgill is about to mutter darkly about the upper classes pulling rank – but he curses instead as he hits his funny bone off a bulkhead in an attempt to remove his dinner jacket.

'I just did that, Guv – if it's any consolation.'

Skelgill grimaces and frantically polishes his afflicted elbow with his opposite hand. But he does not answer, for he has an ear cocked to the corridor – from beyond comes a successive slamming of doors. The night train to Scotland is about to depart.

2. THE LOUNGE CAR

Thursday, 00.15am

By Skelgill's estimation they are not the last to reach the lounge car – for, having counted ten cabins including their own, there could be as many as twenty passengers on board, and only eight are presently ensconced for drinks. There is a main group of six: it comprises a honey blonde woman in her forties, her features regular but just slightly craggy, and dominated by deep-set brown eyes beneath curved brows; a younger woman clad all in black, perhaps in her early thirties – she is strikingly dark, almost raven-haired, with pale skin, cold sapphire eyes and Alice Cooper mascara and (Skelgill decides) a Scandic physiognomy; and four men, the three sharp business suits of the original '*Glenmorangie* party' and the fourth an older male, rotund and balding, perhaps in his early sixties, also besuited, but casually tieless – his doughy countenance and permanently surprised features strike Skelgill as familiar. This little coterie has occupied a u-shaped seating area around adjoining low tables – there is the suggestion that this is a regular haunt of theirs, and that they have moved swiftly to occupy the spot.

Seated separately – alone at tables of standard height – are two more men: one who might be about Skelgill's own age, fairly nondescript, dressed in neat attire, unobtrusively checking his mobile and occasionally sipping from a bottle of mineral water; the second, aged around the seventy mark, is considerably more distinctive, sporting an untidy mane of white hair and a bushy grey moustache; he pores over some densely printed manuscript and has the look of the archetypal academic in his lived-in brown tweed suit. Indeed, as the two detectives take seats towards the bar – a little apart from their fellow travellers – DS Leyton is prompted to quip behind the back of his hand.

'Albert Einstein, Guv – didn't realise he was still alive.'

'Leyton – keep your voice down.' But if anything it is Skelgill's hissed retort that is too loud – for the man raises an eyebrow that might be disapproving – or it might just be something he is reading.

They bow their heads over the table – as if conspiring – but actually out of slight embarrassment. Then Skelgill becomes conscious of a presence beside them. It is the guard – or, rather, he has now divested himself of his jacket and assumed the role of steward, in waistcoat and shirtsleeves; he has not, however, shed the dour expression. Skelgill quickly dismisses the idea of facetiously requesting a cask beer.

'What ale would you recommend?'

'Ah'd recommend *McEwan's Eighty.*' He pauses, as if to see how this goes down with Skelgill. However, before Skelgill can reply, he resumes. 'But we dinnae stock *McEwan's.* After that – Ah should say – *Deuchars IPA* – which we also dinnae keep.'

Skelgill flashes a glance at DS Leyton. *Monty Python's* cheese shop sketch is coming to mind – and he wonders if he dare venture a brand name of his own. But instead he reconfigures his inquiry.

'What ale *have* you got?'

'*London Pride.*' This announcement is devoid of enthusiasm.

'Aye – that's fine – I'll take that.' Skelgill does not wait to see if his choice will be gainsaid. 'Same for you, Leyton?'

'Nah – you know me, Guv – easily pleased – any old cooking lager.'

DS Leyton looks up at the steward as he says this, to convey his order. The man is tight lipped, and replies tersely.

'*Tennent's.* Plain cans only.'

That Ruairidh seems resentful about this latter fact goes over the heads of his clientele, who are too young to recall the bevy of beauties, scantily clad, that once ornamented the packaging of Scotland's favourite 'cooking lager', as DS Leyton puts it. He turns away with a look of disdain – Skelgill wonders if the man is simply congenitally grumpy; or perhaps he considers them to be travelling above their station, out of place in First Class.

Nonetheless, their drinks arrive promptly, though without any ceremony; they are left to pour for themselves, from a brown bottle in Skelgill's case, an unadorned tin in DS Leyton's. Skelgill is glowering, but his colleague endeavours to put a positive spin on the matter.

'That's up your street, ain't it, Guv – good old *Fuller's?*'

'Aye, it's a decent brand – but it's not real ale. You can't get real ale in a bottle – it needs to come out of a cask, still live, at cellar temperature – this is fizzy pasteurised pop, served so cold you can't taste it. Once it's tapped, real ale only keeps a week – this stuff lasts years. It's like the difference between a tomato and a tin of tomatoes.'

DS Leyton vacantly admires the yellow gassy lager that is filling his own glass half with foam; the distinction is somewhat lost on him. However he nods amenably in the face of superior knowledge (albeit he is thinking he is rather partial to tinned tomatoes on toast).

'Cheers, anyway, Guv.'

Skelgill raises his glass – but pauses before he sups.

'Aye, cheers – and well done tonight, marra.'

DS Leyton suddenly looks rather sheepish – and even begins to colour. A rare event is his boss calling him 'marra', Cumbrian vernacular for 'mate' that he reserves almost exclusively for fellow locals; but doubly rare is that which does not come easily to Skelgill in any circumstances, the bestowing of congratulations. It is a scrapbook moment. However, in his typically self-deprecating manner, DS Leyton makes light of the compliment.

'Truth be told, Guv, I feel a bit of a fraud – when there's officers knowingly tackling suicide bombers and mopping up military-grade nerve agents. Being stupid ain't being brave.'

'Happen that's what I told you at the time, Leyton.'

DS Leyton grins equably.

'As I recall, so you did, Guv.'

Skelgill may be about to embellish his mickey taking – but the swish of the sliding door at the far end of the carriage draws his attention.

'Hey up – here's Jones and her new pal.'

DS Jones enters the lounge car ahead of her cabin mate; she has changed into casual clothes, black slim jeans and ankle boots

16

and a close-fitting long-sleeved top, and she has freed her hair from the intricate style woven for the formal event earlier in the evening. Notwithstanding, Skelgill notices she attracts the eyes of the main group, male and female alike – but her unassuming charms are quickly eclipsed as she is followed into the carriage by the taller figure of the pale blonde, who still wears the chic outfit in which she arrived upon the platform. DS Jones spies her colleagues and turns to motion to the woman, as if she intends to introduce her – but there is an intervention.

'Wiktoria!'

The cry of recognition comes from the raven-haired woman Skelgill has labelled as Scandinavian – although even in the single word he hears a Russian inflexion and has to recalibrate his geography. Wiktoria – thus summoned, her name pronounced with a 'V' – shows fleeting annoyance, as if this calling out by strangers is tiresomely familiar – but then recognition sets in and her demeanour becomes amenable if slightly condescending – as though the other woman is not actually a friend, but an acquaintance of some marginally lower standing. All this Skelgill takes in at a glance. His first sentiment is to dislike the woman's attitude – but then she does a more considerate thing – for she reaches to place a hand on DS Jones's upper arm, and leans to confide in her, indicating with her free hand that she intends to speak with the other, and that DS Jones should continue. DS Jones smiles and nods and says something in response. The main group shift around in their seats – indeed the four males all stand to attention – and they make a space for the new arrival. DS Jones proceeds to join her colleagues.

DS Leyton, perhaps taking his cue from the chivalrous act of the other men, rises – but Skelgill remains resolutely seated, as if refusing to be dictated to by the mores of others. DS Jones is unperturbed. She slips into the space beside DS Leyton. He speaks, his voice now more suitably hushed.

'So who's Wiktoria – some kind of VIP?'

'You mean you don't recognise her?'

17

DS Jones speaks with tongue in cheek, as if she doesn't expect him to. DS Leyton makes a face of concomitant bafflement.

'Give us a Scooby, girl.'

DS Jones has her mobile phone, and she deftly taps in a command and manipulates the image on the screen. She places the handset on the table such that both of her colleagues can see the display. DS Leyton leans over with interest; Skelgill is more reluctant – but nonetheless a squint betrays his curiosity. DS Leyton reads aloud.

'"Wiktoria Adamska – former supermodel, fashion designer – third wife of Polish shipping magnate Artur Adamski."' But he shakes his jowls like a dog that has dunked its muzzle too deeply in a bowl of water. 'Never heard of her.'

'She owns the *Million Dollar* clothing label.'

Now DS Leyton shows a flicker of recognition.

'Oh – yeah – reckon I've heard the missus mention that – does what it says on the tin, eh?'

DS Jones smiles wistfully.

'That outfit she's wearing – plus the shoes and handbag – probably the equivalent of an average person's annual take-home pay.'

A whistle escapes DS Leyton's lips and Skelgill can't suppress a kind of scoffing sound that he submerges into his beer. Casually, he glances over – Wiktoria Adamska is seated beside the (now reclassified) Russian brunette, listening calmly to something she is relating. The men are pretending to be in conversation, but are clearly distracted by the woman's majestic presence.

'What's she doing slumming it with us?' Skelgill now mutters scornfully. 'You'd think she'd be on a private jet.'

DS Jones answers evenly.

'She said she needed to travel at short notice – all tomorrow morning's flights are in doubt – apparently Edinburgh airport closed at 8pm this evening due to snow.'

'It's the Baltic Blast!'

DS Leyton's interjection is rather gleefully macabre. Skelgill is quick to take him to task.

'Where do you get that from?'

'Just going by what the missus said, Guv – I phoned her after the dinner. It's what they're calling it on the BBC. Easterly gales blowing all the way from the Baltic – for the next three days. It's gonna be like last year with knobs on. She reckons it's been snowing in the north Lakes since teatime. Just as well we're on the train – the M6 is closed at Shap by a jack-knifed lorry and the A1's all snarled up at Scotch Corner. We'd be snookered if we were driving.'

Skelgill glowers. He turns to the window – the soft suburban neon of Greater London flashes past like a continuous fusillade of silent tracer bullets.

'Looks alright here.'

'Hah – never snows in The Smoke, Guv – else the bookies'd have to pay out on a White Christmas. That's their best little earner after the National – apart from when it's a World Cup year.'

Skelgill eschews the possible digression. He remains sceptical.

'Last forecast I heard, it was going to miss us.'

'Apparently it's coming further down the country, Guv. Something about the jet screen, the missus said.' DS Leyton takes a pull of his drink and exhales with enthusiasm. 'Let's hope we make it.'

The pensive silence that settles upon the trio (during which Skelgill decides he cannot be bothered to correct Mrs Leyton's Chinese whisper) is interrupted by an unfamiliar alert from DS Jones's phone. DS Leyton remarks with a chuckle.

'Tarzan likes your post.'

Skelgill's antennae are twitching.

'What's that?'

DS Jones looks a little discomfited.

'Oh – DI Smart follows my *Instagram* – I put up a picture of the awards.'

'*Tarzan?*' Skelgill's tone is scathing. 'Why do you call him that?'

'Oh, no – that's his own username.'

Now Skelgill tuts. 'And what the hell's *Instagram* when it's at home?'

'It's an app for sharing pictures and videos – it's a good way of keeping in touch with my friends from uni.'

Skelgill gestures dismissively at the handset.

'So what's he saying?'

'It's just a *like*, Guv – on my profile. It doesn't mean anything.'

'It means he's snooping on you. Look at the time.' Skelgill shakes his head. However, his manner becomes a little less belligerent. 'I just don't get this social media lark. Don't folk see they're being exploited?'

DS Jones seems relieved by his shift away from the specific instance. She reaches for her phone and quickly checks something. Then she indicates to the display.

'I understand what you mean, Guv – but, look, Wiktoria Adamska has almost thirty million followers – and no one is forced to follow her. At least whatever she does or says isn't distorted by the press.'

'What's that – press distortion? *Never!*'

Simultaneously they look up in surprise – for they have been joined by the honey blonde with the sunken eyes – she is standing a yard away, drink in hand, swaying a little – although that might be the movement of the train as much as the side effects of the contents of her glass.

'*I* certainly shan't be distorting *your* achievements.'

The detectives exchange puzzled glances – as if to ascertain which one of them must know her. The woman seems to sense their predicament.

'Let me introduce myself – Jenny Hackett?' There is the faintest inflexion of a question – as if the name, at least, ought to ring a bell – but not enough to embarrass her when it does not. Indeed, she continues quickly. 'Crime correspondent for *The Inquirer* – my byline is Virginia. I was at *The Grosvenor* this evening. I witnessed your recognition – it seems you are an intrepid trio – hiding your northern lights beneath a bushel.'

Skelgill is first to react.

'Aye – happen we've not figured out *Instagram* yet.' He grins wryly at DS Jones. 'We only get a phone signal when it's not raining – and that's twice a year.'

If the woman is who she claims to be, she certainly has the brass neck for the job – and now she slides into the bench seat beside Skelgill, close enough to brush against his shoulder, and he notices an intense perfume that reminds him of *Parma Violets*. It almost masks the ketones on her breath – but not sufficiently to dispel the inference of sustained drinking, albeit she does not sound inebriated. She rests her forearms on the table, cradling her tumbler; her nails look artificial – Skelgill is never sure about this kind of thing – and varnished to match a maroon silky blouse that is tight across the bosom, and worn loose over close-fitting black pants. Her outfit is smart and new looking – but unlikely to be what she would have worn for the gala dinner – perhaps she, like them, has changed.

'Sergeant Leyton – congratulations – George Medal – *now with bar.*'

She salutes with affected deference – although the impression is sincere.

Skelgill watches as DS Leyton shrugs self-effacingly – and then looks to him for a lead as to how they ought to respond to a member of the press. But in the hiatus the woman turns to Skelgill and touches his upper arm.

'Not that I wish to diminish your own achievements – Inspector Skelgill – and –' (she nods to DS Jones) 'Sergeant Jones.'

She knows who they are well enough. Skelgill is instinctively on guard – but his inclination is to take the bull by the horns. He indicates with a jerk of his head the group she was with.

'You're obviously not on the train to pump us for information.'

The woman gives a short ironic laugh.

'I certainly should hope to be more subtle about it, Inspector – although if you are willing it would make an excellent feature. How about *Skelly's Heroes?*'

Skelgill glowers, but his subordinates would recognise that the suggestion – despite its rather crass denomination – most certainly piques his vanity. The woman pats his thigh, and he stiffens.

'You'd need to consult the powers that be.'

'I quite understand.'

There is something about her intonation that causes Skelgill suddenly to wonder if she is an Australian, perhaps long naturalised, her accent now more neutral, her voice an amalgam of those in the London-based media amongst whom she circulates. The three police officers remain taciturn; Skelgill's subordinates taking their cue from his stilted advice. Undeterred, Jenny Hackett continues.

'To answer your question – no – I am bound for Edinburgh. There is a financial symposium at the International Conference Centre over the next two days. It is entitled *'Wealth of Nations'* – although that is something of a misnomer – at least the word *nations.'* Now she leans over the table and lowers her voice in a conspiratorial manner. 'The white-haired gentleman halfway down the carriage is the keynote speaker. You don't recognise him? I imagined – in your line of work –'

DS Leyton takes the opportunity to restore a light-hearted note to the conversation.

'I thought he was Albert Einstein – 'till the Guvnor put me right.'

Skelgill now scowls disapprovingly – but Jenny Hackett merely grins.

'Relatively speaking, he is making similarly iconoclastic waves. His name is Mikal Mital – and, if I may mix my metaphors – he promises to open a Pandora's box upon money laundering, so the rumour mill has it.'

That she hints at a more sinister subtext is not given the opportunity to develop, for DS Leyton is ready with a jovial rejoinder.

'Cor blimey – he should have a word with my missus – she's forever giving me grief about washing fivers in me trouser pockets!'

The journalist smiles in an effort to humour him. But it seems she has other matters on her mind. She looks pointedly at DS Jones.

'I see you are an acquaintance of Wiktoria Adamska.'

DS Jones raises her palms in a display of modesty.

'Oh, no – she didn't have a reserved berth – I overheard her arguing with the guard and said it was no problem if she wanted to share my cabin. We leave the train at Carlisle, in any event.'

Jenny Hackett lifts her glass and regards DS Jones pensively over the rim.

'I have colleagues who would give their eye teeth to be in your shoes – your *bed* come to that – and I'm not just talking about the men – you are a delicious specimen. Ask dear Wiktoria!'

DS Jones bursts into laughter – it can only be a shocked reflex – that this woman whom they have only just met has had the nerve to say such a thing – and that she has apparently conflated several risqué intimations. She sees that her male colleagues are speechless – DS Leyton's jaw has dropped and Skelgill stares at her with a look of consternation. However, her response is composed.

'I'm sure my travel companion would be the greater attraction – whatever the motivation.'

The woman laughs throatily.

'Wiktoria might surprise you. Indeed – should you find yourself in a position to pen a *kiss-and-tell* – just tip me the wink. It would be eye-wateringly lucrative.'

DS Jones's eyes have certainly widened. She flicks a glance at Skelgill – as if to suggest that Jenny Hackett is tipsier than they have judged. But now there is the intervention of the steward – who, on reflection, may have been eavesdropping.

'Same again, sir?'

Skelgill notes that, inexplicably, he has been elevated to the title *sir*. He wonders if it has something to do with the presence of the two females – perhaps even their perceived attitude towards him. But he looks questioningly at DS Leyton – whose expression of ambivalence morphs into a twitch of agreement.

'Aye, why not.'

'I too shall have the same again, Ruairidh!' Jenny Hackett mangles the man's name, confounded by the Gaelic spelling on his enamel badge. 'A large *Glenmorangie*.'

'It's *mor*angie, Madam – and Mr Bond has already reserved that for his and Sir Ewart's party.'

'Oh – I'm sure Eck will spare me a couple of fingers! *Hah-ha!*' This quip she obviously thinks hilarious, and presses hard on Skelgill's thigh to communicate her mirth. 'Just tell him from me.'

The steward gives no indication he will do any such thing. He turns to DS Jones, his lips twisted as though he has bitten into a lemon.

'Just a tonic water for me, please.'

'Oh, have a vodka with it – live dangerously!' Jenny Hackett reaches to press her hand insistently.

'No – it's fine, really – just plain tonic, please.'

The steward disappears behind his counter and into whatever compartment lies beyond. There is no public access to the rest of train – for the 'Midnight Express', as it is known, in winter is largely a mail and parcel service – rather like a freighter that takes on an exclusive contingent of paying passengers to supplement the income from its cargo. But at less than the cost of a London hotel room, it can be an efficient facility, killing two birds with one stone. It gets the long-distance traveller home before breakfast, with a night's sleep thrown in. Well – of the two – home at least is generally guaranteed.

'Which one's Eck?'

It is DS Leyton that quizzes the journalist. Jenny Hackett regards him with mock reproach.

'You do lead cloistered lives. Sir Ewart Cameron-Kinloch. Former Conservative Home Office minister. He famously introduced the Golden Visas scheme – it led to a flood of foreign investment and fuelled the London property boom.

Sadly he failed to detect the nationalists creeping up behind him – they swiped his Edinburgh seat at the last election. Ambitions of becoming PM were put into abeyance. Now of all things he hosts a current affairs show on *VoxNews*. A travesty.'

She regards each of them in turn, as if to assess their individual political persuasions; but perhaps she is disappointed. She reins in her voice, though the note of bitterness that conveyed the word *travesty* remains.

'Do you know who is behind *VoxNews?*'

DS Jones is first to respond.

'Isn't it sponsored by the Russian government?'

Jenny Hackett's tone becomes somewhat caustic.

'Setting aside editorial control – it is Bogblokinov – the oligarch who owns what little of Mayfair that the Duke of Westminster doesn't.'

There is a brief silence – but now DS Leyton rejoins the debate.

'What's a Tory toff doing working for the communists?'

'Ah, the romance of the rouble.' Jenny Hackett wags an admonishing finger. 'But since when was Russia controlled by left-wing ideologues?'

'It's still quite a coup.' This is DS Jones.

'Absolutely. They certainly got their man.' Jenny Hackett glances at the group beyond DS Jones's right shoulder. 'Someone from Labour – or a loony left nationalist – would not have the same credibility. He is what Lenin called a Useful Idiot.'

Skelgill, also looking at the man in question, now realises he must have seen him on the TV. And the name he has certainly heard, albeit he doubts he could have put it together with the face. He calculates that 'Eck' must be a contraction of his initials, rather than the more usual Scots diminutive of Alexander (first reduced to Alec, and thence simply Eck).

'Who are the rest of that crew – are they all with the TV channel?'

Jenny Hackett twists so that she faces Skelgill, as if to conceal that she is talking about them.

25

'Oh, no – just his handler.'

'Handler?' DS Leyton cannot contain himself. 'It gets more sinister by the second!'

Jenny Hackett chuckles. 'Oh, I say it in jest, of course. The black-haired woman, Ivanna Karenina – officially she is Eck's producer.' Now she hesitates, her voice lowered. 'But since she previously worked as a senior executive at *VoxNews* headquarters in Moscow, we sceptical journalists rather suspect her declared status here in the UK is something of an artifice. Think of her as the ventriloquist and wee Eck as her dummy.'

DS Leyton looks like he is desperate to swivel around. Skelgill, for his part, can't help staring – and now Ivanna Karenina meets his eye. She plies him with just the tiniest hint of a knowing smile – and he finds himself lowering his gaze. Meanwhile, DS Leyton seems enthused by the growing conspiracy.

'Cor blimey, Jenny – sure you're not working for the spooks?'

She laughs throatily again.

'Perhaps the distinction is not always so great.'

But, rather than elaborate upon this cryptic remark, she continues to answer Skelgill's inquiry.

'The other three males – I have only just met. The spray-tanned he-man character is called Richard Bond – he wasted no time in telling me he is ex-Special Forces. It seems he is some kind of private venture capitalist, and the two sycophants are his junior colleagues, they were introduced to me as François and Egor. I leave it to you to determine who is who.'

She chuckles mischievously. Skelgill considers her challenge. The two men in question are a decade younger than their boss – one of boyish Mediterranean appearance, with dark eyes and long black hair; the other is apparently of Eastern European provenance, with a broad, round face, high cheekbones, cropped fair hair and pale grey eyes. It is apparent that Richard Bond is vying to hold court. He waves a bottle of Scotch whisky – and seems particularly keen to top up the glass of the former cabinet minister. Skelgill sees that the latter reclines rather smugly, as if he knowingly holds the strings of power within the company.

However, he is plainly distracted. He has an arm draped along the upholstered bench seat, behind Ivanna Karenina – but he glances uneasily from time to time, for she is engaged in a prolonged *tête-à-tête* with DS Jones's celebrated cabin mate, Wiktoria Adamska.

Sporadic laughter emanates from the group – but Skelgill notices that it is Richard Bond himself, his voice deep and resonant, that first guffaws at his own aphorisms, aped dutifully by his acolytes. And now his voice booms out, "Ruairidh, my good man – another bottle – your esteemed compatriot Sir Ewart is dying of thirst here." Eck deigns to acknowledge his importance with a superior smile.

'That only leaves the enigmatic American. You don't happen to know who he is?'

Skelgill, lost in momentary reverie, finds himself nudged in the ribs by the sharp elbow of the journalist.

'What?'

'The preppy type – pretending to be engrossed in his phone – watching the others. Good looking, in a dull way.'

Skelgill shrugs rather indifferently.

'We're not regular travellers – not on the night train.'

'But you are detectives – surely it is second nature to be inquisitive?'

'You should see my in-tray. Inquisitive's the last thing I need to be. You're thinking of journalism.'

The woman makes a purring sound in her throat. She drains the contents of her glass.

'Touché.'

Without warning, she now rises. Once more, it is impossible to judge whether the serpentine motion of the train is the cause of her unsteadiness. They watch as she employs one hand on the seatbacks and tables to return to the main group. It seems a fresh bottle of whisky has been procured. She picks up an unused glass and obtains a measure in both it and her own from the overtly gallant Richard Bond. But when he entreats her to sit beside him she rather airily declines – and instead totters across to the man she described as the American. Peremptorily she drops into the seat opposite him and slides the spare drink under his nose. Without raising his head he lifts his gaze. He seems unsurprised, rather like a poker player who knows that a meditative state conveys the fewest clues to one's opponent. But Jenny Hackett has her back to them – and whatever she now says is subsumed beneath the clatter and rumble of the rails, and the ululating chatter of the group. However – it seems she successfully engages the anonymous traveller in conversation – for after a few moments he takes up the glass, signals cheers, drinks – and then responds to what must surely be her question about his identity and purpose in life.

'She's bonkers, Guv.' DS Leyton stares at Skelgill for a moment and, getting no reaction, turns his head to look at DS Jones. 'And what was all that about the broad you're shacking up with?'

Now it is DS Jones's turn to shrug. She is slow to reply – perhaps because she is replaying in her mind a moment in their cabin she has not related: when Wiktoria Adamska asked if later she might try on the dress that she so admired.

'I – think – that was her just being provocative.'

'I reckon that was her being three sheets to the wind!'

DS Jones seems content to go along with this explanation.

'I'm sure you're right. I suppose when you consider it, the drinks reception began almost seven hours ago. But I get the feeling she wouldn't be slow in coming forward at the best of times.'

'She hit us like a flippin' tornado.'

DS Leyton's remark leads to a few moments of silent contemplation – interrupted when the steward brings their drinks – although he seems harassed and does not dwell in depositing the cluster of glasses on their table. DS Leyton dishes them out.

'There you go, girl – get yourself sobered up on that.'

DS Jones smiles good-naturedly.

'Actually – I only had one cocktail – after that I stuck to water. They filled my wine glasses up at the table, but I never touched them. I didn't want to take any chances for the morning.'

28

She refers to the fact that they left her car near Carlisle railway station; it will be their means of getting back to Penrith, where they rendezvoused before setting out together. DS Leyton chuckles.

'Right enough – it would be a bit of a bummer to fail a breath test the morning after you've picked up a bravery award!'

DS Jones nods – but now Skelgill is prompted to speak.

'What time do we get into Carlisle?'

Although DS Leyton is the keeper of their tickets, it is DS Jones that knows the answer.

'It's just before 5.30am, Guv. Then the train stops at Edinburgh at 6.44am before it heads for the Highlands.'

Skelgill suppresses a yawn and stretches his arms above his head – and DS Leyton seems to take a cue from his action.

'I'm bushed, an' all, Guv. I'm not normally up this late. Apart from most nights.'

DS Jones is amused by his contradiction.

'Nah – what I mean is – we go to bed about ten – then, sure enough, one of the nippers'll have us up for something or other. Sore throat. Bad dream. *Jammie Dodger*. The nights I sleep through – I wake up in the morning and think they must have been kidnapped by Peter Pan!'

Skelgill is checking his watch – the time is approaching 1am.

'I've half a mind to do the all-nighter.'

But his bravado does not sound convincing. It has been a long day, requiring an early start, delays on their journey to London, nerves and adrenaline during the awards ceremony, speeches and formal dinner, and now the unfamiliar and challenging company on the night train. DS Leyton probably speaks for them all when he puts a counterpoint to Skelgill's proposition.

'Even a few hours kip – you'll feel better in the morning, Guv. Reckon I'll sleep like a log.'

3. BUMP IN THE NIGHT

Thursday, 4.45am

There can be little more frustrating than trying to get to sleep knowing that the window for slumber is rapidly drawing shut. Not that Skelgill had any difficulty in dropping off – more that 'dropping off' in a literal sense was what has woken him – the feeling that he is at any moment likely to be sent tumbling from his narrow bunk, the train driver unaccountably slowing and speeding up, when smooth progress is called for (and surely is achievable on an empty track). Once disturbed, Skelgill would always claim he never gets back to sleep – but this cannot be entirely true, for he wanders fitfully in the no-man's land between true sleep and full wakefulness, where conscious thoughts and dreamlike images intertwine, and like a child's model train set these confused ideas orbit repeatedly, further confusing the befuddled brain and distorting any sense of time. As a twist on counting sheep he has imagined the train's steady progress through stations he knows to be on their route up country: Northampton, Rugby, Nuneaton, Tamworth, Lichfield, Stafford, Crewe – Midlands towns accompanied by curious images perhaps dredged from his memory and modified by his rewired brain: Northampton, worn brown leather boots; Rugby, an old-style stitched oval football (also brown leather); Nuneaton, a baker's window jammed with pies (none eaten); Tamworth, a giant ginger sow with sagging udders; Lichfield, a three-spired cathedral; Stafford, medieval villagers armed with poles wading across a river; Crewe, sailors lined up in salute along the platform as if it were the deck of a carrier sliding out of port – but progress never seems to get beyond Crewe before they are back at Northampton (misleadingly named, a mere sixty miles from London) – and each time at Tamworth, the grunting of the pig – which has a familiar face and can only be DS Leyton beneath, blissfully dead to the world and experiencing no such nocturnal torment.

And amidst this disconcerting maelstrom in which time both stands still and leaps in stages there are other external stimuli that enter the kaleidoscope of his subconscious mind and blend with the incomprehensible drama. There is the pressure blast of tunnels, a sense of interminably holding one's breath under water. There is the shriek of another train – like two great beasts jousting at high velocity at the very margin of their territories yet incredibly not colliding. There is the banging of doors and sliding of bolts – wakeful travellers using the washrooms? And there are voices – real or imagined? Are these words from dreams or words from the corridor? There are shambling footsteps and dull thumps of shoulders off bulkheads as if drunks stagger about. There is a hushed conversation in some unintelligible language – yet in his dream-state he invents a translation – it concerns the extortionate excise duty imposed on Scotch whisky and a means of laundering the raw liquid through the oil pipeline in the Firth of Forth. There is a woman's voice, raised and sharp – is that, "Go away!" he hears her hiss? Perhaps someone has opened or tried the wrong compartment? And there is a woman's laugh, throaty – sexy, even – drawn out, and then smothered in some way – by a kiss?

And then – a big bump.

'Struth! Cor blimey!'

Skelgill is suddenly wide awake. His sergeant's voice – and alarm – is real. And the only reason he has not joined him on the floor of the cabin is because the two vertical restraining straps that run between the frame of the upper bunk and the ceiling have done their job. There is no such luxury for DS Leyton in the lower bunk, where this protection is deemed unnecessary. He hears his sergeant scrabbling for his reading light.

'I thought you'd shoved me out of bed, Guv.'

'Leyton, we've stopped.'

'We ain't meant to stop that quick, Guv. Just as well I landed on me bonce. No damage done.'

Skelgill reaches to release the window blind. It clatters up.

'Stick that light off a minute.'

31

DS Leyton does as bidden. Skelgill stretches his frame and presses his nose up against the glass. But there is only pitch darkness beyond – not even any light from the train cast upon the surroundings. But what he does see is so close as to be out of focus – the immediate accumulation of large flakes of snow, pressed onto the window by the easterly wind. It is Mrs Leyton's much-vaunted Baltic Blast.

'What time is it?'

'Er – quarter to five, Guv – near as dammit, anyway – 4:47.'

Skelgill shakes his head in an effort to expel the lingering fragments of his imaginings. 'I dreamt we were trapped in some loop in the Midlands – like the points were stuck and we were going round in circles. We must be in Cumbria by now. Maybe Kendal neck of the woods. Somewhere in the eastern fells.'

He jumps down from his bunk and begins to pull on his jeans and shirt. He starts as he is confronted by his reflection in a hitherto unnoticed mirror and he gives his hair a vigorous rub, to no obvious effect.

'I'll find out what's going on. Check Jones is okay. Knock first, mind.'

'Roger, Guv.'

While DS Leyton fumbles for his clothes and gasps as he pulls on his socks Skelgill slips out into the corridor. It is dimly lit by a series of bulkhead lights, but otherwise deserted. He is a little surprised – but he has acted promptly and supposes the other passengers are gathering their wits – although he thought he heard the sound of a compartment being opened and closed. As he approaches the vestibule the automatic dividing door slides open and he feels an icy draught. He rounds the washroom to be confronted by an incongruous sight – one that might even hark back to his nightmare. A muscular, tanned figure – naked but for boxer shorts, Richard Bond, the 'he-man' so-called by Jenny Hackett – has the left-side external door of the train open and is squatting and half hanging out as if he is preparing to leap.

'What are you doing, man?'

32

Richard Bond swings around – his features contract into an expression of self-reproach – perhaps that he has been caught unawares.

'Ah – just assessing the danger we're in.' He rises, and hesitates for a moment. He holds out large hands, palms upwards. 'In case we need to bail out.'

Skelgill is grimacing doubtfully.

'And?'

Richard Bond begins to speak in short staccato bursts, with a military precision. He appears distracted – as if he is counselling himself as much as Skelgill.

'The situation looks stable. But the visibility is under three metres. It won't be light for three-and-a-half hours. We're sitting ducks for an avalanche. Snow depth increasing rapidly. Need to establish if there's been an engine fire – explosion – whether it's an act of terror.'

Skelgill appears unperturbed by such speculation – but he is concerned that here is a man inclined unilaterally to take charge of a situation.

'You'd better close that door. The drift builds up on the leeward side.'

Richard Bond looks sharply at Skelgill. His features briefly contract into a mixture of suspicion – that Skelgill has said something knowledgeable – and perhaps regret that he has not said it himself. But sure enough snow is swirling back into the open portal as the wind sweeps relentlessly over the top of the carriage and creates a low-pressure vortex beneath. He slams shut the heavy door with some ease. He is about to speak when the intercom crackles. It heralds an announcement – as does the clearing of a throat, and then comes Ruairidh's voice – guttural and rolling its r's even more harshly than before, as if he too has been rudely awakened.

'Ladies and gentlemen – this is yer guard speaking. Fae yer own safety please remain in yer cabins. A further announcement will be made shortly.'

Skelgill steps away from Richard Bond.

'I'm going to have a word with the driver.'

'I'll come with you.'

Skelgill ponders for a moment. He senses the time is fast approaching when he must pull rank – but for the sake of mere irritation there is little merit in making an enemy of Richard Bond. Brash he may be, he looks competent – and as things stand Skelgill has no idea of just how difficult is their predicament. There is Lyndon B. Johnson's principle of inside and outside tents, and all that.

'You better put something on.' Richard Bond is about to object. 'You might give the driver the wrong idea.'

Whatever Richard Bond thinks Skelgill means by this (and Skelgill is not sure himself) it seems to provoke second thoughts.

'Just a moment.' The man steps away, then he suddenly swivels on the balls of his feet, lightly for someone of such bulk. He extends a firm hand to Skelgill. 'Bond, Richard Bond, former captain, SAS.'

Skelgill hesitates – not intending to delay the handshake – but uncertain of how much information to impart. He settles for giving his surname – it seems to suffice, as if that is pukka form in establishment circles. Then, as he strives to match the power of the man's grip – a disadvantage for him, having a tendency towards sinistrality – a notion strikes him.

'What was your specialism?'

For a fleeting moment the confident big-boned face crumples – but then it swiftly regains its determined set.

'Desert warfare – but – there are similarities.' He breaks away and treads silently. He calls in a whisper over his shoulder. 'One minute, max.'

While he waits Skelgill crosses to the other side of the vestibule. Snow is rapidly building up on the window. He thinks about lowering it – but there is little to be gained. He saw enough on the leeward side of the train to begin to understand something of the conditions. There was no bare ground visible, not even protruding rocks, which tells him the fallen snow is already seven or eight inches deep. It is coming down thick and fast, and the drifting is rapidly coating the train. But he is encouraged that at least the power is on; he can feel the vibration of the diesels, so they have heat and lighting for the time being. He hears Richard Bond returning, and now leads the way into the next carriage, the lounge car. To Skelgill's surprise they find a troubled-looking Ruairidh standing in discourse with a young woman who wears a similar uniform. Simultaneously the pair present anxious faces to the new arrivals. From behind Skelgill, Richard Bond calls out.

'We intend to consult with the driver.'

Both staff members react with a furrowing of brows – as though this is some kind of mini-mutiny by the passengers. The woman breaks away from her colleague and bars the aisle. She is small and slender, her blonde hair is tied back, her features a little plain but pleasingly regular. Her uniform together with a determined glint in her blue eyes belie her size.

'Happen I am the driver.'

At his back Skelgill hears an intake of breath – a female in charge is plainly not what Richard Bond had in mind. But Skelgill merely grins; the woman has a local Cumbrian accent.

He decides, however, to cut to the chase – for the crew look in no mood to accommodate pushy members of the public – he can see they have enough on their plate. He slips his police warrant card from his back pocket, and holds it so that the woman only can read it.

'I'm travelling back to Carlisle with two colleagues. They'll be along in a moment. Anything we can do?'

It seems he is correct in assuming the driver is the more senior of the pair – and she appears to appreciate that the Detective Inspector has established a kind of private understanding between them. She glances at the guard and then looks back at Skelgill with a faintly helpless grimace.

'We've run into a massive snowdrift – it was like a wall of snow. Everything went pitch dark – it's buried the entire loco and part of the first goods van. We've lost all traction. Forward and reverse.'

'Do we need to abandon?'

35

Skelgill says this with reluctance – but the driver nods to acknowledge that the greatest risk to a train that makes an unscheduled stop is that another one smashes into it.

'No – so long as the signalling is not down entirely. As soon as Control sees we've not left this sector they'll activate red lights behind us – in any event Penrith will miss us in a few minutes. Besides, the next train northbound is the local service from Lancaster, not until 5.56. I reckon the line behind us will be impassable long before then.'

But Richard Bond picks up her initial point. He pushes forward, crowding alongside Skelgill in the aisle.

'What do you mean, madam, so long as the signalling is not down?'

The driver glances doubtfully at Skelgill – as if for his approval to share information with this stranger – Skelgill gives a barely discernible nod.

'We've got no radio signal. The transmitters hereabouts must be iced up.'

'We can use mobile telephones.'

Now the woman brings her handset out of her shirt pocket. She glances at the guard and then waves it uselessly in the air.

'We're on different networks – we've got nothing.'

Skelgill's phone is in his cabin – but Richard Bond produces his own – and growls.

'So, it seems, have I.'

'This is always a dead stretch. Besides, the embankment's sixty foot at its highest.'

Skelgill's expression becomes hopeful.

'You know where we are?'

'I think we're in Shake Holes cutting.'

'At Shap summit?'

There is a note of concern in Skelgill's question, and it is mirrored by the woman's severe expression. The climb over Shap Fell is one of the most isolated sections of the entire West Coast Main Line.

But Richard Bond pounces on the uncertainty.

'You only *think?* Surely you have better systems.'

Skelgill looks a little irked. He turns to the man.

'You've seen it outside – you said yourself, the visibility's not above ten foot.' He reverts to the driver – like the guard, she wears a badge that displays only her Christian name, and now he uses it. 'Laura – go on, lass.'

She appears unmoved by Richard Bond's implied criticism.

'I'd say we passed through Oxenholme fifteen minutes before we hit the drift. There's a snow fence to protect the cutting, but it was part demolished by gales in October. They said it wasn't a priority to reinstate because it was only the east side that was damaged.'

Skelgill nods grimly. But the Baltic Blast has defied the prevailing winds and is blowing *from* the east. The driver continues.

'I felt the snow on the rails – there must be a gradual accumulation as the drift gets worse with altitude. Normally we can deal with up to a foot. But the gradient on Shap is 1 in 75 – and it's a continuous ascent of a thousand feet – so we were barely making fifty – I realised we were fighting a losing battle. But at least it brought us to a controlled stop.'

Skelgill grimaces wryly.

'My oppo fell out of bed. He wouldn't recommend the uncontrolled version.'

Skelgill can sense that Richard Bond is itching to speak; if he were a schoolboy he would be jabbing his hand urgently skywards for attention. But he can contain himself no longer.

'You say we're on a steep incline. And the track behind us is clear of trains.' He does not wait for the driver to reply. 'We can detach the rear carriage. Roll back to safety.'

This suggestion elicits a strangled ejaculation from the guard, which causes all eyes to fall upon him. Though when he makes a recovery his tone is suitably deferential.

'Ye've been watching old movies, sir – the slip coach was phased out in the Sixties. There was a special coupling that could be released frae inside the carriage, and the guard used a manual brake tae bring it tae a halt.'

'We can let the adverse gradient do that job, my man.'

37

Skelgill has raised an eyebrow – albeit he has to admit to a small if reluctant pang of admiration for Richard Bond's *up and at 'em* attitude. However, he is not surprised when the driver moves to quash the idea.

'We don't have the equipment to uncouple a carriage. Even if we were able to – without brakes we could derail on a bend. And there's always the likelihood of workers on the tracks, de-icing points. It would be too dangerous. I couldn't do that without clearance.'

The driver's objections are comprehensive. Richard Bond brims with frustration. Skelgill can feel his muscular form flexing, as though he is imagining himself singlehandedly shouldering the train into motion. And, frankly, if push came to shove Skelgill is sure that between them they could probably find a way. It is his inclination, too, to respond to their dilemma. But Richard Bond is treating it as a military training exercise, a challenge to be overcome by brute force and lateral thinking, and to hell with the consequences.

On this particular score the driver is right. The relevant authorities will soon be alerted – as with planes, at least there is a system in place for trains to be monitored. That the same cannot be said for automobiles, however, raises a problem for the passengers stranded on board the Midnight Express. If the forecasters' prophecy of three days' snow proves accurate, there will not be the resources to come to their aid. Priority of rescue will be given to hundreds if not thousands of motorists trapped in their cars, some no doubt with ill or elderly or very young passengers. And, even if the means of access were clear, the train is stranded in a near-wilderness area. Country lanes and farm tracks will be impassable. Helicopters will be grounded. One small aspect in their favour is their lack of communication – central command will want to know the degree of danger they are in. But, as a longstanding volunteer in the mountain rescue, it is plain to Skelgill – what would the emergency services actually do if they came in on foot with a satellite phone? Call to say all was well and stay until the *Glenmorangie* ran out?

The train driver is watching him closely. She seems to know his thoughts. She glances briefly at the guard, and then returns her gaze to Skelgill.

'We think we're safest on board. We've power – heating – food supplies – and,' she grins wryly, 'flush toilets.'

Skelgill is about to remark – but it is perhaps just as well that at this juncture the sliding door announces the arrival of DS Leyton, followed by DS Jones – both looking a touch dishevelled. Skelgill catches DS Jones's eye – and she gives him a little nod to indicate all is well. He suggests they take seats in the area where Richard Bond had formerly held court. He makes the relevant introductions. At this point it becomes apparent, to those who do not yet know, what must be their occupation. Richard Bond addresses Skelgill – quite respectfully, as though conditioned by martial protocol and perhaps assuming that Skelgill effectively ranks above him.

'Excuse me – are you British Transport Police?'

Skelgill shakes his head.

'We're common-or-garden detectives.' He pauses. 'But as it happens we're based about ten miles from here.'

DS Leyton cannot help intervening.

'C'mon, Guvnor – you're doing yourself down.' He holds out an arm towards Skelgill as though he is introducing him to the three civilians. 'He's in the mountain rescue.'

Skelgill frowns as though annoyed by the revelation – but he can sense that Richard Bond is eager for commensurate recognition. He makes a similar sweeping gesture as that employed by his sergeant.

'This fellow – Mr Bond – has military experience. I reckon he knows a thing or two about sticky situations.'

Richard Bond's reaction is an even less convincing affectation of modesty than that exhibited by Skelgill.

'Please – just call me Richard – I rather feel Bond might unrealistically raise your expectations.'

He brays at what must surely be an old chestnut as far as he is concerned – but then his face falls when he does not get quite the response he anticipated. Skelgill instead launches into a

39

succinct and somewhat terse assessment of their circumstances, in order to bring his colleagues up to speed. Characteristically, it falls to DS Leyton to make light of the matter.

'Cor blimey, Guv – I'll be in the doghouse if I'm not back for Christmas Eve. The missus will never pass for Santa!'

His riposte generates a ripple of polite and slightly nervous laughter – for many a true word is spoken in jest, and perhaps the prospect of spending several days together begins to sink in. The strained hilarity tails off. But a strident electronic bleeping abruptly punctures the little bubble of pensive silence that envelops them. Its source is above the bar area. Skelgill looks questioningly at the driver.

'Laura – what's that – a smoke alarm?'

But she has risen to her feet and is shaking her head.

'Carbon monoxide.'

'What – in here?'

'I don't know. The alarms are all connected in series – when one goes off, they all do. I'll be able to tell from the control panel in the cab.' She has her hands on her hips, emphasising her small frame and narrow waist. Her features are creased anxiously. 'But I'll need to shut off the diesels. It's a safety regulation. It's potentially life-threatening.'

Skelgill curses under his breath.

Richard Bond slaps a hefty palm on the low table before him.

'The exhausts must be blocked by the snow. Do you have shovels on board?'

All eyes have turned to him – but now the driver inhales to speak and regains their attention.

'The exhausts discharge directly above the engines.' She glances at the guard for corroboration; he nods, though his expression is doubtful. 'From the glimpse I got as we plunged into the drift, it's at least the height of the train again. You could be talking fifteen foot of snow on top of the loco.'

Skelgill is thinking it is probably too risky to tunnel into a deep snowdrift, even if there are shovels and they were able to scale the streamlined fuselage in the raging blizzard. Meanwhile the alarm continues to bleep, like a timer counting down their decision time. He presses the driver.

'Have you got a back-up system?'

'A bank of auxiliary batteries. Fully charged they last four to six hours.'

'What about if we just heat this carriage?'

'Maybe twelve - fourteen?'

There is no reason she would know. Skelgill scowls broodingly. Richard Bond rocks to and fro in his seat, as if formulating his next scenario for escape. Skelgill has a further question.

'What temperature was it reading outside?'

'Minus eight Celsius as we came up Shap Fell.'

DS Leyton splutters.

'Cor – if that ain't brass monkey weather, I dunno what is.'

Skelgill's brows are knitted, such that an uninformed observer might wonder if he is calculating the heat transfer coefficient of a modern railway carriage. In fact a more practical task occupies his thoughts: the unfolding of his mental map of Cumbria.

'Laura – what bad weather kit have you got on board?'

The woman glances at the guard and then again at Skelgill.

'There's two drysuits and gaitered boots. They're standard issue – kept on every train, in the brake van.' She inclines her head towards the front of the train. 'They're one size – way too big for me.'

She suddenly looks a little guilty, as if realising her conclusion makes her sound uncooperative. But Skelgill is unperturbed.

'Happen that's what I wanted to hear, lass.'

He turns to Richard Bond, who looks like a dog that has overheard the word 'walkies'. Indeed, before Skelgill can speak, he blurts out a proposal.

'If we strike due east into the wind we'll eventually meet the M6. Even if the road is closed we can call in assistance from the nearest emergency telephone.'

He regards Skelgill eagerly, imploring his approval. While Skelgill knows this is not the worst plan it paints a picture in his mind fraught with uncertainty. The nearest point on the M6 is

41

two miles away, across treacherous moorland. As DS Leyton related, the M6 was closed hours ago; the exposed stretch over Shap Fell will be blanketed by snow; at best they will find stranded vehicles, possibly abandoned, their occupants rescued. If the national grid is down, the emergency telephones will not be working.

DS Jones can see that her superior is conflicted.

'What are you thinking, Guv? Do you want to try to dig out the exhausts?'

But Skelgill shakes his head.

'I doubt we could do it – the drift would collapse on us.' But he glances at Richard Bond, and bows his head as if to make some concession to his latest suggestion. 'I reckon we need to get out of here, right enough – once our power's gone we could freeze to death if we're stuck long term. Down in this cutting, the whole train could become entombed. But if we're right about our position, there's a possible answer.' He looks now to the driver – for a moment she is distracted, staring anxiously back down the carriage to where the alarm continues to sound. But his words penetrate her thoughts and she turns her eyes to him, her expression hopeful. 'There's a hotel – *Shake Holes Inn* – it's in the middle of nowhere – like us. It's probably under a mile. Happen it'll be cut off itself – but they'll have oil-fired boilers, plus open fires and plenty of timber. It would be a safer place to be.'

DS Jones is quick to identify what may be Skelgill's most pressing concern.

'How would you find it?'

Now he again looks interrogatively at the driver.

'Laura – do you remember – before we stopped – did we pass the footbridge over the cutting?'

The woman looks momentarily alarmed – but then she nods eagerly.

'Aye – it were just seconds before – then we hit the bank of snow – and I were thinking it were virtually the same height as the bridge.'

42

Skelgill is nodding slowly. Again it is DS Jones that attempts to join up the dots. It seems she can envisage something of the solution.

'Are you thinking of one person at a time – with a guide – since there are two outfits?'

But now Skelgill shakes his head.

'*Shake Holes Inn* does outdoor activities. They provide gear for their guests – for quad-biking – that sort of thing. They've got sledges and whatnot for kids.' Skelgill looks pointedly at Richard Bond. 'There's a bridleway that goes over the footbridge into a pinewood. The hotel sits on the far side of the plantation – the path ought to be sheltered. We could drag enough kit back here. In the process we'll beat down a decent track. Then set out together in close formation. We'd have the wind at our backs. Even taking it steady we ought to cover a mile in half an hour.'

Bond is nodding. In fact he is compelled to rise to his feet. He rubs his large hands vigorously together. 'Ready when you are.'

The train driver is becoming increasingly agitated.

'I need to turn off the diesels. The black box will be recording everything – I'll be failing in my duty if I don't respond to the carbon monoxide warning.'

Skelgill regards her earnestly.

'We'll get this kit on. No point letting the grass grow.' He turns to DS Jones and DS Leyton and the guard, Ruairidh. 'You'd better get everyone up and organised. Tell them to put on warm sensible clothes, if they've got any. Assemble in here – keep the interconnecting doors shut as much as you can. Brief them on the plan.'

The driver moves swiftly, she is light and agile on her feet, followed by Skelgill and Richard Bond. As they weave through the serving area Skelgill hears DS Jones ask the guard if he has a manifest of passengers.

4. RECONNAISANCE

Thursday, 5.30am

As he leaps into the dark Skelgill recalls Richard Bond's expression about bailing out – it had seemed curious at the time, but on reflection it was perhaps not so inappropriate, as stepping out of an aeroplane at night would maybe not feel so different – at least for the half second before his borrowed boots thump into the thick snow, and his momentum causes him to tumble forward onto hands and knees. The overall is not a bad fit, everything considered. Skelgill has a lean frame; but Richard Bond, despite being of about his own height, must weigh a good three stones heavier and the snug suit cannot be so comfortable. They each have a rubber-armoured flashlight – but as Skelgill gets to his feet it becomes immediately apparent that these are as much a hindrance as a help; the beam reflects off the swirling snow that chokes the ether, and offers no distance penetration, merely the impression of a cocoon of whiteness at arm's length.

Skelgill has briefed Richard Bond on his plan. They follow the railway line back to the footbridge. They scale the embankment – wherever it is least overgrown with briar. Once on the bridge, they locate the bridleway that runs into the pinewood on the west side of the railway. Provided they can stay on the track, it will guide them to the vicinity of *Shake Holes Inn*. He was impressed by the way the man paid attention – he listened intently – and then asked just two questions, employing bullet points, what was a) the bearing and b) distance of the hotel from the footbridge?

What is also plain to Skelgill is that they have to get everyone out of here as soon as possible. As he had drawn to the attention of Richard Bond – that the snow is accumulating in the lee of the train – the cutting likewise is filling up from the east; there is a ramp of snow that sweeps down over the southbound track, a cliff sliced through by their train before it hit the main bulk of the drift only thirty minutes ago. As such, the northbound track on which they are stranded is comparatively clear. Although the rails are already covered again, their profiles are visible, and the snow between them about eight inches deep. It reassures Skelgill that his method ought to be foolproof. By reference to fixed features – rail track, bridge and bridleway – he can effectively navigate blind.

Thus the first challenge is not to blunder past the footbridge. Having conferred in more detail with the driver, Skelgill's estimate is that it is at least two hundred yards south of the train – and not more than four hundred. They have agreed initially to walk in single file to beat a path. Richard Bond had offered to go ahead, but Skelgill had merely responded with an exhortation to measure two hundred paces, and set off. As he counts rhythmically, and the process slips into his subconscious, he begins to wonder how to spot the bridge. If it were constructed for vehicular purposes it would have great piers of blue engineering bricks with their foundations at the trackside – even in the restricted visibility something that would be hard to miss. But a narrow footbridge will likely have its footings high on either embankment, veiled by the blizzard and beyond reach of their meagre torches. He is still turning this over in his mind when Richard Bond cries "Two hundred!" – his eager tone suggests he is pleased to be first.

Skelgill half turns and shouts beneath the wind that they should 'fan out'. As a military command it seems Richard Bond needs no further instruction. They go more slowly – each at one margin of the track, trudging in deeper snow – but to Skelgill it still seems impossible that they will see anything. When train driver Laura glimpsed the underside of the bridge just prior to the impact, she was seated in a cab raised a good six feet higher, and had the benefit of immensely powerful headlamps. Though they are separated by just three or four yards, Skelgill can only see Richard Bond as a shimmering glow. He is directing his flashlight up the embankment – but surely to little avail. Skelgill has his to the ground. And now he calls out.

'Wait!'

'What is it?'

45

Richard Bond struggles across to him. Skelgill indicates the area at his feet.

'Look at the change in depth – there's a ridge right across the tracks.'

'Good show – we must be under the deck.' There is a note of excitement in Richard Bond's voice. 'I'll go up – do a recce.'

Before Skelgill can object Richard Bond takes a line perpendicular to the tracks and Skelgill can see the halo of his torch rising; it disappears as he successfully scrambles up the side of the cutting. Skelgill feels frustrated by his own inaction – but he realises it is essential now that he does not move from the spot. And barely a minute later the pale glow reappears, and Richard Bond comes slip-sliding, half on his backside. As he reaches track level he stumbles forward and Skelgill has to brace to support his heavy bulk. His face is close to Skelgill's; he is a little breathless.

'A-okay. There's a barred timber fence at the top – no problem to scale – I mean for the ladies.' He squats on his haunches and begins to gather armfuls of snow. 'We must mark the turn-off.'

'Do it on the way back. We can bring something more obvious – a pole.'

Each time Skelgill employs a tone that resembles an order Richard Bond seems automatically to acquiesce.

'Roger.'

But he is keen to lead the way back up the embankment. As Skelgill follows, he considers what may be the most fraught aspect of their task – to get the party up to the bridge. The banking is steep and the snow unstable – but Richard Bond has already ploughed something of a furrow, and their passage now, and again on return, should see them compress rudimentary steps into the snow. It is a lung-bursting climb – perhaps double the height of a house. But in due course they reach the fence to find themselves at the western end of the narrow footbridge. Now they are exposed to the full force of the gale – and it *is* a gale, eight on the Beaufort scale, Skelgill estimates – forty knots that would certainly drive him off Bassenthwaite Lake; though these conditions are more reminiscent of the bleak mile between Great End and the summit of Scafell Pike in the depths of winter.

The bridge itself offers some protection. Its sides are constructed of steel panels welded onto a box framework, up to chest height, and they withdraw into the mouth of this corridor to take stock. There is absolutely no indication that, only yards ahead, the railway ought to be bordered by a tall stand of conifers. Like a misguided bat a fluttering doubt invades Skelgill's thoughts. What if this is the wrong bridge? What if the driver were mistaken and this is not Shake Holes cutting, but another one altogether? But he detects that Richard Bond seeks leadership, and he knows he must act before the man makes up his own mind. Striking a parallel line from the footbridge Skelgill leads the way into the void that is both black and white. And, sure enough, after a dozen paces there is the sense that something is changing. The constant barrage of the wind in the ears begins to relent; instead, overhead it acquires a new resonance, a surging oceanic roar – and Skelgill realises it is the interface of substance in its different forms, air forced across the rough plane of the treetops. Their pace quickens – for the conditions underfoot are improving rapidly. The dark matter that permeates the spinning galaxy of flakes seems blacker, the flurries less intense, and their torches begin to pick out the ranks of conifers on either side of the descending track.

This is of course what Skelgill had subliminally imagined – but had not allowed himself the luxury of visualising. The dense plantation serves as a windbreak, and the declination is curving away from the wind; meanwhile the progressively layered canopy is capturing the bulk of the snow. Yes, a *whump* close at hand reminds him it will dislodge in weighty clumps – perhaps accompanied by the odd weak bough – but it is a benign environment compared to the exposed crest of the cutting. Heading east to the M6 would have been foolhardy. As the path takes a turn to the south, Richard Bond echoes Skelgill's unspoken assessment.

47

'Frankly, this is a cakewalk for the likes of us. What about taking a bearing off the wind and yomping down through the woods? Save ourselves a few minutes.'

It pains Skelgill to shy at the gauntlet. He requires a moment's thought to contrive a plausible rejoinder.

'I reckon it's better we check the exact route we'll be bringing the others. Besides – it's riddled with shake holes hereabouts – the bridleway's the best way to stay safe.'

He senses that Richard Bond is stymied; indeed, the man's reply is somewhat oblique.

'I am forgetting this is your old stamping ground.'

It is hardly the case. They are a long way from Skelgill's "old stamping ground" as Richard Bond has put it. He is a Cumberland lad; this is Westmorland. He knows it only from a couple of visits, exploring, and one time a mountain rescue training exercise across the bleak moorland to the north and east. Indeed, this district borders on the Yorkshire Dales – where the obscure geological features he has referred to are more prevalent.

'You know what shake holes are, aye?'

'I have not heard the term – I presume we are talking caves?'

'Sinkholes. This is a limestone escarpment.' Skelgill casts out a conciliatory hand. 'Right enough – the madcap cavers dig out the boulder clay in the bottom to see if there's a pothole worth exploring. But they can fill with drifted snow – they're like the mantraps the Romans used to dig round their forts.'

'Lilia, yes?'

Now it is Skelgill's turn to confront his ignorance; he guesses that Bond, with his public school accent, would probably know this sort of thing. Before he can speak, however, his companion asks a follow-up question.

'How deep are they?'

Skelgill is content to expound.

'Most are just up to your waist – others a dozen, twenty foot – as much as forty. If you're really unlucky, like I say – there can be a pothole disappearing into the rock. They're a constant hazard for sheep. Walkers, too. Especially when they've filled with bog and look like solid ground.'

'You must show me if we pass one.'

'Let's hope we don't find one by accident.'

'Hear, hear.'

On such a theme they now each sink into something of a brown study as they march, falling into step through the crisp snow. Skelgill reflects upon what Richard Bond has said – certainly it is true that this is not a particularly challenging expedition for either of them. But he is wondering who else is on the train – it occurs to him that among the passengers hitherto unseen might be the elderly or infirm. He ought to have established this fact before setting out – and now he has no means of contacting his team for confirmation. In his desire to act – perhaps under pressure to stay one step ahead of Richard Bond and thus hold him in check – he has overlooked a basic principle. But now his torch catches a shadow in the terrain where there is a small clearing at one side of the track, and a round snow-filled depression about ten feet across.

'I reckon that's a shake hole. That's why it's not planted.'

They halt for a moment.

'It could be a bomb crater. The size of a half-decent mortar, wouldn't you say?'

Skelgill wonders if this is a kind of subconscious one-upmanship, that Richard Bond can't help it, and that his questions of this nature are to all intents and purposes rhetorical. Thus he does not respond, and following a few seconds' contemplation they move on. In these conditions Skelgill would expect to cover a mile in fifteen minutes, and the way through the woods is barely two-thirds of that. Accordingly, they encounter a marked deterioration in visibility as they emerge from the western fringe of the plantation. With nothing to guide them Skelgill's fears resurface – is this the right route after all? He racks his memory – when last he perused the map, how far was the hotel? Surely it was adjacent to the pale green segment with its little stick-drawn conifers? And his concern is short lived – for they have taken barely thirty tentative paces before the building looms up before them. Of course – this place was a traditional coaching inn, and an ancient route now largely

49

forsaken has aided them. His rejuvenated spirits, however, are tainted by an absence of parked cars, or even tyre tracks buried in the snow; the surroundings are pristine. No light shows from any window; indeed their torches reveal the old building as stark and desolate; there are fissures in its white stuccoed walls, and the window jambs, sills and lintels picked out in black are flaking extravagantly. Above the recessed portico are painted the fading words *'Shake Holes Inn'* – he notices that the ascender of the first letter 'h' is worn away, so as to suggest 'Snake' to the uninitiated.

Skelgill is not ready to accept that the place has been abandoned. Yet, by this time of the morning – approaching 6am – he would expect the first stirrings of staff, even in a modest hotel such as this; and somebody must live-in, even if the majority of workers are dailies. And, given last night's conditions, it is possible that bar and kitchen staff would have been obliged to stay over.

But he can reach no conclusion, and while he is shining his flashlight in search of a bell-pull Richard Bond strides forward and hammers upon the heavy oak door. Skelgill cannot help thinking this is ham-fisted (never mind that it literally is so) – for it smacks of a police raid to bang aggressively at such an ungodly hour. If there are occupants, they will surely not be enamoured of their appeal for assistance. But he is reminded of the Shap summit memorial – not too far from here, beside the old A6 trunk road – its inscription commemorating the local people that *"gave freely of food and shelter to stranded travellers in bad weather"* – and he holds this tradition in mind as there comes a scrabbling of locks and chains from behind the door.

It swings open wide enough to admit them, almost as though their arrival has been anticipated. And, as for tradition, the impression of bygone times is enhanced – for before them stands a Dickensian apparition, a slight young woman, pale of complexion, clad in a flowing white nightdress. Long dark tresses spill in rivulets over her shoulders and breast; dark eyes glitter beneath arched brows in the flickering light of the candle that she bears in an old-fashioned brass holder.

'Quickly. You must come in.'

She steps aside to allow the two men to pass; they must seem tall and bulky to her, yet she shows no sign of feeling intimidated and presses shut the door. Could it be their matching railway-issue drysuits with their reflective stripes and panels convey some sense of officialdom? Accordingly Skelgill finds himself skipping formalities with a question an official might ask.

'Is there a power cut?'

The girl – she must be in her early twenties – still does not appear fazed.

'Yes – but we have a generator – it is turned off for the night to conserve fuel.'

Though she is articulate Skelgill realises her accent is not British – but such a thing can be a rarity in the hospitality business these days.

'What about your guests?'

'We have no guests – there was a –'

'Sam – what is going on?'

It is another foreign accent (the word 'what' pronounced with a 'v' sound). German, or Dutch, Skelgill thinks. The voice is male, commanding, gravelly, and it comes from above them, from the darkness beyond the hallway in which they stand – perhaps the man is leaning over a balcony. Skelgill short-circuits any further preamble.

'Cumbria CID, sir.' He does not distinguish between himself and Richard Bond. 'We've got folk stranded on a snowbound train – we need to bring them here for their own safety. We'd like to borrow some of your outdoor gear.'

The man makes an unintelligible exclamation – unintelligible to Skelgill, that is – but Richard Bond promptly responds.

'Is jy 'n Afrikaner?'

There is a brief pause – as if the invisible man is evaluating his options – and perhaps the realisation that he cannot hide his feelings behind an alien tongue.

'Ja. Jy?'

'Namibiese. Ek praat Afrikaans. Hou by Engels assebleif.'

Richard Bond leans close to Skelgill and hisses rather loudly.

'He's South African – I have instructed him to speak English.'

51

Skelgill wonders what else Richard Bond told him – something about his own provenance that doesn't quite ring true?

'He didn't sound too chuffed.'

'Never fear – like I say, he's South African.' Richard Bond chortles heartily at his private joke – and now seems to have no qualms in directing his flashlight upon what proves to be a heavily built man in his late forties with a broad head and unkempt black hair trailing over a swarthy, twisted countenance, who is descending with the aid of a stick a wide staircase and attempting to fasten one-handed a tartan-patterned dressing gown over flannel pyjamas. 'Here he comes.'

At the moment only the single candle held by the girl otherwise lights them. She seems to appreciate this, and she extends it at arm's length and the four of them converge around it as the man approaches. He glares; his features are noticeably lopsided.

'I am Joost Merlyn, landlord.'

Skelgill introduces himself by his title and surname, and his companion simply as 'Bond', which he detects meets with the latter's approval.

'Samanta is my housekeeper.'

Skelgill and Richard Bond duly nod towards the young woman. It strikes Skelgill as an outmoded job title; but he turns back to the owner.

'First, I'd like to use your phone, sir.'

'Ach – the lines were brought down last night. Nor do we have a mobile signal in this dale.'

Skelgill clicks his tongue in frustration.

'But I gather you've got your own power.'

He gives a tip of his head to indicate that the girl has communicated this fact.

'Ja – we have a generator – it is sufficient for the lights. There is plenty of oil for heating. And no shortage of timber, naturally.'

Skelgill is nodding implacably. He begins to speak but realises that what he is about to relate is incomplete in his own mind.

'There's – approximately – twenty people.' He senses Richard Bond wants to interject, the man inhales – but Skelgill continues quickly. 'It's not a difficult walk – under a mile, with a favourable slope – but we need protective gear and boots or wellingtons. Then a couple of big rucksacks if you've got them – otherwise maybe holdalls, and sledges that we can drag them on.'

'We do not have rucksacks.'

'The canvas laundry bags.' This is Samanta. She looks hopefully at Skelgill. 'We have our sheets and towels delivered in them. They have a large capacity. I can show you. The linen store is beside the tack room.'

She reaches out and lightly touches Skelgill's sleeve – then she glances apprehensively at her employer; it is as if the greater powers of the two arrivals have usurped his authority, and she is torn between whom she must serve. But it seems Joost Merlyn grudgingly acquiesces.

'The toboggans are in the old stables. It is easiest to reach them from the front door. Turn to the right and again under the archway into the courtyard.'

'I'm on it.' Richard Bond immediately strides away, clicking on his torch. He calls out more loudly without turning, 'Depending what you've got we can probably stack them and take several each.'

Skelgill regards Joost Merlyn and at the same time gestures with an open palm towards the girl.

'Is it just the two of you that's here right now?'

The owner grimaces sourly.

'Yesterday afternoon the other staff were sent home. Last night we were expecting a company from Glasgow for their festive celebrations. They had booked out the hotel for exclusive use up to Christmas Eve. They called at about 5pm to say they could not risk the journey. I am not anticipating they will arrive now – not at all.' In the flickering light of the candle the heavy

53

creases in his countenance seem to deepen. 'It was an important piece of business for us.'

Skelgill inhales in the manner that precedes informed pontification.

'Play your cards right, sir – this is your chance to make a railway company look good for once.'

The hotelier appears to grasp the intimation that he will not be out of pocket for whatever now unfolds. Albeit without enthusiasm, he summons a note of cooperation.

'I shall go and fire up the generator.' He turns and begins to limp into the darkness, his stick tapping erratically on the stone flags. He mutters, half to himself, still with a hint of bitter irony in his voice. 'And, of course, we have ample provisions.'

'Shall we go?'

The girl again touches Skelgill's sleeve, this time taking a light grip.

'Aye – lead on.'

Initially she follows in the footsteps of Joost Merlyn. But whereas he has melted directly into the gloom she takes a sharp right turn along a corridor that opens up beside the staircase. Skelgill's boots echo, yet the girl moves noiselessly. After twenty or so paces she stops and tugs at a door on the left – it is a walk-in cupboard, the shelves stacked with neatly folded white linen and towels. On the floor beneath lies a heap of the bags to which she referred. While she illuminates with the candle Skelgill stoops to inspect them. They remind him of the slings in which rocks are lowered upon the fells by helicopter in order to repair damaged footpaths.

'Aye – a couple of them should do the trick.'

'Then please take them.'

Skelgill gathers up two of the bags. As he rises, behind the girl some low-level lighting flickers into life in the corridor.

'Ah – Mr Merlyn has turned on the generator.' She blows out her candle and places the holder in a niche in the wall. 'This way, please.'

She leads Skelgill to a further door, the last on the left. She presses a switch as she enters and fluorescent strips flash and pop and flood the room with their stark light. Blinking, it is an image that Skelgill recognises – to the extent that he has perused the *Shake Holes Inn* brochure, plucked out of boredom from the tourist information display while kicking his heels at Tebay motorway services. True to the photograph – and his recall – there is a rank of wellington boots, and *Barbour* jackets on a long row of pegs – but what most catches his eye is a wheeled hanging rack of all-in-one overalls. They resemble his outfit – other than their camouflage design (which perhaps Richard Bond will covet). Attached to each hanger is a protective facemask and pair of gloves.

'These look like the ticket.'

'Mr Merlyn has recently introduced paintball. Since we are next to the forest.'

'Beats blasting pheasants, I reckon. And you can shoot your boss.'

She grins nervously.

'Oh, yes – I have not tried it yet.'

She pauses and then inhales as if to add something – but it seems she suffers a change of heart. Skelgill considers her more carefully. He realises now the cause of her silent steps is that she is barefooted; and still she wears only the long nightgown. The air in the room is icy – it has double barn-style doors that are by their nature poorly sealed. Though he is warm enough, he can see his breath, and the girl's as it comes in rapid puffs that seem to belie her calm exterior. She gazes at him suppliantly, her face tilted to reveal the smooth pale flesh of her throat. To his alarm he suffers a sudden flashback to a vampire movie watched in his youth. He starts.

'Are you not cold, lass? – I can manage this now.'

'Oh, no – I am from Vilnius.'

'What's that – Latvia?'

'Lithuania.'

'Sorry.' His features contract with affected contrition.

She smiles patiently.

'Most people do not get as close as Latvia. Or even the Baltic.'

55

Skelgill makes the connection with the prevailing storm. He grins wryly, a little relieved.

'You've brought the weather, right enough.'

'It is a little like home, yes.' She seems consumed, perhaps by a memory – and for a moment once again appears about to speak. But she gives the faintest shake of her head. 'Please – tell me what you would like and I shall help.'

Skelgill realises he is lingering – and that shortly Richard Bond will be breathing down his neck – and, besides, until the passengers are safely back here, he has no cause to dwell.

'Aye, right. I'd say if you can stick all the adult-size wellies into one bag – I'll put these suits in the other. That should do us.'

The girl works quickly and in only a minute she has the job done. While he is finishing off, and before he can object she has the bag over her shoulder and is ready to haul it away – he realises she must be stronger than she looks. Skelgill is hoping that the sledges will be suitable – it is not so much the weight of the bags but their awkward bulging shape. Although he suspects if necessary the ex-soldier will offer to lug both singlehandedly.

Back in the entrance hall there is no one about. But as they deposit their loads the main door flies open to reveal a beaming Richard Bond. He looks like a schoolboy bearing news to the dorm that he has discovered the tuck-shop unlocked.

'Inspector, come and see what I've found!'

With the return of electrical power an external light above the porch has activated. In the fleeting moment that Skelgill hopes for a snowmobile a lusty whinny recalibrates his expectations – a small horse! It is already harnessed to a four-wheeled box trailer stacked with half a dozen plastic children's sledges and what appears to be a golf flagpole.

In most circumstances this would be a bizarre sight. But Skelgill is getting used to Richard Bond's methods. He can picture the scenario: parachuted behind enemy lines, Captain Bond and his unit improvise with the cooperation (or otherwise) of a local farmer. However, even in this genuine peacetime crisis, to press-gang the animal into service in such adverse conditions seems lacking in sentiment. Except – and Skelgill immediately recognises the breed – this is no show pony but a superb specimen of the Lakeland Fell variety. Adapted for life amongst the Cumbrian mountains, with its stocky build, shaggy black coat and great sweeping russet mane it is as hardy a beast as can be imagined; he has heard tell of individuals surviving for months trapped by snow, able to scrape for food with their powerful hooves. It probably beats a snowmobile hands down – and, if his amateur reading of equine body language is anything to go by, it is champing at the bit.

'I've put a couple more ropes in the trailer. We'll be able to use her to pull that fence down.'

'Steady on, man.'

Skelgill can see that Richard Bond's enthusiasm is again getting the upper hand. It seems he plans to take the pony all the way to the train. He'll have them riding rollercoaster in the trailer down the embankment! But Skelgill decides to tackle each hurdle as it arises. Thus a small moment of generosity comes upon him.

'Nice work, Richard.' The man's broad chest swells with the praise. 'Let's load this kit and get our skates on.'

Skelgill turns to the girl, who begins to lift her bag and heave it towards the door. He puts a halting palm on her shoulder. 'That's enough lass – leave it to us. The best help you can be is to get a decent-sized public room nice and warm – where we can thaw everyone out with a hot cuppa. Give us ninety minutes max.'

'Would you like bacon rolls?'

'Make that sixty minutes.'

5. EVACUATION

Thursday, 6.45am

As Skelgill and Richard Bond reach the rear end of the train they are required to divert through the deeper drift at its side. More ponderously, they pass beneath the glow of the lounge car, its windows steamed up and, even in the lee, becoming coated with snow. They each draw a stack of three sledges, a bag of gear roped on top. Their progress has been uneventful; the pony pulled the trailer without a murmur and is now stabled contentedly upon the sheltered deck of the bridge. Skelgill had gently persuaded Richard Bond that this was the optimum strategy, and gravity took care of delivering sledges and laundry bags to the trackside. Experiencing an attack of devilment Skelgill briefly entertained the idea of tobogganing down, and then of building a snowman 'caddy' to hold the golf flag – but his mountain rescue training kicked in, and basic rules such as avoiding gratuitous injury, and unnecessary timewasting, held sway. In the event they settled for rolling a ball in which to plant the marker beneath the footbridge, whence the equipment was easily towed up the more modest incline of the cutting.

Now he checks his watch while Richard Bond thumps on the door of the vestibule situated at the front end of the lounge car; it seems it has become his job so to bang. Skelgill nods with some satisfaction – the return trip has taken them twenty-two minutes. Though conditions are becoming progressively more difficult – in particular the depth of snow – they should get out in good time. And as the sound of the door being unfastened reaches their ears, the intrepid explorers might each secretly be expecting some version of a conqueror's homecoming.

It is Ruairidh the guard who opens it. His expression seems unreasonably hostile – but Skelgill puts that down to a truncated repertoire, a spectrum from dour to disparaging. But when he retreats and DS Jones steps into the breach, Skelgill knows her well enough to understand something is badly amiss. But

Richard Bond is already launching into jokes and guffaws as he heaves first one and then the other bag on board, and scrambles up behind them. Skelgill hangs back in the vestibule while Richard Bond enlists the guard to help him manhandle the gear round into the lounge car, where he might receive the plaudits he seeks. His departure heralds the appearance of a worried-looking DS Leyton. Skelgill turns to DS Jones. She takes a deep breath.

'Guv – there's one passenger missing. And one dead.'

What seems a long silence but which can only be a second or two is broken by DS Leyton.

'Would you flippin' Adam an' Eve it, Guvnor?'

His words might seem facetious – however his tone is anything but. He lifts his broad shoulders and lets them drop with a great sigh. Questions begin to swirl in Skelgill's mind like the flakes caught in the light beyond the glass. But he stares grimly at DS Jones, knowing that at any moment she will provide a far more orderly briefing.

'The dead passenger is the elderly man, Mikal Mital. After you left, the guard knocked at all the compartments, but two people never came to the lounge car.' She glances at DS Leyton for corroboration. 'I went back with him. He used his master key. Compartment one was completely empty and has not been slept in. At that point we assumed the occupant was elsewhere on the train – in the toilet or something. Mikal Mital's is the next cabin, number two. He was in bed, lying on his back – peacefully asleep, it looked like.' She pauses. 'And it appears to be natural causes, Guv.'

Skelgill has been inadvertently holding his breath. Now he exhales between bared teeth.

'And the missing person?'

'Named on the passenger list as Mr Harris. The guard has done a full search of the train. He checked the man on board at Euston. But the thing is, Guv – there's no luggage – and the compartment looks untouched.'

'What about signs of exit?'

DS Jones shakes her head.

59

'As best we can we've looked outside all of the vestibule doors. Apart from where you and Richard Bond jumped out there's no indication of marks in the snow.'

'Who else knows about all this?'

'The guard, obviously – and then just the driver. She's up in her cab. I said we three would come along as soon as you got back.'

'Right – let's go.' Skelgill takes a step but then halts abruptly. A second thought has struck him – it comes back to Lyndon B. Johnson's principle. 'Leyton – bring Bond, will you? Fill him in – top line.'

'Righto, Guv – I'll be with you in a jif.'

Skelgill and DS Jones make their way to the front of the train. Skelgill is a little shocked when he enters the driver's compartment to see the windows entirely encased in snow. The sense of entombment intensifies the news he has been met with. The young woman swivels around in her seat. She is about to speak but Skelgill holds up a palm to silence her.

'I know the story. I shan't beat about the bush. There's some investigation we could usefully do – and procedures we need to follow. But the first priority is to get everyone to safety.' He gestures to include DS Jones. 'We can come back here as necessary – it's not that difficult a hike. And we'll get a message out to summon back-up – I reckon we'll get some priority given the new circumstances.'

The driver nods; she looks drawn and anxious, but before she can respond the sound of voices signals the imminent arrival of DS Leyton and Richard Bond. Skelgill can tell from the latter's animated features that he is apprised of the situation. He immediately addresses Skelgill.

'Do you want to extract the casualty? We can rig up a field stretcher. Carry him between two of us – then use the pony and trailer.'

At this suggestion the two sergeants' eyes fall apprehensively upon Skelgill.

'There's folk better qualified than us to deal with that.' Something about his tone implies a deeper meaning – which

Richard Bond seems to get – and, besides, Skelgill has issued it as an order. He turns to DS Leyton, but puts a hand on the upper arm of Richard Bond. 'Can you pair brief everybody. Leyton – you cover the little difficulty – keep it low key – Richard, you get them organised into the gear. Get their bags down onto the track and roped onto the sledges. Be ready to move out in – what' (he looks at his watch) 'fifteen minutes?'

Richard Bond almost salutes. He is revelling in being part of the official team. DS Leyton puffs out his cheeks, his features somewhat hangdog, the short straw being a familiar outcome.

'One low-key-difficulty briefing coming right up.'

He and Richard Bond depart. Skelgill recapitulates with the driver his plan; they agree she will turn off the electrical power once they are all ready to leave; then they will move together as a body as swiftly as possible, and keep going to minimise the risk of anyone suffering from the effects of cold. Now he asks a belated question of both the driver and DS Jones.

'How many of us are there?'

It is DS Jones who replies.

'Thirteen, Guv – excluding the deceased – and the missing passenger.'

Skelgill furrows his brow. He regards the driver doubtingly.

'I thought it would be more than that.'

She shakes her head, but all the same casts a worried glance at DS Jones.

'We've been through the manifest, Guv. All ten cabins were taken but only three of them were shared. That's six people. Another seven for solo occupancy makes thirteen – minus two. Then add back Laura and the guard.'

Skelgill is now nodding. He makes a face that suggests some small relief.

'There's plenty of choice of kit, then.' He looks at the driver appraisingly. 'Happen you should grab a set that fits – put the same aside for my sergeant. You're not far off the same size.' He turns to DS Jones. 'I take it you've got the master key?'

She nods.

'Show me.'

61

'Sure, Guv.'

As they enter the lounge car the mood is subdued – obviously there is the shock news of their fellow passenger's untimely demise, albeit he was presumably unknown to most of them. Richard Bond is still dispensing advice about fitting gear and packing belongings. They move through inconspicuously. Skelgill notices that the two Russian women are helping one another into their suits, and he catches a snippet of their conversation.

'This is so unbecoming.'

The woman refers to the man-size overall that is inevitably bulky around her tall and slender model's figure.

'Think of it as a fashion opportunity, Wiktoria. I expect to see a creative interpretation on the slopes of St Moritz next season.'

This raises a laugh from Wiktoria Adamska.

'Ivanna, at least I have my *Cartiers* to protect my eyes from the blizzard.'

Skelgill also takes in that 'Eck', Sir Ewart Cameron-Kinloch is glancing slyly at the pair as they dress, while the American Bill Faulkner, quietly getting on with his own business, in turn watches the former government minister, his expression dispassionate. The detectives pass through the interconnecting vestibule into the sleeping car. The ten cabins have their doors on the left as they look.

'Do you want to see the empty one?'

Skelgill hesitates; it feels like an unnecessary diversion.

'Aye, may as well.'

But it is a quick job; there is little of note other than what Skelgill already knows about the layout and facilities. It looks simply like a compartment made ready for occupancy. There is no indication of any disturbance. He merely sticks his head around the door for a few seconds.

'Okay. Next.'

DS Jones is more circumspect in opening number two. She checks the corridor as if for prying eyes before unlocking the door. They shuffle inside.

DS Jones's expression is anxious – and she seems almost relieved to find the body still in its resting place – indeed in its resting pose, as she has described.

It is a policeman's lot to encounter this kind of sight – and much worse at times – but familiarity makes these first few moments no easier – and the presence of a fellow human, expired, has both of them descending into contemplative silence – for here is somebody's relative, friend or loved one.

'Have you checked under the covers?'

'Superficially, Guv. He's wearing pyjamas. There's no sign of blood or obvious injury.'

Skelgill bends and stares more intently.

'How old do you reckon?'

'Seventy-one. There's an American passport in his attaché case.'

Skelgill pulls back.

'American?'

'He must be naturalised. It gives his place of birth as Prague. That would have been during the post-war communist era.'

Skelgill makes no response. Of his many weak suits at school, history rarely pricked his interest unless reference were made to the various annexations of his Celtic homeland – Roman, Viking, Norman – which simply raised his hackles, despite his obvious part-descent from at least one of these tribes.

He removes his gaze from the deceased man and makes a superficial inspection of the compartment. It is much as he would expect of an organised traveller having settled in for the night. The thick tweed suit is on a hanger. Worn but good quality brown leather brogues are pushed together beneath the bunk alongside a small trolley bag. On the shelf at the foot of the bed stand a plastic glass still in its sealed bag and half-drunk bottle of mineral water with the lid off. There is a wash bag on the folding shelf above the sink. And behind the door, opposite the head of the bed is the worn leather attaché case to which DS Jones has referred.

'The light was off, aye?'

'It was, Guv.'

63

Skelgill rotates slowly on his heel. He knows his sergeant is equally if not more eagle-eyed than he – certainly her attention to detail far outstrips his own. Yet his sixth sense tells him he is looking at something that is not quite right. He inhales through clenched teeth, in the way of an ex-smoker scarred by his habit. But if something is wrong... *what is it?* He exhales, hissing with dissatisfaction. He indicates with a jerk of his head that they should go.

'Nowt's going to change here in a hurry. This place will be like a deep-freeze in no time.'

DS Jones is nodding as they step out into the corridor and she makes sure the lock has engaged automatically.

'Guv – just in case a rescue party makes it to the train – I've written a note with timings and details of what has happened and where we are going – it's on the driver's control panel. I figured that would be the first place anyone would look.'

Skelgill, with his back to her, grimaces in silent self-reproach. This basic principle he has overlooked in the greater melee. As he knows from bitter experience, there is little more exasperating than to be summoned to a spot only to find the 'casualty' has walked – leaving mountain rescuers ignorant of his or her fate. At least, as he strides on, he remembers to acknowledge his subordinate's common sense with a thumbs-up sign.

They return pensively to the lounge car to be greeted by an eager Richard Bond.

'All present and correct. Luggage roped on sledges, ready to go. The six younger men, including us, to haul them.'

Skelgill takes in that everyone seems to have on a paintball suit; they stand clutching their masks and gloves in nervous anticipation. In the camouflage material they look like raw recruits awaiting their first parachute jump and wishing they had visited the rest room. Laura, the driver, comes forward with an armful of gear for DS Jones. While she is dressing, Skelgill approaches Richard Bond and speaks quietly.

'You lead. Take it steady. I'll bring up the rear.'

Richard Bond nods decisively; he likes the idea of breaking trail.

'Inspector, I propose a human chain to pass the luggage up the embankment. There ought to be enough of us to span the distance.'

Under some circumstances this would be a reasonable suggestion – a summer's day, perhaps. Skelgill's face reveals his objection. While he has no doubts about the capabilities of DS Jones, of the other four females he cannot be so confident; the cutting is steep and slippery underfoot. Sir Ewart Cameron-Kinloch is decidedly tubby and in his sixties; at the moment he looks like a lost schoolboy, with his pudding face and surprised expression. Neither does Ruairidh the guard strike Skelgill as particularly agile.

'Why don't you go up first with one of the ropes? That means you can start as soon as you reach the flag. Anchor it to the fence. Then everyone can use it to climb. Up top, get them to gather in the shelter of the bridge. I'll tie on the bags – you can haul. I'll send the sledges last of all – may as well hang onto them.'

'Roger.'

It seems Richard Bond needs no convincing – he is programmed to respond to a plan. Skelgill clears his throat and calls out.

'Ready?' The reaction is muted, the atmosphere heavy with apprehension. 'This is not a difficult walk. It's three minutes to the bridge. Follow the tracks in the snow and keep close to the person in front of you. You won't see far, but by all means use the torch on your mobile. There's a short climb out of the cutting and after that it's downhill through the shelter of the pinewoods. Hot cocoa awaits.'

'Hah – how about a hot toddy!'

This is Jenny Hackett that chirps up. But her rejoinder raises only a half-hearted ripple of appreciation.

'Happen we'll know to look in the bar if we lose you in the woods.' Skelgill grins wryly. He raises an arm to indicate towards the forward vestibule. 'Okay – follow Mr Bond.'

As the passengers variously leap, clamber and are helped down from the open door into the swirling snowy darkness and

65

keening wind, Skelgill finds himself last aboard with his two sergeants. The power now goes off and a moment later the driver appears. DS Jones switches on her mobile phone light. Skelgill first addresses his colleagues.

'Mingle as you see fit. Keep your eye on the ladies – make sure no one drifts off course.'

He hands his colleagues down to the trackside to do as bidden. DS Leyton takes up the reins of a laden sledge, making the joke that his kids will be envious when they hear about his adventure. He moves off together with DS Jones; she goes quickly ahead to catch up with the main party. Skelgill assists the driver and then helps her to close the heavy door. It is plain she is distressed.

'What's up, lass?'

'I feel like a captain abandoning ship.'

'Don't fret – you're doing exactly the right thing. Once these folk are safe at the hotel you'll be fine.'

'But – it's – the body – leaving it – alone –'

In the ambient light of his torch Skelgill sees her resilience crack – and without warning she lurches at him and he has no choice but to embrace her. He gets it – this is beyond what can be expected of her rank. He gazes apprehensively over the top of her head, but of course there is no one to see them. He feels her life force, coiled, hot almost, reminiscent of a wild creature, a rabbit extracted from a cruel snare, a ripe cushat blown down from its precarious platform of twigs, a pike even, unhooked and beginning to gasp. But she seems content in his clutches.

'Hey up, Laura – I've had my knuckles rapped by a few Cumbrian lasses in my time – you're tough as they come, you lot.'

But it takes a few moments for her tension to be conducted away, for her to nod and thus indicate that she is ready to stand unassisted. He releases her and takes a step back. 'Come on, lass – we'd better not have them waiting in the cold.' He points with his torch. 'Howay – catch up while I get this sledge.'

*

Initial progress is not as swift as Skelgill has hoped. Though he suspects Richard Bond will be setting a challenging pace at the front, someone – or ones – in the party is decidedly tardy, thus Skelgill has to plod laboriously at the tail. He supposes, for folk unaccustomed to the outdoors, it is a test of their mettle. Even the skiers amongst them are unlikely to have ventured out in darkness into a bullying blizzard; and from what he has gleaned of the sport it is designed to eliminate exercise proper. They must feel more like evacuee submariners, wading in cumbersome diving suits along the seabed, such is the sensory deprivation and the constant buffeting of the gale.

But they make it to the bridge where those most advanced cluster around the marker. He sees that Wiktoria Adamska and Ivanna Karenina are clinging to one another, shivering. Jenny Hackett seems to be consoling a flagging Sir Ewart Cameron-Kinloch. DS Jones and DS Leyton circle like good sheepdogs. Skelgill stomps across to the foot of the embankment, finding the disturbance in the snow where he and Richard Bond have made a track – as he does so a rope comes snaking down; he knows that the ex-soldier will not have tossed it until it is secure – he gives two tugs and feels two in return.

Now he calls out for the group to line up; he sends a protesting Wiktoria Adamska first, followed by Richard Bond's young colleague Egor – and continues with each female chaperoned by a competent male. Again progress seems painfully slow – but he understands that the unknown intensifies their trepidation. Eventually he despatches his sergeants and waits alone until the rope first becomes limp and then two more sharp tugs tell him it is clear for the bags. He might have made an argument that luggage should have been abandoned as an unnecessary luxury that could hamper their safe escape – but, frankly, he wanted his own gear – and should they be marooned for any length of time at the hotel, personal belongings will provide some small comfort. Besides – it has not been so difficult thus far, and now Richard Bond hauls at a prodigious rate; in short order Skelgill is sending up the six plastic sledges nested together, and setting off behind them. The sledges slip from sight, and a few moments later the rope unfurls once more – Skelgill, a quarter of the way up – avails himself of its extra stability, wrapping it around his left forearm. He feels Richard Bond, with good touch taking up the slack and indeed pulling him skywards with impressive strength.

He reaches the shoulder of the cutting to find the group huddled in the comparative shelter of the bridge. The trailer is already loaded with their luggage and the sledges stacked on end. Richard Bond has the rope coiled and slung diagonally over one shoulder; now he attaches it to the rear of the trailer, while DS Jones holds the reins, a calming hand on the unruly mane of the Fell pony. Richard Bond detects Skelgill's scrutiny and calls across to him.

'Inspector – your sergeant has offered to lead. I shall act as brake.' In the light of his torch Skelgill detects a flash of self-reproach in the man's expression – as if he has diagnosed an act of insubordination on his own part. 'If that's okay with you?'

'Aye – let's crack on.'

Skelgill realises that Richard Bond makes a good point – downhill through the forest there is little to stop the trailer running away on the steeper sections. He strides across to DS Jones and with his torch indicates the tracks in the snow that will take them into the woodland. He has to raise his voice to be heard above the wind.

'Keep straight – after a minute the route takes care of itself.'

Skelgill counts them away – a full suit of thirteen beating hearts, his own included; what would he be – the King, the Ace – or the Knave, more like? But as they descend into the tunnel of the bridleway and the conditions moderate, he detects a corresponding lifting of spirits. Sensing the worst is behind them, hunched figures begin to straighten and play their lights upon their surroundings. There is even some cheerful if ghoulish banter, a debate likening their predicament to *Babes in the Wood*, trumped first by the suggestion of *Deliverance* and finally *The Blair Witch Project*. Skelgill speculates that they look more like pilgrims of old, lanterns lit for morale, journeying through the snow in anticipation of hearty respite at the old inn. It might almost be a scene from a Victorian engraving.

The pony is making good speed, and the party begins to string out. Skelgill is not perturbed – the dense pines on either side of the bridleway hem in his charges. It strikes him that if the firm that had booked the hotel had made it to Cumbria, once the storm abated they might have enjoyed a few days' good fun. But, for his 'company', any such frivolity lies over the present horizon – it is not in his nature to count his chickens. On cue, there comes an ear-splitting shriek.

In the darkness ahead forms a sudden conflation of flickering lights and shadowy movements and raised voices; the torches converge – and Skelgill realises the focal point is the snow-filled shake hole over which he and Richard Bond had brooded. He breaks into a jog – and then accelerates as the most prominent cries (they are of a woman) become increasingly desperate.

'I'm sinking! Help – I'm sinking!'

Skelgill does not wait to take in the precise circumstances – he calls out to Richard Bond – shining his flashlight to where he and DS Jones have brought the pony and trailer to a halt. Richard Bond responds – he stoops to untie the rope from the back of the trailer. Skelgill reaches the crowd at the edge of the shake hole. The plaintive voice continues in its despairing appeals. It belongs to the journalist, Jenny Hackett. She is up to her neck in snow.

Skelgill sees now that a prone DS Leyton, at full stretch, has a one-handed grip on her fingers – and he would be falling into the shake hole himself if it were not for the American, Bill Faulkner, who has his sergeant around the waist, and is lying half on top as if he has rugby-tackled him. In turn, Richard Bond's colleagues, Egor and François each have a grip on one of Bill Faulkner's legs. They appear to have reacted instinctively – and have succeeded – but at best it is a holding position. Skelgill swivels to see Richard Bond now approaching – the standing section of the rope is still coiled over his shoulder. Skelgill snatches the working end, passes it around his waist, ties what is probably the

69

quickest bowline he has ever knotted in his life – and plunges into the pit beside Jenny Hackett.

He, too, sinks up to his shoulders – and immediately is reminded of the suffocating properties of drifted snow. But he knows he can rely on Richard Bond – and gains confidence as he feels the slack taken up. From close behind the stricken woman, he embraces her beneath the armpits and forms a double wrist-hold. She is wriggling furiously, and he tightens his grip. Instantaneously Richard Bond begins hauling them out – up and past DS Leyton, who in turn has to be judiciously dragged back, an inch at a time, by the human chain. Skelgill rises, lifting Jenny Hackett to her feet and passing her into the custody of the other females.

Only DS Jones is not amidst the throng at the lip of the shake hole. She has squinted anxiously from the darkness, keeping the pony in check. Skelgill calls out to her that all is well. People are variously reassuring Jenny Hackett, and gingerly patting her down to remove loose snow, and restoring the zip and Velcro fasteners of her suit, which have come undone. Richard Bond struts about barking instructions, but these are merely statements of their situation. Jenny Hackett sounds to be none the worse for her dramatic if brief ordeal.

'I'm fine – I'm fine. Silly me – I just stepped too close. The edge gave way. What a troublemaker you must think me.'

Skelgill beats the snow from his own suit. When satisfied, he sidles across to DS Leyton. He lowers his voice.

'Did you see what happened?'

DS Leyton is still recovering his breath.

'Nah – just heard her scream – I ran towards the sound – someone was shining a light – just managed to reach her hand before she went any deeper. Lucky enough some geezer got hold of me by the goolies – else I'd have been eating snow. There should be a warning sign – that's a flippin' death trap, Guv.'

Skelgill decides now is not the moment for a lecture on the geology of the area. He pats his sergeant on the upper arm.

'Good job, Leyton.' But the praise must seem faint as peremptorily Skelgill turns and calls out to the group. 'Let's move before we start getting cold. Ten minutes and we'll be there.' He adds a rider. 'Don't stray from between the tracks made by the wheels of the trailer.'

As they file away the party remains close now, as if for safety in numbers, their chatter more subdued. Skelgill waits before bringing up the rear. He directs the beam of his torch onto the snow around the curved rim of the shake hole – but there is little to be gleaned; the snow is heavily trodden, and sloughed where he and Jenny Hackett were hauled out and DS Leyton pulled clear. But he ponders grimly for a moment, and the words of DS Jones's ominous revelation echo in his thoughts. *"Guv – there's one passenger missing. And one dead."*

*

Rather ironically, as it turns out, *Shake Holes Inn* boasts fifteen public bedrooms, so it could have accommodated even a full complement of travellers. Ranged around the first floor, these are reached by a single 'square' corridor that traces the quadrangle, its windows overlooking the stable yard. As he presses his nose against the warped antique glass Skelgill watches mesmerised. In the winter dawn he sees that the sheltered courtyard is generating a vortex, akin to an eddy that betrays a deeper pocket in the bed of a stream. The flakes swim tirelessly before his eyes, like an immense shoal of fish. He speculates that in bygone days, for travellers muffled senselessly in greatcoats and blankets, it must have been an uplifting moment to hear the clatter of hooves upon the cobbles. For the horses, too, there was respite after an energy-sapping pull across the stony tracks of the windswept fells. That said, their little Fell pony had been reluctant to return to her stall, and had to be tempted with a nosebag of oats. Skelgill had observed DS Jones's gently persuasive manner with the animal, while he and several of the men were handing the luggage into the tack room.

Together he and DS Jones had been last to reach the residents' lounge – bedecked for Christmas with a tree and twinkling lights – to find the travellers ranged around a crackling log fire, immersed in contrasting aromas of pine resin and fried bacon, and furnished with piping hot tea from an urn. Skelgill had noted that Wiktoria Adamska and Ivanna Karenina merely nibbled at dry biscuits. The option of brandy had been called for – perhaps not unreasonably now in the case of Jenny Hackett – and several members availed themselves of its fortifying properties. Skelgill had contemplated tipping a measure into his tea – but why would you spoil a decent cuppa? The thought causes him to snap out of his trance – for in one hand he bears a recharged mug, and in the other a somewhat dog-eared *Ordnance Survey* map extracted from the library.

The party safe, breakfast and room allocation completed, Skelgill's priorities have moved on. A clock somewhere is striking three-quarters, and he pulls himself away from the view of the courtyard and turns to the door immediately opposite – on which he knocks.

'Just come in!'

The main landing running around the inside of the building, the bedchambers accordingly offer external views, as it happens almost precisely to each of the four points of the compass. In the case of this room – allotted to DS Jones – its windows face due east, and Skelgill sees that the sill and the mullions are piled high with snow, filtering the twilight, and his colleague has switched on the bedside lamps. There is an air of cosiness, enhanced by the muted sough of the wind. DS Jones herself is kneeling beside the nightstand on the far side of her bed, twiddling with the knobs of an old-fashioned analogue radio.

'I feel like we've been transported back in time, Guv.'

Skelgill stands at the door, his expression pensive. When he scrutinised the hotel brochure he had been more struck by the lack of fishing as an activity, when hereabouts numerous little trout becks spring from the limestone. But now he recalls an unpunctuated quotation that had boasted: *"no WI-FI no MOBILE no TV no STRESS"*. On reflection, this might be a case of

72

making a virtue out of thrift, for investment does not appear to feature large in the present management's marketing strategy.

'They say it does you good.'

DS Jones understands his remark to be rhetorical, if a little sarcastic in tone.

'Even this old wireless set, Guv. It's just long and medium wave. If they're all like this we shan't be able to get Radio Cumbria.'

'Let's hope we've made the national news, then.'

Skelgill places his mug on the adjacent nightstand and casts about the room – but he decides the double bed is the best place for his map; he flicks it out with the practised ease of a chambermaid spreading a fresh sheet. He balances with one knee and both hands on the counterpane and leans rather precariously over the newly revealed landscape.

'That's the BBC – I'll turn it up when we hear the pips.' DS Jones clambers lightly onto the foot of the bed and settles into a side-saddle position. She is sockless and Skelgill notices the meticulously silver-painted nails that had complemented her head-turning cocktail outfit of the previous evening. 'Where are we, Guv?'

Skelgill has to steady himself before he can raise a hand. He makes a series of downward sweeping movements, lines that run in parallel to the eastings of the grid.

'M6. West coast main line. A6.' He indicates to a spot near the centre of the map. 'There's the pinewood – there's the hotel.'

'What's the scale?'

'Two-and-a-half inch – to the mile. Probably makes things look further than they are.' He glances at the window. 'Then again, in these conditions, can't be too careful.'

'The journey was less demanding than I expected, Guv.'

'Aye – the trick is not to be lost.' He turns his head to regard her, his expression strained. 'Lost – that's another kettle of fish altogether.'

DS Jones nods reflectively. Then she brightens and casts a hand over the map.

73

'What are you thinking, Guv?'

Skelgill is silent for a few moments, his expression still grim. He stares at the patchily coloured sheet, although his gaze seems to be clouded.

'While it's like this, we sit tight. I want to hear the forecast as much as the news.' He measures out with his left thumb, like a tailor estimating cloth. 'There's farms within a mile or two – but if they're in the same state as us – no communications, maybe no power – there's no point struggling there. Okay – they might have a quad or a tractor – but there's a limit to what they can cope with. Our best bet's Shap village – there's a manned Fire Station – but you're talking seven mile. If the A6 is blocked, you could just end up stranded half way.'

'I could ride, Guv.'

'Ride what?'

'The pony. There's a full set of tack in the stable. They must use her for trekking.' DS Jones points to their position on the map. 'If you could guide me to the A6 – I could surely follow the route safely?'

Skelgill regards his colleague with consternation.

'I used to ride every week as a teenager, Guv. I only stopped when I went away to uni. I can jump fences, you know.'

Skelgill finds himself scrabbling for an objection.

'Aye – but can you jump a ten-foot snowdrift? Even a Fell pony's not going to get you through that.'

DS Jones is about to respond but suddenly she performs a deliberate tumble onto the rug and reaches to turn up the volume on the radio; she has heard the time signal.

'That's nine a.m.'

One thing that can be relied upon – there might be an asteroid about to strike the Earth and the President of the United States might have stolen a rocket and escaped to the Moon – but give the British a chance to talk about the weather and it will relegate all other items to the category of minor news. Foreigners accustomed to extremes rarely experienced in Britain's benign climate must be perplexed that audience ratings can be so boosted by commonplace meteorology – but there it is.

Cynics will argue it is a free hit for the lazy media, but perhaps the public welcomes the respite from political angst, all the same. Thus Skelgill and DS Jones settle to listen introspectively to what is a news report entirely dominated by the weather.

In a nutshell, the Baltic Blast has licked like a great tongue across the north of England and southern Scotland to bring the region to an almost total standstill. Schools are closed, public transport is cancelled; fistfights have broken out over bread and milk. Virtually all roads are impassable, and motorists are warned not to undertake any journeys. The experts now say that the strong easterly winds and accompanying snow will continue for at least the next twenty-four hours. The army has been mobilised to rescue stranded travellers and move them to the nearest places of safety – but it is believed many hundreds of people may be trapped, with no way of knowing who and where they are, a situation exacerbated by damage to power lines and the cell phone network. Aerial surveillance is presently impossible.

At the conclusion of the bulletin a well-spoken announcer intones, with no apparent hint of irony, "And now we present, music for your pleasure, *Desert Island Discs*."

There has been no mention of the train.

Skelgill loosely punches a fist into the opposite palm. DS Jones has been reflecting on what she has heard.

'Just as well you got us here, Guv. Without your knowledge and expertise we could have been in serious trouble.'

Skelgill hams modesty.

'I expect Bond would have thought of something.'

DS Jones smiles knowingly, but does not contradict him. Instead she rises and then resettles herself on the clear side of the bed and rests her head on the pillow. She stretches, catlike, and closes her eyes.

'But probably not as good as this.'

Skelgill seems rather captivated by her actions – but perhaps they bring home to him what they have been through – he in particular – a rude awakening at 4.45am and four hours of responsibility and physical demands. After a moment he pulls

75

the map away and lets it float onto the rug. He rolls onto the bed beside DS Jones and regards her for a moment; she remains unmoving. Her naturally streaked blonde hair is a little dishevelled, but her strong features and smooth olive skin combine to present a picture of serenity. Skelgill grunts as he slips his hands behind his head. The room is warming up as the central heating kicks in – an old-fangled cast iron radiator gurgles and ticks beneath the long window.

'Aye – a nice little mini-break.' Now he, too, closes his eyes. 'If it weren't for a missing passenger and a corpse on the train.'

DS Jones inhales sharply – but she does not yet speak, nor open her eyes. Perhaps she is reminding herself of Skelgill's – of *their* – pressing duty to get a message out about their situation. She inhales again, as though she may now say something – but Skelgill begins to snore.

*

'Er – sorry to butt in, Guvnor.'

DS Leyton clears his throat rather melodramatically. He takes a tentative step inside the room. DS Jones sits up abruptly on the bed, rubbing her eyes with the heels of her hands. Skelgill takes a few seconds longer to wake, he lies blinking.

'Not Crewe again?'

His colleagues look at him with a mixture of amusement and alarm, unsure whether he is clowning. But his apparent confusion clears, and he drags the fingers of both hands through his hair, as if to comb out recalcitrant fragments of his dreams. DS Leyton waits a few more seconds before announcing the purpose of his intrusion.

'What it is, Guv – that reporter, Jenny Hackett – she's insisting on seeing you. She's claiming someone pushed her into that snake hole thing.'

6. THE INN

Thursday, 11am

'It's shake, Leyton – not snake.'

'It says *"Snake Holes Inn"* over the front door, Guv.'

'Aye – it does now – but it started out as *Shake* – take my word for it.'

DS Leyton for a moment looks like he wishes to contest his superior's rather belligerent attitude. 'Snake hole' seems to make far more sense with reference to his metropolitan lexicon.

'Well – she's shaken up about it, that's for sure, Guv. *Hah!*' Characteristically he opts for appeasement.

In any event, Skelgill's mind has moved quickly on.

'Who pushed her?'

Now DS Leyton looks rather blankly at his superior.

'Dunno, Guv. I didn't like to pile in. I thought you'd want to question her. I've told her to come to the library at 11.30 – reckoned you might need a few minutes to get sorted.'

Skelgill is staring out of the window. In the two hours since he nodded off the only evident change in conditions is a partial lifting of the twilight; but still there is a preternatural gloom beneath the constantly shifting shroud of snow; it is the impression of the proverbial 'nuclear winter', when sunlight is banished from the Earth.

'What are the rest of them doing?'

DS Leyton makes a gesture with open hands towards the bed with its crushed pillows and creased coverlet.

'Having a kip, I suppose, Guv. As far as I know everyone's in their rooms.'

Skelgill pats the breast pocket of his shirt; he is feeling for his own room key. He rubs one hand against the emerging stubble on his chin – and then for more accurate confirmation of the time he refers to his wristwatch.

'Twenty minutes – alright?'

77

*

Why Skelgill wanted twenty minutes is not apparent when he joins his colleagues a little behind schedule, for he remains unshaven and wears the same *Levi's* and check shirt; by comparison, on the evidence of her damp hair, DS Jones has showered and has changed back into her skinny jeans, trainers and a college-style hoodie. DS Leyton is poking at embers that smoulder in the hearth – unproductively in Skelgill's estimation. He is about to take charge when he notices on the wall furthest from the door a framed map of the immediate vicinity that he had overlooked on his previous visit, when instead he had made a beeline for a stack of folded maps and local guides, that included several well-thumbed *Wainwrights.*

The library is ostentatiously decorated in a concoction of deep wines and burgundies (a misguided 1980s refurbishment that pervades much of the establishment), albeit imbuing a certain vulgar cosiness. There is a firm-looking chesterfield sofa beneath the window, another to the left of the door; otherwise winged armchairs each with an occasional table arranged around the fireplace accommodate four people – so it is more of a snug reading room than a traditional reference library such as might be found in a stately home; there are a couple of bookshelves mainly populated with doorstopper paperbacks which Skelgill suspects guests have abandoned unfinished. He saunters across to the map; it is dated "1959" and he notes there is no motorway to the east; the A6 was the only route north when this region was surveyed. It is *Ordnance Survey* at its finest level of detail, in monochrome on aged sepia, a scale of 1:10,560 or six inches to one mile, sufficient to represent the inn with its stable yard drawn. There is no trace of the coniferous plantation, just some deciduous woodland that forms its present-day fringe. He peruses the landforms with a critical eye, and as is his wont is becoming absorbed when a self-assured female voice penetrates his thoughts.

'Good morning, Cumbria CID – so glad to have you on the case.'

Skelgill starts but resists the inclination to swivel around; his innate obstinacy rails against such presumption on the part of Jenny Hackett, despite that she speaks in jest. He waits a moment while DS Jones organises a seating plan. DS Leyton gives up on the fire and calls to his superior.

'Want me to sort some tea, Guv?'

'Aye.' Skelgill taps the map decisively with the index and middle fingers of his left hand and turns a self-satisfied grin on the group. He does not elaborate upon what little triumph he may have achieved. Now that DS Leyton has retreated he takes up a poker and ruthlessly attacks the embers in the grate, before tossing on a trio of split pine logs taken from a tarnished brass log box embossed with the image of a running fox. Almost immediately flames begin to lick hungrily at the fresh, dry timber. 'May as well make ourselves comfortable.'

DS Leyton reappears promptly – it seems he has encountered Samanta the housekeeper nearby and has placed their order. He takes the remaining available chair, nearest to the fire. Jenny Hackett casts about the room – Skelgill can't help wondering if she is checking for a drinks trolley – but perhaps it is just to verify that DS Leyton has closed the door, for now she assumes the conspiratorial manner of the previous evening, hunching over as if inviting them into a confidential exchange. Her tone becomes strained.

'How deep was that hole, Inspector?'

It is not the question that Skelgill has been expecting. He makes a face of discontent.

'There's no knowing. Happen it were deep enough to swallow you up – I didn't feel the ground under my feet. The snow supported us to some extent – but flail about and you start to dig your own grave.'

'An uncompromising prognosis.'

She inhales between clenched teeth – and then plies him with a grateful smile. He thinks she looks older this morning, the crow's feet at the corners of her deep-set eyes more pronounced, her hair lacking structure and its colour suggesting a grey undertone; it is as if her ordeal has taken some toll – but maybe she had been 'dolled up' for the posh dinner, and this is her more regular appearance.

'I did not get chance to thank you properly – you were marvellous – such quick thinking. Didn't I tell you – *Skelly's Heroes!*'

Any emergent preening on Skelgill's part rapidly dissipates. That she might pen such an article seems to be a growing threat. He glowers darkly.

'You've since told Sergeant Leyton that someone pushed you.'

'In the heat of the moment it seemed inopportune to mention it.'

'Why?'

Jenny Hackett shrugs – and makes to answer – but she refrains because the door opens and Samanta enters bearing a tray. Skelgill looks up frowning; the girl detects his displeasure and appears fearful – but she cannot know they are in the throes of a sinister revelation, and his expression softens, indeed becomes something of a belated grin. Now attired in a long charcoal tube dress that clings sufficiently to show her slender, even skinny form, there is a pathos about her demeanour, and dark shadows beneath her eyes and a red mark on her left cheek that had escaped his notice earlier. But she moves efficiently amongst them, dispensing their refreshments and making a subtle exit before he can take in much more, closing the door carefully behind her.

It is Jenny Hackett's cue to resume where she had left off.

'At the time I couldn't believe it – that someone would have pushed me – and then, as I began to regain my senses – well, I suppose it felt rather unworthy, to cast aspersions when several of you risked danger to rescue me.'

Now she looks generously at DS Leyton. He seems a little abashed, unaccustomed to praise from members of the public. But it is Skelgill who replies.

'You definitely were pushed?'

The woman sits more upright and folds her arms – but she nods decisively.

'A sharp shove between the shoulder blades, Inspector.'

Skelgill is regarding her interrogatively.

'Can you describe what actually happened?'

Jenny Hackett relaxes her pose. She looks from one to the other of the detectives as though to assess the quality of their attention. The professional in her appears to have processed and packaged the story ready for consumption.

'When Richard Bond briefed us about the trek that we were to undertake, I suspect he tried to scare us into submission by highlighting the dangers of wandering off course – primarily of getting detached from the party, and lost – but then he warned us about these terrifying 'shake holes' that swallow up sheep and humans like this is some sort of predatory landscape from a Tolkein fantasy. However, once we reached the woods and the conditions eased, I think we were all becoming blasé – you may recall there were jokes about *Babes in the Wood* and suchlike – and when someone identified what could have been a shake hole we were enticed by the thrill of the unknown.'

'Who spotted it?'

'Of that – I am not certain.' She speaks more slowly – and now her tone becomes less assured. 'You see, I was walking – I think – closest to Wiktoria and Ivanna – and they both exclaimed, something like, *"Ah – yes!"* – as though someone else had said it first. There were lights flickering about – and the hole was only – what – a couple of yards off the path? Else no one would have noticed, I suppose. We had hold of one another – in trepidation – as we went to the edge.'

'So it couldn't have been either of them?'

'I don't think so – I don't know.' She inhales – that she vacillates strikes Skelgill as an unhelpful contradiction. 'I wasn't really concentrating – and it was basically pitch black – and there was the crashing of the wind in the branches. Anyone may have crept up behind without my realising. I'm sure both girls made a grab for me as I fell.'

Skelgill persists with his narrow line of questioning.

'Have you mentioned this – have you asked the two ladies – what they saw?'

81

'Good heavens, no.' She smiles in a way that might be apologetic, yet tinged with reproach. 'In my game one doesn't so glibly let the cat out of the bag, Inspector.'

Skelgill begins to gnaw at the corner of a thumbnail. It seems she is seeking to preserve some journalistic angle. And perhaps she reveals an ingrained distrust of those around her, knowing that everyone eventually talks, at a price. The flames that lick upwards over the logs in the grate capture his gaze; a movement from DS Leyton suggests some physical discomfort. It seems to prompt Skelgill to change tack.

'Ok – so we don't know who. But why, then?'

'Last night I spoke with Mikal Mital and this morning he was dead.'

Her riposte seems indecently forthright.

'What are you suggesting?'

Jenny Hackett glances sharply at Skelgill – as though she suspects his question to be disingenuous.

'He was about to spill the beans at the Edinburgh symposium.'

It takes Skelgill a moment to respond.

'Aye – you'd mentioned that. Did he tell you what exactly?'

The journalist shakes her head dismissively, as though this is in fact a poorly considered question, and that she would not be beating about the bush if she knew otherwise.

'Of course not, Inspector. But he was observed by all those present to be in conversation with me.' She gestures loosely to indicate the three detectives. 'This was after you had retired. He had been reviewing a manuscript. The rumour mill has it that he was writing a book and an unseemly scrum of publishers have been brandishing blank advance cheques.' She looks about as though she is in need of something; but she sighs and shrugs. 'He would have considered it to be more of the same, filthy lucre – I believe he was a communist of the old school.'

'Did he show it to you – this manuscript?'

'He slipped it into his briefcase the moment that I sat down.'

'Did he know who you are?'

She nods unhesitatingly.

'Naturally.' She flutters her lashes in a small act of immodesty. 'You might say we represent opposing factions of the same alliance. He seemed to hold no grudges against me personally.'

'What do you mean by that?'

Again she plies Skelgill with a penetrating glance, her head tilted so that her eyes are only just visible beneath her prominent brows.

'Do you read *The Inquirer*, Inspector?'

Skelgill's journal of choice is *Angling Times*, in which political debate tends to be restricted to whether it is ethical to use boilies for carp and boobies for trout; but he knows vaguely of her newspaper's uncompromising reputation.

'Is that why he wouldn't talk to you about his work?'

'It is usually only whistleblowers who will speak freely to me – under conditions of extreme confidentiality.'

'But you're saying he's a whistleblower of a sort.'

'That may be partially correct. But he is not an insider – which I think is a requirement of the designation. Besides, he had the reputation for an extraordinary level of secrecy. He did not operate online, or even own a computer. He was renowned for a prodigious memory.'

Again she takes a moment to look at each of the detectives. DS Jones responds to what she reads as an invitation to treat.

'But, surely – how would he conduct his research?'

Jenny Hackett regards the younger woman rather forgivingly.

'When your enemies have the entire apparatus of a modern state at their command I imagine they can hack into anything – your laptop, your phone – your fridge, even. But not yet a manual typewriter.' She hesitates, perhaps realising she has not directly answered the question; she waves a hand aimlessly. 'He was alleged to be furnished by a network of contacts with intelligence from all corners of the globe. No system of course is foolproof. Telephones can be tapped. Mail can be intercepted. Meetings can be eavesdropped upon. And, yes, individuals can be nobbled.'

Skelgill seems to be absorbing her analysis; though his expression remains doubtful.

'What *did* you talk about?'

'Oh – I was making a pitch of my own. At my paper we are hard-wired to unmask the great and the good. Our readers feast upon such tales. I suppose I was hoping he might drop me a few crumbs in advance of his speech. In return he would receive a glorious fanfare.'

'But he didn't – drop you any crumbs?'

Skelgill wonders if a jolt from the woman's conscience fleetingly clouds her features.

'Oh – merely his general thesis.'

'And what would that be?'

'Has it not occurred to you, Inspector, that the majority of the world's super-rich – this crude new class that has been unleashed upon us in the past couple of decades – hail from failed states with economies that leave most of their populations languishing in poverty? How can that be? How come half of Knightsbridge is owned by offshore companies nested like Russian dolls to hide their true beneficial owners – obscure bureaucrats from countries of which most people have never even heard? How come presidents wear wristwatches that cost more than their annual salaries – and sail in private super yachts that could build a dozen provincial hospitals? Mikal Mital's shadowy network comprises loose-tongued facilitators and financiers who enable the billions extracted from national budgets and state-owned companies to be laundered.'

Jenny Hackett looks around her audience – perhaps a little pityingly.

'Need I go on?'

An awkward silence prevails. Skelgill appears especially conflicted. He swallows, as though there is a lump in his throat – and he reaches for his tea and drains the cup. It falls to DS Jones to muster a structured rejoinder.

'It would be fair to say that this offence is increasingly receiving coordinated attention from the relevant authorities. We have the instrument of the Unexplained Wealth Order since the Criminal Finances Act, for instance.' Jenny Hackett is nodding – but her narrowed eyes betray a deeper sentiment, of cynicism. 'Are you saying, madam, that Mikal Mital was about to expose a particular individual – or organisation – or government?'

Jenny Hackett snorts, rather unbecomingly.

'I'm certain he was.'

'Some geezer on the train?'

All heads swivel to look at a red-faced DS Leyton. He can generally be trusted to point out the elephant in the room, even when wondering what it is himself. DS Jones appears shocked. Jenny Hackett, excited. But Skelgill is scowling ever more deeply. And now he intervenes decisively. He addresses the journalist.

'Madam – *Jenny.*' His affable correction comes too late to conceal that he has formal police procedures in mind. 'If you could leave us for now – we need to discuss how to take this forward – your allegation of being pushed.' Now he curses inwardly, for still his language smacks of officialdom. It must be plain to her journalistic instincts that he does not intend to air his concerns in her company. But, perhaps to his surprise, she opts not to dig in her heels – and graciously she rises to take her leave.

'Certainly, Inspector. I shall be at your disposal. Perhaps in the bar.' She regales him with an enigmatic smile. 'Bearing in mind our illustrious passenger list, I shall feel safer in full public view.'

Her peal of sardonic laughter seems to resonate about the library even after she has closed the door. Skelgill's subordinates wait expectantly. The fire is growing in intensity – DS Leyton is beginning visibly to perspire – and he wipes his brow, flicking aside his tousle of dark hair. It seems he can hold back no longer.

'Cor – what do you reckon, Guv?'

'About what?'

It is immediately apparent that Skelgill is being capricious – something that no doubt has its roots in his own inner turmoil,

85

for he resents being pressed for a perspective when he is disoriented.

'Well – I dunno, Guv – I suppose she's saying someone's out to get her. If she's right – she's still in danger, ain't she?'

'What if she jumped, Leyton?'

'*Whoa!*' DS Leyton is wide-eyed. 'Into the snake hole?'

Skelgill ignores both the persistent descriptive error and what is a perfectly reasonable objection. He glares into the rising flames.

'Think about last night, Leyton. She was all over everyone like a rash. The main crowd when we arrived – then us three – the American – and Mikal Mital after we'd gone to bed. So now she wants us to rattle their cages so she can watch the feathers fly.'

DS Leyton's bewilderment grows – it seems to him that his superior is being unreasonably cynical, irrationally so.

'But, Guv – she nearly came a cropper.'

Skelgill perhaps shows a hint that he might relent – that he recognises his flimsy hypothesis is borne out of petulance. Indeed, it is not even his custom to make such wild assertions. His tone becomes more measured.

'Leyton – if she *were* pushed – aye, like you say, she could still be in danger. But what's the logical conclusion?'

'I'm not sure where you're going, Guv.'

'What does it say about Mikal Mital – *that he was killed?* That's a big leap to make. We can't just cook up a murder investigation on the say-so of a scrawny old hack who's scratting about for a scoop.'

Skelgill's words are perhaps unintentionally cruel, signalling his underlying discomfiture. A silence descends, but for the logs that spit like discontented cobras. Eventually DS Leyton, his cheeks burning in the face of the now ferocious blaze speaks, his tone philosophical.

'It's out of the frying pan and into the fire, Guv.'

His idiom might be inspired by his proximity to the heat source – but his words surely reflect their collective sentiments; there they were, speeding home for Christmas, only to be headed off by the Baltic Blast. While they have circumvented the worst of the storm, they find themselves pitched into a quandary of another magnitude altogether.

DS Jones is next to speak. Her tone, however, is decidedly more buoyant.

'Guv – what about Mr Harris?'

'Come again?'

'The missing passenger.'

Skelgill grimaces – as if there isn't enough on his plate. Not believing in the supernatural, or teleportation, or invisibility, he has somewhere along the line relegated the fact of the absentee to an administrative or observational error on behalf of the guard. Why worry about something that may never have happened?

'If he existed.'

DS Jones persists.

'But, Guv – what I mean is – whether he exists or not – it provides us with a plausible excuse to interview everybody.'

DS Leyton now perks up.

'What if he's been hiding, Guv – followed us – what if he were the cove that sneaked up and pushed her in?'

Like a terrier discombobulated by half-a-dozen rats simultaneously breaking cover in as many directions, Skelgill can think of so many practical objections that he can't answer – other than rather disdainfully to ignore his sergeant. He sits muted. Then he rises and stomps across to the large-scale map from which he was earlier torn away. After a minute's perusal he clears his throat. He turns to face his colleagues.

'Fine – we'll talk to them.' He seems to be looking hard at DS Jones – but perhaps she is just in his line of sight, for he speaks as if to himself. 'But first – there's something I need to do.'

'What's that, Guv?'

Skelgill looks startled.

'Go back to the train.'

DS Jones's neatly curved eyebrows rise imploringly.

'Can I come with you?'

87

Skelgill's countenance remains severe – but it belies his reply, which is suddenly casual.

'Aye, alright.'

'What about me, Guv?' There is a note of trepidation in DS Leyton's voice and he glances anxiously at the window.

'Leyton – you said it yourself. Someone needs to make sure one of the others doesn't murder Jenny Hackett.'

DS Leyton does not look entirely disappointed, although his outlook may be about to change.

'But – what should I do, Guv?'

'I don't know, Leyton – use your imagination. You're the one with bairns. Keep them entertained – think up some parlour games.'

7. THE TRAIN

Thursday, 12pm

'I'm not sure I've ever heard of a shake hole, Guv. Sink hole, swallow hole, yes. I chose history over geography. We all had a crush on the teacher.'

Skelgill eschews the temptation to be led off script and stares broodingly at the small round crater. He replies, speaking slowly.

'I don't know much about geography. Mostly I've learned from experience, out on the fells. Swallow hole – that means it's got a beck disappearing down into it. Sink hole – aye – except that's a general term – that can be a mineshaft or a sewer that's given way. A shake hole's what you get in limestone – the rain filters through the acid bog and dissolves the joints between the rock fragments and eventually there's a collapse. There's hundreds of them in this neck of the woods.'

'Are there many – actually in the woods?'

DS Jones does not intentionally take literally his idiom, but he responds regardless.

'Bear in mind this plantation's nobbut forty year old. The shake holes are mostly ancient – though some of them are still forming, you can tell where the vegetation around the banks is torn. Folk used to think they were caused by surface mining – but pits dug by humans always have spoil heaps nearby.'

'It doesn't look much – covered in snow. You wouldn't know it was dangerous.'

Skelgill continues to glower.

'Aye – happen Bond should have kept his trap shut.'

'I wonder if anyone will admit to being the person who pointed it out.'

Skelgill glances sideways at his colleague.

'Most likely it was Bond himself.'

But DS Jones furrows her brow.

'I'm not sure about that, Guv. I was quite close to him. I think I would have heard if he'd called out a warning.'

Skelgill does not look convinced. He rubs a hand across his eyes.

'Come on, lass. Time and tide.'

It is an apt simile – for new snow is progressively eradicating the tracks made by the collective comings and goings, much as the first ripples of a flow tide erase footprints from exposed sands. Once in the open, subjected to the full force of the gale, they draw in their hoods and, blinking away snowflakes, slip-slide into the comparative shelter of Shake Holes cutting. Here too their tracks are almost obliterated, and the going is challenging. When the rear carriage of the express looms into sight, they are shocked by the rapid progression of its of entombment. In the hours since the train embedded itself in the main snowdrift, a good eight inches have settled upon its roof – but much deeper drifts have accumulated along the flanks and they have to wade through thigh-high powder to reach the first available entrance. DS Jones is prompted to call out.

'I feel like the train is going to disappear altogether.'

'Happen it will if the forecast is right. Then what did they say – it's to stay below zero for a week? None of this'll be going anywhere – snow or train.'

Skelgill wrenches open the door and prises himself inside, then rotates and gives a hand up to his colleague. She could make it easily enough, but she accepts his assistance. They stand close for a moment. In the stillness of the carriage their steamy breath fuses in the air between them.

'You were right about it being like a deep freeze, Guv.'

'Aye. At least that's one thing we don't have to worry about.'

DS Jones makes a face that reflects the gruesome aspect that overshadows their task: that Skelgill refers to the mortuary-like conditions. They have entered the train between the guard's van and the sleeping car, and now they make their way along the corridor to compartment number two. DS Jones has the master key, and she rips open the *Velcro* of her suit to reach an inner zip pocket. She unlocks the door but hesitates for a second, perhaps steeling herself. She steps inside, glances briefly to her right at the corpse, and then partially closes the door – before re-emerging with Mikal Mital's attaché case. She transfers it to Skelgill's grasp. He re-presents it at chest height while she lifts the flap and delves inside.

'The passport. Text books. Newspapers. *Private Eye*.' She shakes her head. 'That's it, Guv – no manuscript.'

Skelgill stares implacably at his colleague.

'He might have slept on it.'

For a moment she thinks he is using the figure of speech – then she realises what he means – she makes a resigned face and nods. Skelgill puts down the briefcase and they shuffle into the compartment.

'It's potentially a crime scene, Guv.'

'Aye – but what can we do – we need to know if it's here or not. Get ready.'

Skelgill raises each end of mattress, body and all – while DS Jones peers beneath. It is all clear. Skelgill checks that the bundle of papers could not be concealed within the covers. Then DS Jones takes a series of photographs on her mobile phone, and they make a search – but Mikal Mital's trolley bag contains only spare clothes and personal effects, and there is no cupboard space – only the top bunk folded away, and it yields nothing. Skelgill tries the sliding door that enables paired cabins to adjoin – for instance, were compartments numbers one and two engaged for the use of a single family. But it is locked.

They rather stumble out into the corridor. Both inhale and exhale more deeply than normal, as though the sinister claustrophobia of the cabin has inhibited their breathing. After a moment DS Jones indicates to the door of Mikal Mital's compartment.

'Guv – when we went in previously – when I first showed you the body –' Her inflection is inquisitive and she hesitates, uncomfortable to be querying her boss. 'Did you pick up the water bottle from the shelf at the foot of the bunk?'

'Don't reckon so.'

DS Jones's expression becomes strained.

'When I entered – I mean just now – the label was turned away. The first time – I'm sure it was facing outwards.'

91

Skelgill is scowling; but his disquiet is aimed inwardly – he is wondering if he did inadvertently lift it.

'What made you notice that?'

'This morning – in my cabin – Wiktoria Adamska mentioned she only drinks mineral water – she complained that it was a cheap Scottish brand. Actually, I've always thought of it as being a bit pricey. I suppose it stuck in my mind. It was in my line of sight when the guard opened the door.'

Skelgill raises an eyebrow but does not offer a rejoinder. DS Jones regards him insistently.

'Guv – the manuscript is gone. We know it exists because we saw Mikal Mital reading it. What if someone drugged him by putting something in his water? They stole the manuscript – and switched the water bottle.'

Skelgill steps sideways and raps with his knuckles upon the door of compartment number one.

'Open this up, lass.'

DS Jones does as he bids. Skelgill enters and immediately tries the interconnecting door to Mikal Mital's cabin. It remains locked. He retreats to sit on the unslept-in bunk. 'Have a pew.' He pats the bed to indicate DS Jones should settle likewise.

'Listen. When you went in with the guard – obviously that was a shock, right?' DS Jones nods – the discovery of the dead man was not what she had expected. 'But you had the presence of mind to check him over – search his belongings – you looked in his briefcase for ID and found his passport. Think – what about the manuscript?'

But DS Jones is already shaking her head, consternation clouding her hazel eyes.

'I know what you're asking, Guv. I was looking for a wallet or similar – and the passport was in the pocket on the front, under the flap. The main section was full of stuff like it is now. I didn't go through it – there was no need. I certainly didn't notice the manuscript – but I couldn't swear either way.'

Skelgill makes a hissing sound between bared teeth. He flings a hand in the direction of the interconnecting door.

'These locks — they're child's play to anyone who knows what they're doing. Never mind if you've got hold of a master key.'

'And for egress, Guv. Someone coming out of here into the corridor would look far less suspicious if they were seen. And by relocking the interconnecting door it's not obvious that entry may have been gained to the next cabin.'

Skelgill leans forward, his forearms upon his thighs and stares pensively at the shiny grey bulkhead a few inches from his face. He is a little alarmed by the many unevidenced permutations that they could probably concoct. But the mysteriously empty compartment and its convenient location seem to be straws driven on the same wind of conspiracy as the missing manuscript, Jenny Hackett's claimed shove between the shoulder blades, and now DS Jones's observation that there has been tampering in Mikal Mital's cabin. He makes a sudden contemptuous expiration of air.

'What is it, Guv?'

'If someone took that manuscript — I've made a nice job of shipping it out for them. And now they've had four hours to find a hiding place.'

DS Jones shakes her head.

'We could never have anticipated the manuscript being stolen, Guv. Not unless we had clear grounds to believe that Mikal Mital was murdered.'

'Which there isn't.'

'I know, Guv.' DS Jones spreads her palms in a gesture of exasperation. 'How do you find a pathologist in a blizzard?'

'That sounds like one of Leyton's jokes.'

DS Jones chuckles.

'It is certainly a conundrum. If only we knew who or what Mikal Mital was about to expose. We might have a suspect in our sights.'

'Why would some international high-flyer get their hands dirty?'

DS Jones turns to look at her superior.

'You mean a hitman?'

'Hitman, hitwoman.'

DS Jones eyes Skelgill warily; if he is being flippant he appears indifferent to her scrutiny.

'Do you think Jenny Hackett has the manuscript, Guv?'

The suggestion prompts another scoff of disparagement from Skelgill.

'Doesn't matter what I think – but I reckon *someone* might think that.'

'If she's telling the truth about being pushed?'

'Aye. Get her out the road – inspect her suitcase at leisure.'

'If so, it proved to be an inadequate method of assassination.'

'It was an opportunity. Desperate person – their plans awry – needs must. Who knows? Besides – if she'd have gone under, sunk deeper – who's to say we'd have pulled her out in time.'

Skelgill clicks his tongue in what might be a rueful manner. DS Jones is pondering his words. She taps together the tips of her slender fingers and then intertwines them, resting her wrists upon her lap.

'To murder Mikal Mital – in the first place it would have required premeditation.' (Skelgill shrugs as though he does not consider this to be a hurdle worthy of concern.) 'If there were drugs or poison involved – that would stack up – the planning, I mean.' However, she frowns. 'But surely they would need to know his travel arrangements?'

'Which is an argument in favour of it being opportunistic – a rival of whoever he was going to expose – a potential blackmailer – or a journalist.'

DS Jones nods pensively.

'Thing is, Guv – in virtually all of those scenarios, it's most likely the perpetrator would be best served if Mikal Mital were dead.'

Skelgill looks like he might disagree. He rocks his head from side to side.

'I reckon Jenny Hackett would have settled for a sneak preview. She made no bones about wanting the scoop – or that she was pumping him for a story. All she needed was to beat his announcement by a day. If it were her that caused his death, then it must have been an accident – a Mickey Finn that was too strong for his system – or, it were a coincidence, natural causes.'

But now Skelgill stands up and flexes his troublesome spine. He exhales and groans simultaneously. It is part frustration that prompts him – he has an inbuilt alarm that sounds when there are too many 'maybes' in a conversation. Then he proceeds to break his rule.

'Happen one of the passengers saw something that'll shed light on it.'

'Maybe one of them saw Mr Harris, Guv.'

Skelgill makes a face of doubt – but it is an expression that changes to disbelief – and he glances at DS Jones to meet her own gaze of alarm. She nods. They have both heard a mechanical clunk.

Skelgill steps closer to the open compartment door and listens. More noises, faint at first, begin to reach them. It sounds like someone is now aboard the train – and moving in their direction. He jerks a thumb, indicating that he believes the intruder is coming from the rear. And now it is certain, as sharp footsteps begin to approach along the corridor.

'Get ready.' Skelgill whispers, the faintest hiss. And he stands, pressed against the bulkhead so that the approaching person will not see him until the last second.

The footfall comes at a steady pace. The person seems to be intending to pass through the sleeping car rather than try any of the doors. But as they near they slow – heightening Skelgill's state of alert. He is coiled – he waits for another step – and pounces like a great tarantula darting from its burrow to snare his unsuspecting prey.

'Police!'

As he cries out simultaneously there is a piercing shriek and too late he realises it is a woman no bigger and heavier than DS Jones – but his momentum is committed and he dumps her unceremoniously upon the bunk. She has an arm above her head for protection – Skelgill starts back and raises both hands to indicate he means her no harm – and DS Jones steps in to place a calming palm on the shocked woman's shoulder.

'Cumbria CID – it's okay, madam – but what are you doing on the train?'

Perhaps that DS Jones uses the polite term 'madam' conveys that they are not some latter-day highway robbers – and the woman lowers her guard – though consternation still creases her features. Skelgill has fished out his warrant card and her pale blue eyes focus upon it and then rise to engage his own with a disconcerting degree of penetration. He guesses she is around his own age. She has short fair hair cut stylishly, and smooth tanned skin, regular features with blonde eyebrows, a small faintly retroussé nose and full lips that glisten with a protective layer of *Vaseline*. The tip of her nose and her cheeks are flushed from exposure to the cold. She is clad in a long Australian-style waxed-cotton riding coat that covers her in its entirety, down to the ankles of polished black leather boots caked with snow. Her breathing is rapid and shallow and she inhales more deeply to speak. She chooses not to answer DS Jones's question – but instead comes out fighting, commensurate with the look in her eyes.

'Is it your regular practice to manhandle innocent members of the public, Inspector?'

Her accent is refined, with no trace of northern vowels.

'It was for your own safety, madam – there has been a fatality on the train. We have evacuated the remaining passengers to *Shake Holes Inn.*'

Skelgill's formally enunciated explanation is somewhat irrational, and his manner unapologetic. But there is a distinct softening of her demeanour.

'Oh – I see.' She sniffs and raises a cuff momentarily to her nose. 'I saw what must be your flag beneath the footbridge – and tracks in the snow. I thought it possible that the train was abandoned.'

Skelgill regards her more forgivingly – it seems he has won the little battle of wills. Now DS Jones repeats her entreaty.

'Madam, can you tell us, please – who you are – and why are you aboard?'

The woman shudders, and sighs rather defeatedly – it might be a delayed reaction to the rush of adrenaline that she has experienced.

'My name is Lucinda Hobhouse. I run an equestrian centre near Ulphathwaite. I heard that the London sleeper was believed to be trapped on Shap Fell.'

Skelgill is looking at her dubiously.

'Ulphathwaite is five miles away. How did you get here?'

'Nicholas Mistress.'

Now the woman smiles; her composure seems restored, and her eyes glint with the knowledge that she is being abstruse.

'What?' Skelgill struggles to process her unexpected words.

'Surely you have heard of him – he won the Stayer's Hurdle at Aintree four years ago. He might be retired– but he has lost none of his steeplechaser's stamina.'

Skelgill is still scowling but DS Jones butts in.

'You mean you came on horseback?'

'That is exactly what I mean, officer. My trusty steed is tethered to the rear of the train.'

Skelgill's tone remains sceptical.

'What route did you take?'

'The railway passes through my land. It seemed the expedient approach – under the circumstances.' She regards him calmly and then looks at DS Jones. Perhaps she is half expecting that they might accuse her of trespassing, but when no such reproach is forthcoming she continues. 'And to answer your question – I am trained in first aid – and I have some basic medicines.' She pats a pocket of her coat. 'Since the emergency services are stretched to breaking point – I thought I might do my bit.'

Skelgill has heard enough to satisfy himself of her bona fides. He seizes upon the implication of her statement.'

'Do you have communications?'

'Not as such. I am snowed in at the stables with three of my staff and four guests. We are entirely offline, as far as internet and telephone is concerned. But we can reach the village on horseback. There is an operational landline at the post office. That is where I picked up the news about the train this morning.'

97

Skelgill can sense that DS Jones is staring at him; but when he does not reciprocate, she takes matters into her own hands.

'What kind of saddle do you have?'

Lucinda Hobhouse regards the younger woman with surprise.

'A bareback pad, as a matter of fact.'

DS Jones does not waver.

'I'd like you to take me to the post office.'

Skelgill glances in alarm at DS Jones – clearly irked that she has not consulted him. But he stays any further reaction, conscious of Lucinda Hobhouse's inquisitive gaze. Indeed, she rises and they each step aside to make room, as though she is now one of their cohort.

'Well – certainly it will be satisfying to know that my expedition has not been in vain. I'm only sorry I could not bring the buggy – else I could have driven you both. But I think three of us would be too much even for Old Nick – a big chap like you, Inspector.'

She briefly places a palm on Skelgill's chest. He makes an involuntary movement, to recoil, but is restricted by the bulkhead at his back. He frowns. He does not think of himself in such terms – he is just a couple of inches above average height, and rangy of build – the shorter DS Leyton must weigh a good deal more than he. Rather gruffly, he coughs up a reply.

'Don't worry, madam – one of us needs to go back to the others.'

The woman rocks forwards on the balls of her feet as if she is keen to move – but then she hesitates.

'What about – if you don't mind my asking – you said there was a fatality?'

Once again Skelgill can sense that DS Jones is watching carefully for his reaction.

'An elderly gent – he may have suffered a heart attack.' Skelgill makes a face of displeasure. 'We've had to leave the body here on the train. Obviously that's why we need to inform the relevant authorities. Under the circumstances there are procedures such as notifying the Coroner. And there's the likes of next of kin to think about.'

'Of course.' Lucinda Hobhouse looks from Skelgill to DS Jones. 'In which case, oughtn't we hightail it?'

DS Jones reacts by taking a step towards Skelgill, but he is blocking the door and seems reluctant to give way. His expression is unnaturally blank but in his grey-green eyes there is an anxiety aimed at his colleague, as though he is trying through telepathy to communicate some coded message. But DS Jones seems unperturbed. She squeezes past Lucinda Hobhouse and places a hand on Skelgill's arm, applying enough pressure to get him to begin to back out of the compartment.

'Don't worry, Guv – I know exactly what I need to do.'

8. INTERVIEWS

Thursday, 2pm

'Just come in, Leyton!'

Skelgill's raised voice follows several attempts, knocking and calling, by his sergeant to gain his attention. But when DS Leyton enters the room it appears empty, although Skelgill's railway-issue overall lies discarded upon the counterpane, spread-eagled in an action caricature of its erstwhile wearer.

'Whoa!'

DS Leyton's exclamation (and that he rears, almost spilling the contents of the tray that he bears) is caused by the sudden appearance, naked to the waist and jack-in-the-box like, of his superior, who springs to his feet on the far side of the double bed.

'Cor blimey, Guvnor – I nearly touched cloth.'

Skelgill merely winces by way of response. He reaches for a shirt from the back of a chair, but offers no explanation as to what he was doing – as far as DS Leyton is concerned it could have been executing push-ups, snatching forty winks or searching for a discarded pipe cleaner. In fact the latter would be in the right proximity, and Skelgill casually presses shut the open drawer of a mahogany desk that sits beneath the window. DS Leyton now rounds to the desk to deposit his tray.

'Saved you some cheese-and-pickle sarnies, Guv – before those flippin' gannets finished 'em off. They act all posh but they ain't half got sharp elbows. Fraid they nabbed all the smoked salmon. And there's tea in this flask – nice and hot.'

Skelgill casts a hungry eye over the small feast that his sergeant has salvaged.

'See, Leyton – I told you, you have your uses.'

DS Leyton simpers rather affectedly.

'Truth be told, Guv it was the housekeeper – young Samanta's idea. She tipped me the wink that you'd slipped in via the tradesman's entrance. She's a decent girl, eh? Bit spooky looking, though – glides about this gaff like my old great granny's ghost.'

Skelgill is already biting into a sandwich and with his free hand trying to screw off the lid of the thermos. While he is unable to speak DS Leyton continues.

'Er – DS Jones, Guv – I just knocked on her door to see if she wanted to join in the picnic – couldn't get an answer.'

Skelgill shakes his head and waggles his sandwich to indicate the futility of his sergeant's quest. He checks his wristwatch as he swallows his mouthful.

'With a fair wind – she'll be getting a message out any minute.'

DS Leyton gawps.

'Struth, Guvnor – what are you saying – she's not here?'

Skelgill pours himself a mug of tea and piles several sandwiches onto a plate and settles down in an armchair. In as few words as he can muster between bites he proceeds to enlighten his colleague about the events on the train. DS Leyton looks at once relieved and bewildered.

'Is this horsey woman going to bring her back?'

'We didn't discuss that – but I reckon Jones'll come up with a solution.'

DS Leyton runs the fingers of one hand through his dark hair.

'*Phew* – that'll take the pressure off all round, Guv – once they know everyone's safe.'

But when DS Leyton looks at his superior he sees Skelgill's features are creased with doubt.

'Safe from what, Leyton? Frostbite, hypothermia, aye. Now you've been babysitting, have you changed your mind about the murder threat level?'

'Well – not exactly, Guv – but I reckoned if you'd found anything critical you'd have rocked up swinging.'

'Leyton – all you need to know is the manuscript has gone. Leastways – gone from Mikal Mital's possession. Which makes the Jenny Hackett incident doubly worrying – whether she's got it squirrelled away somewhere, or not.'

DS Leyton ponders for a moment. Then he indicates with a downward motion of the hand.

'You weren't just looking for it under your bed, Guv?'

'Not exactly, Leyton – but you're not so wide of the mark. Somebody has been.'

'What do you mean, Guv?'

Skelgill looks reluctant to elaborate. He contrives a partial clarification.

'Things have been moved.'

DS Leyton's expression becomes more puzzled.

'Was your room locked, Guv?'

'Leyton – I don't reckon we're dealing with someone who's put off by basic door locks.'

DS Leyton shrugs.

'Could have been Samanta, Guv – doing a bit of a tidy. She was telling me she's a jack of all trades, working here – and her a trained interpreter – she speaks five languages –' DS Leyton tails off, seeing that his superior disapproves of this diversion. 'How could you tell, Guv?'

'Come off it, Leyton – don't tell me you don't know when your missus has been checking out your secret stash of *Mars* bars.'

'Stone me – how – *aha!*' DS Leyton points an accusing finger at Skelgill – that he has caught him out. 'I prefer *Kit Kats*, actually, Guv – the missus buys 'em in bulk for her WI ladies' coffee mornings. Trouble is, try hiding anything from our nippers, little varmints, they are.'

DS Leyton abruptly falls silent and Skelgill, assiduously working his way through the sandwiches and tea, glances sideways at his colleague to see that his features are rather forlorn. Of course, his family Christmas is at present in jeopardy – an anxiety compounded by the irony that, as the crow flies, they are within easy striking distance of their home railway station of Penrith; so near and yet so far.

'Leyton – it's unlikely we'll get out of here tomorrow – but if the forecast's right and the snow stops, back by Christmas Eve is a realistic possibility.'

DS Leyton starts from his reverie. He regards Skelgill guardedly – surely his superior is not becoming sentimental? For a moment he brightens.

'Cor blimey, Guv – it's like that there whodunit, the flippin' *Mousetrap* – where they all get stuck in a country house in the snow.' But again there is a flicker of melancholy in his dark eyes. 'I took the missus out west to see it when we were courting – trying to impress her, I was. Told her at the interval who the culprit was – me being the smart Alec bobby, like. She was determined it was someone else – I couldn't help but laugh. Except, come the end – she made a right monkey out of me – she only went and got it right!'

'Happen you'll have more success this time, Leyton.'

Skelgill's tone seems unreasonably irritated – it prompts a more businesslike rejoinder from his subordinate.

'It sounds to me like we need Forensics to give us a steer, Guv – but I guess that ain't gonna happen any time soon.' (Skelgill is shaking his head grimly.) 'But I've got 'em all primed for interviews – I told 'em at lunchtime that as soon as you and DS Jones had properly searched the missing geezer's cabin we'd speak to everyone individually. Who do you want to start with, Guv?'

'The guard, I reckon. He's supposed to have checked in the elusive Mr Harris.'

'Righto, Guv – I'll organise it for the library again, shall I?'

'Aye.'

DS Leyton rises, but somewhat ponderously, and instead of setting off on his mission he loiters and looks apprehensively at the tray. One sandwich remains and Skelgill has drained the flask.

'I may as well take that down, Guv – drop it back to Samanta.' He hesitates. 'You don't want that last sarnie?'

Something in his manner causes Skelgill to regard DS Leyton sharply. Then he glares at the tray and it registers with him that there are in fact two more mugs and side plates, and his sergeant's words upon arrival about *DS Jones* and *picnic* come to mind. A small note of alarm creeps into his voice.

103

'Have you eaten, Leyton?'

'Er – well – not exactly, Guv – but I mean – you've done five trips this morning – I didn't like to –'

'You donnat, Leyton – you should have said.' Skelgill looks more annoyed than remorseful; the latter is not an emotion he would experience when it comes to competition for food. 'Get Samanta to put you up some more bait.'

DS Leyton grins self-reproachfully.

'I'll be alright, Guv – I've got an emergency stash of *Kit Kats* in me suitcase.'

*

'Ruairidh Angus McLeod.'

Skelgill glances to one side; squinting, he can just read his colleague's notebook, and that DS Leyton has written 'Rory'.

'Would you like to spell that, please, sir.'

While the man does so, and DS Leyton, ever fastidious in his note-taking makes a correction, Skelgill scrutinises him. He is still wearing his railway-issue outfit, other than having swapped his blazer for a mottled grey cable-knit sweater that has leather patches sewn onto both elbows. With his untrained ginger eyebrows and ruddy complexion he could pass as a fisherman from one of Scotland's myriad ports. His small blue eyes dart from one to the other of the detectives; there is a superficial belligerence in his manner, but it is plain that he is unnerved, like a gaoler usurped by a prisoners' uprising. Skelgill senses he expects to be accused of failing in his duty, of losing a passenger. And perhaps, therefore, to the man's surprise, and without particular deliberation on Skelgill's part, he opts for a collaborative approach.

'We'll all get it in the neck if we sit on our hands and it turns out there's something we should have done about this Mr Harris.' Ruairidh McLeod regards Skelgill suspiciously as he gestures to indicate himself and DS Leyton. 'Besides – this is our patch. It would have been one of us sent out to investigate in the normal course of events.'

'Ah cannae be held responsible for people deciding tae leave the train.'

It seems the man's instincts for self-preservation for the moment prevail. Skelgill maintains an amenable tone.

'Correct me if I'm wrong – we didn't stop between Euston and when the train hit the snowdrift?'

The guard shakes his head.

'Aye – we didnae.'

'The only scheduled halt before Edinburgh is Carlisle, right? Where we were due to disembark.'

'Aye.'

DS Leyton is looking rather perplexed. This is perhaps because Skelgill has not begun with the more obvious explanation – but now his superior does so.

'Could the person – this Mr Harris – have changed his mind at Euston? Got off again?'

Ruairidh McLeod hunches his shoulders.

'Ah would have seen him. Ah was on the platform until we departed.'

Skelgill does not contest the man's assertion. Instead he gestures to DS Leyton, who has the manifest obtained originally by DS Jones. He hands it to his boss. Skelgill examines the list of passengers, their designated cabin numbers, and ticks made in biro in the left-hand margin.

'Mr McLeod – we were cutting it fine – and Mr Bond and his team, and Ms Adamska – they were hot on our heels.' (The guard nods sullenly.) 'When did Mr Harris arrive?'

'Ah deal with hunners of passengers every day. It's nae my job tae remember individuals.'

'But you recognised Mr Bond – and he called you by name.'

'Aye – he's a regular on the sleeper – and Sir Ewart.'

'And that goes for their colleagues?'

'Aye – I suppose so.'

Skelgill taps the paper with the back of his right hand.

'Could you have ticked off Mr Harris by accident?'

The guard shakes his head with determination; his reply, however, is more ambiguous.

105

'The first group of passengers all came together – they'd been waiting for the gate tae open.'

Skelgill consults the list.

'That would have been Sir Ewart Cameron-Kinloch – and Ms Ivanna Karenina – who you already knew.' Skelgill glances up and the man nods warily. 'Plus Ms Hackett, Mr Mital, Mr Faulkner – and Mr Harris. Only four strangers – it's not exactly a lot to remember.'

The guard's intransigence seems to resurface as Skelgill's assertions become more probing.

'Like Ah say – they made a rush at me. My job's tae get them checked on board with nae fuss.'

'What did Mr Harris look like?'

It could be the heat of the small library with its rekindled fire, and that the man is wearing a thick sweater, but his face is becoming increasingly flushed.

'Late thirties. Medium height. Average build. Short dark hair.'

Now Skelgill's brow creases.

'It sounds to me like you're describing Mr Faulkner, sir.'

The man glowers obstinately but offers no defence. Though the universal description would fit several million citizens, Skelgill opts not to press the point further.

'Okay, Mr McLeod – after the train departed – what did you see of Mr Harris?'

'I didnae see him. He must have went tae his bed.'

'Is that unusual?'

The guard shakes his head.

'Some passengers just want tae sleep. It's under seven hours tae Edinburgh. Plus they get woken up forty-five minutes before we reach Waverley.'

Skelgill nods pensively.

'Just remind us about the locking of the compartments, sir.'

'When a passenger arrives on board their cabin is open. They can lock it on the inside. If they go tae the toilet or the lounge car they can leave it on the latch – or if they set the lock I have tae let them back in.'

'So somebody locked compartment number one.'

It takes the man a moment to process Skelgill's logic, but when he does he nods vigorously. It seems he believes this vindicates his resolution that there was a Mr Harris.

'Aye – Ah had tae unlock it for your lassie.'

The man grins – a little salaciously, Skelgill would judge, if it were not for the gravity of the subject. He shifts in his chair and tugs at the back of his shirt, as if he needs a physical distraction in order to realign his thoughts. There is nothing yet to convince him of the existence of Mr Harris. It can only be that a man displaying the powers of Spring-heeled Jack might explain whatever crimes have been committed which keeps him from dismissing the matter entirely. But folklore is not the answer, and it is only in the movies where villains subvert the laws of physics, while a willing audience is suckered into suspending disbelief.

'Look, Mr McLeod – this can't be the first time something like this has happened. What's your theory?'

'He could have been a jumper.' The guard is quick with his response.

Skelgill narrows his eyes.

'You mean a suicide?'

The man shrugs.

'Aye. It's the only possible explanation.'

Skelgill remains sceptical. The vast majority of rail suicides occur from platforms; to have boarded the train in the first instance seems a peculiarly intricate modus operandi. Moreover, his colleagues found no signs of such an exit having been attempted.

'Putting that to one side – did we ever slow down such that a person could have safely leapt from the train?'

'Ah wouldnae say so – maybe forty miles an hour. But ye wouldnae ken what ye'd hit – in the pitch dark.'

Skelgill tries not to show his frustration – and though he feels like he is trapped in a hopeless loop he finds himself returning to the beginning.

'You're absolutely certain a Mr Harris got on the train?'

'Ah might not remember his face – but Ah wouldnae forget the name.'

'Why not, sir?'

'Ah come frae Harris.'

'What – the *Isle* of Harris? Where they make the tweed?'

'Aye.' The man looks like he is expecting an objection – perhaps that his accent does not match this explanation, albeit that he has a Gaelic given name and indeed a common Western Isles surname. 'When I were a bairn Ma gave birth tae triplets – we had tae move the weans for hospital care – I grew up in Gorgie.'

'Edinburgh.'

As the man nods tersely Skelgill recalls his recommendation, of ales hailing from the Scottish capital, indeed the traditional brewery quarter that he has mentioned. While he is silent for a moment, DS Leyton chips in.

'Mr McLeod – could someone have tricked you at Euston?'

'What dae ye mean?'

'Pretended to get on – got back off. Climbed out the other side.'

'On tae the tracks?' Ruairidh McLeod appears bewildered. 'Why would anyone dae that?'

Skelgill is not keen that DS Leyton should involve the guard in a discussion of motives – not least because of his antipathy to the hypothetical, but also there is the risk of revealing what underlies their ostensibly innocent investigation into a missing passenger. However, DS Leyton responds before he can intervene.

'To make it seem like they'd travelled to Edinburgh. There's no ticket inspections once you've checked people on board, right?'

'Aye.'

DS Leyton nods with satisfaction – but now he senses that Skelgill is glaring at him with barely contained irritation. He soldiers on, looking rather hamstrung.

'Would the blind side of the train be covered by CCTV?'

The guard appears doubtful.

'Ye'd need tae contact British Transport Polis. But the 05:31 Glasgow express was alongside us. It would have blocked the view.'

DS Leyton makes a humming sound, perhaps an acknowledgement – but he turns artlessly to Skelgill, as though to hand over these findings to his wiser superior. Skelgill is evidently displeased, and it takes him a few moments to muster a response. He regards Ruairidh McLeod in a somewhat strained manner.

'We expect to be getting a message out to that effect shortly.' He does not elaborate upon their method. 'In the meantime, we'll do what we can to establish whether or not there were any sightings of Mr Harris on the train. What about after we went to bed – myself and my two sergeants? That was about 1am. How long did the other passengers remain?'

The guard reverts to his defensive posture, hunching his shoulders.

'Ah cannae mind. Ah dinnae keep a register, ken?'

Skelgill, still holding the manifest, flaps it with apparent frustration. He squints at the list.

'There was Mr Mital, who was reading. Ms Hackett was talking to Mr Faulkner. The rest were sitting round together – Mr Cameron-Kinloch and his colleague Ms Karenina, and Mr Bond and his two male associates.'

He looks up interrogatively at the guard. But DS Leyton interjects.

'And Ms Adamska, Guv.'

'What?'

Skelgill looks accusingly at the document. Then he is reminded – she was not a scheduled passenger.

'I was coming to her, Leyton.' He addresses the guard. 'You must be able to remember roughly when they turned in, sir?'

Ruairidh McLeod shifts charily in his seat.

'Maybe half an hour after youse, I went tae the guard's van. When I came back they'd all gone.'

'Well, what time was that, sir?'

'Two-fifteen, two-twenty.'

109

'What did you do?'

'Cleared away the empties. Tidied the galley and the washrooms. Went back tae my van. Stayed there until we came tae a halt.'

Skelgill inhales pensively.

'So, you didn't see anyone after 1.30am?'

'Aye.' But the man's brow creases – it seems there is some recall. 'Wait. Ah saw someone – when Ah went back tae clear up. Ah glimpsed a woman at the end of the sleeping car – she must have went intae the toilet.'

'Which woman?'

'Ah dinnae ken.'

Skelgill tilts his head back, a little disbelievingly.

'Ms Adamska – she's tall – blonde. Ms Karenina, medium height, black hair. Ms Hackett, smallish, fair hair. They're all very distinctive.'

'And DS Jones, Guv.'

Skelgill glares at his sergeant. But he transfers his disapproval to the guard – personal observation is not proving to be his strongpoint.

'You're sure it was a woman?'

Skelgill's tone might almost be sarcastic, but the man has an immediate retort.

'Aye – she had on a red dressing gown.'

It seems the issue of gender is settled by the colour of the garment, categorically so, going by the man's intonation. Skelgill, who has subconsciously eliminated DS Jones, cannot imagine his colleague to be the person concerned – a red dressing gown? But she may have visited the washroom – indeed, during the wee small hours there were surely multiple comings and goings to this effect; and he had been disturbed himself. Moreover, there is something about the guard's account that disquiets him. He feels strongly disinclined to take Ruairidh McLeod into their confidence (a bridge he has yet to cross with the driver) and has formed a low opinion of his reliability as a witness. But there are more questions he should ask.

'Had any of the passengers locked their compartments – that required you to open them so they could turn in?'

The guard shakes his head.

'No, they didnae.'

'Who makes up the beds and puts in the welcome packs?'

'There's a housekeeping team that comes on board at Euston.' The man scowls disparagingly, as if this is a task below his station. 'Foreigners – dinnae speak a word of English.'

Skelgill raises an eyebrow at the unintended irony of this complaint.

'What if someone wants more drinking water in the night?'

'They just ask me – Ah've got supplies.'

'As a matter of interest – did anyone request water – or whatever?'

Ruairidh McLeod again shakes his head – although perhaps there is a moment of hesitation.

'Folk had only been in bed a couple of hours when we stopped. Usually if they want extra water it's when they get their morning call.'

Skelgill considers this proposition by reference to his own archives.

'Depends how much you've had to drink.'

He means alcohol – and it prompts a quip from DS Leyton.

'They were certainly knocking back the old *Glenmorangie*.'

The sergeant in his Cockney brogue mispronounces the brand name to rhyme with 'Angie' – which clearly jars with the Scotsman. He scowls – but unlike the previous night does not correct the speaker.

'Aye – there's a couple of the regulars that like tae get intae the spirit.'

Former traumas cause Skelgill to wince inadvertently. There is nothing so brutal as a whisky hangover – especially if compounded by the regret of yielding to a beverage that tastes like a peat bog when there was still good cask ale on offer.

*

'What do you reckon, Guv?'

Skelgill expels a lungful of air in a manner that verges upon the flabbergasted.

'I know what I think, Leyton – I think he made a mistake. There was no Harris and he's too pig-headed to admit it. Harris is flapping around like a red herring on platform nine-and-three-quarters.'

'Some geezer must have locked that cabin next to Mikal Mital's – you said it yourself, Guv.'

Skelgill glowers. The act, at least, must have been tangible – and DS Jones witnessed the situation. The natural state of affairs, had there been no Mr Harris, and no tampering, would have seen the door remain unlocked. So there is a small possibility – that supplements DS Jones's observation about the water bottle – that someone failed to conceal their tracks. And, there is no denying that – while they do not know the cause of Mikal Mital's death – the manuscript is gone. Skelgill growls.

'It's this pussy-footing around, Leyton – it's no way to conduct an investigation – I don't know if I can stand asking another nine folk pointless questions.'

DS Leyton regards his boss a little warily – perhaps wondering if this choice of words is code for the passing of the buck. But the sergeant's altruism – and perhaps the gloomy prospect of twiddling his thumbs for the rest of the day – gets the better of him.

'I can do it – if you want, Guv.' He spreads his palms, large hands for a relatively short man. 'Quick round of interviews – just ask 'em about Harris, get everyone's personal details – you never know, someone shows their hand – you can give 'em the good old third degree.'

Skelgill rises and approaches the hearth. He takes up the black cast-iron poker and fences extravagantly with the logs, sending sparks flying up the chimney. He ponders for a few moments. While he has his own knack of appearing disinterested when questioning a suspect or witness, it is an affected manner and not always convincing, his unique blend of capriciousness and recalcitrance lurking never far below the surface, liable to be agitated by obduracy. DS Leyton, on the other hand, innately ingenuous, need not flatter to deceive; he is the friendly fireside Labrador to Skelgill's fell-wise Border Collie. While the perspicacious would suspect at any moment that Skelgill might snap, from DS Leyton the worst would be a slobbery lick. Skelgill, if not exactly envisaging such a stark contrast, turns to his sergeant with a wry grin.

'Aye, fair enough. Happen you'll make a better job of it than us.'

DS Leyton is taken aback that his speculative offer has borne fruit; his eyes widen and he looks momentarily alarmed.

'What'll you do, Guv?'

Skelgill stretches out his arms and bares his teeth, as though it is with the effort of pushing at invisible pillars at his sides.

'You know me, Leyton – unless I've got a fishing rod in my hand I have the devil's own job to stay in one place.'

*

With snow still falling and the wind a remorseless roar that marauds amongst the treetops like a great winged wolf pack, what little afternoon twilight remains seems inconsequential as Skelgill picks his way up the wooded fellside, albeit he is in the bare deciduous fringe on its sheltered western flank, where Shake Holes Beck tumbles in a series of falls and small steep cataracts to its confluence with Ulpha Beck beside the old inn. The sub-zero temperatures have been too short-lived to freeze the ground water that percolates from the limestone escarpment, and the stream cuts a slick black sliver through the white terrain, winding beneath precipitous cornices and dividing to pass around boulders capped by domes of snow. Wafts of sulphur reach Skelgill's dilated nostrils, and he is reminded that in Victorian times the inn served as a spa, where the great and good gravitated to take the pungent waters.

He pauses to gaze at a raft of saucer-sized ice plates that gently jostle one another in the slack water downstream from a plunge pool; the latter looks deep and must be tempting in

113

summer, just the spot he sought out as a boy, creeping up, always hoping to disturb a fell sprite indulging in a secret moment of mischief. He expects to see no one now, spirit or human – or animal come to that – and yet he feels no trepidation about losing his bearings. The old map on the wall of the library is sharp in his mind's eye – the lie of the land, the becks, the clusters of shake holes (albeit he cannot recall each one individually). And the patch of forest – mostly post-survey plantation – provides a finite border, and the relentless easterly gale the compass he needs to navigate. Besides, his purpose is not especially to find out anything – unless, that is, the distraction enables him to learn from his own subconscious what hitherto has not been revealed to him. In the absence of fishing, the present combination of mechanical activity and sensory overload might form the preconditions for such a revelation. But as he stares unseeing at the frozen platelets he experiences only a logjam; there is not yet the critical mass to break out and release a stream of cognisance.

Skelgill dislodges a drip from his nose with a sleeve and moves on. His commandeered railway-issue overalls were still damp with perspiration and melted snow, and he has raided the tack room for an alternative outfit – rather ironically he has settled upon a long waxed-cotton riding coat similar to that worn by the horsewoman, Lucinda Hobhouse, topped and tailed with a wide-brimmed hat of a similar material to the coat, and equestrian wellingtons that grip his calves just below the knees. It is far from his ideal outdoor garb, but his ambitions for mobility are modest – he is happy to trudge, and the outfit protects him without compromising his senses. It strikes him that he would not appear out of place astride a horse – although upon the stocky Fell pony he would look plain daft, if the headstrong beast would even stand for it. The thought prompts him to consider the whereabouts of DS Jones – a small doubt clouds his mind – but he tells himself that she is in a better place – a village post office with a working telephone – there is no great logic in her returning to *Shake Holes Inn*, by whatever

114

means. But it would be good to know that their predicament has been communicated to the authorities.

Having followed the beck north, he takes a right angle and ducks into the wind, and begins to pick his way through the coniferous plantation. The snow is not so deep here, held up by the canopy, but underfoot the going is just as onerous, beneath the crust a decaying underbrush, a springy spiky matrix of fallen branches and twigs that has accumulated over the decades. Then there is the persistent obstacle of the annual rings of dead branches that climb each trunk like the spokes of successive cartwheels, inhibiting passage and always ready to poke out an eye. Skelgill has acquired a heavy club, a shillelagh-like branch, and uses it to smash off those twigs that impede his progress or threaten his face. He reaches a tiny circular clearing, and sees that it is a shake hole – and he is reminded of DS Jones's query about these hollows being scattered through the woods.

Skelgill circles the snow-filled depression and slips back into the trees. It is suddenly darker, but he is confident that if he holds his bearing into the wind he will reach the bridleway – and, sure enough, ten minutes find him doing just that, and he emerges onto the now familiar track. Visibility beneath the premature dusk is barely fifty yards – but it is sufficient for him to recognise ahead a bend in the bridle path around which lies the shake hole of greater notoriety. He mutters to himself – was that only this morning – and today the same calendar day of the train crash? He approaches, stopping just short of the rim. *Jenny's Hole*, he calls it under his breath. He determines to come back here in spring – to see just how deep it really is; the majority of these collapsed shafts are inconvenient rather than treacherous – but then again he never felt terra firma. Now it occurs to him that he did not ask Ruairidh McLeod where he was, or what he saw or heard, in the prelude to the incident – but such a blatant question is bound to set alarm bells ringing. Right now gut feel tells him that the idea of a deliberate assault on Jenny Hackett is a scenario best kept under wraps. Moreover, if someone did push her – what are *they* thinking? There have been

115

no explicit repercussions – does the culprit suspect she is keeping mum because she has something to hide?

Standing stock-still Skelgill stares severely into the shake hole. He might almost be testing himself – to see if he succumbs to some urge to leap. But that is not the action he now takes. It is less predictable – and connected to his wide-brimmed hat (for, had he been beneath the hood of his railway overall he would not have heard the crump of snow compressed underfoot close behind him).

In one smooth action he swings his club two-handed to his left at shoulder height and makes a half-turn at the hips – the pose that of a baseball batter – and indeed he swings hard, only to pull the hit at the very last possible instant – inches before the club makes contact with the head of a person – who recoils and topples backwards, spluttering a protest.

'Good heavens! It's you, Inspector!'

'Jeez – you donnat! I could have brained you! What are you doing, creeping up on us?'

The 'donnat' is Richard Bond – and if the colloquialism, like the club, goes over his head he can be left in no doubt by the expletives edited for the purposes of public decency that Skelgill has temporarily suspended the convivial relationship built up during their rescue. Richard Bond clambers gingerly to his feet and pats himself down to dislodge a liberal dusting of snow.

'Sorry – sorry – I wasn't creeping up on you – I mean to say – I didn't think it was *you*, Inspector.'

'Who did you think it was?'

'Well – I don't know.' The man seems suitably chastised, avoiding eye contact and not at all offended that Skelgill almost scalped him. 'I saw some gear was gone – and fresh tracks crossing the stable yard. It obviously wasn't Joost Merlyn – no limp – and the prints too big for any of the ladies, I should say. I was pretty sure you were interviewing – I haven't had my turn yet – so I didn't realise you weren't in the library. Since there's this business of Mr Harris – well – I thought – maybe it's him. May as well follow – see what he's up to – thought you'd be chuffed if I solved your mystery for you.'

Skelgill opts to respond to this practical explanation rather than backtrack into an awkward exchange of apologies. Besides, Richard Bond, it seems, in good military tradition does not hold a grudge for a dressing down.

'It could have been one of the other blokes.'

'Well, you say that, Inspector – with the greatest respect – but it could not have been either of my team – absolutely no reason for them to wander off – in any event I'd left them in the bar. The American, Faulkner, he's rather reserved and doesn't strike me as the sort to venture out alone – and clearly not Sir Ewart.' Richard Bond affects a diplomatic cough. 'Frankly both he and the guard are badly out of condition. In due course – when I caught sight of somebody – it didn't occur to me that it was you in that rather pukka riding outfit.'

Richard Bond grins, and so ingenuously that it can surely only be heartfelt embarrassment that underlies his efforts at mollification.

'You nearly got a reet twatting there, marra.'

Richard Bond seems to detect a lightening of the tone, and he appears to get the gist of Skelgill's descent into Cumbrian vernacular.

'Oh – it wouldn't have done any damage.'

'Aye – that's what I tell folk. Except in my case it's true.' The man does not attempt to gainsay him – and he rather suspects that Richard Bond's big-boned skull is so dense that a blow from a knobkerrie would likely not floor him. 'Still, can't be too careful.'

When Skelgill does not elaborate upon this latter remark, Richard Bond makes what may be a tentative inquiry.

'Your Sergeant Leyton explained earlier that you went back to search for clues to the disappearance of Mr Harris. I would have accompanied you – but, er – well –'

Richard Bond suddenly appears rather crestfallen, like a schoolboy who is reminded he has not made the First XV, and is still troubled by the shock of rejection. Skelgill feels a small pang of guilt – without his collaboration the evacuation to the inn would have been a considerably more challenging prospect.

117

Only DS Jones among the others could match his athleticism – but she is probably half the weight of Richard Bond and at times it was his sheer brute strength that was the deciding factor.

'Not to worry, Richard – we were treating it as a police matter – it might look a bit awkward in the reports later if a civilian were involved – if sommat went wrong, like.'

'Naturally, Inspector. This is your command.' Richard Bond looks away, as if casually noting their surroundings. 'And did your return visit shed any more light on the missing passenger?'

Skelgill beckons with his head that they should start walking – they move away from the shake hole and begin to march briskly in parallel, each taking one of the partially in-filled tyre tracks made by the trailer.

'There's no indication he was on the train.' Skelgill glances sideways at his companion. 'When I saw you hanging half-naked out of the door I thought for a second someone must have jumped for it.'

Richard Bond looks a little perturbed. His eyes narrow and his brow creases.

'There were certainly no tracks – as I think you saw. I was merely getting the lie of the land. First principles – secure one's retreat, you know?'

Skelgill treats the question as rhetorical.

'I take it you didn't see him at the station or on the train – I mean, another male who's no longer in the party?'

'I did not. Of course, one assumes there are always fellow passengers who keep themselves to themselves.'

Skelgill delays for a moment before he responds.

'That's a regular little drinking club you have in the bar, is it?'

Richard Bond's tone regains something of the pompous stridency that first caught Skelgill's ear on the platform at Euston station.

'There's a coterie of frequent travellers – company CEOs, politicians, PR types – we like to put the world to rights over a whisky or two. But Christmas has depleted the numbers. There was just myself and my boys and old Eck and his – er – female colleague. And we were joined by the journalist – and the attractive Russian model – what?'

The man's inflexion seems to invite a locker-room comment about Wiktoria Adamska, but Skelgill declines to be sidetracked.

'So, what's the Edinburgh connection?'

'Well, of course, Eck's Russian crowd have their studios there – gets them under Ofcom's radar, so they think.' He suddenly guffaws, in a way that suggests he assumes Skelgill will understand what he means. 'Then we do a decent amount of business with the Charlotte Square mafia – Edinburgh still has a fair bit of financial clout – we have a corporate apartment in Thistle Street – you know it, Inspector?'

'In the New Town, aye?'

The Rose and the Thistle, the King in the middle, the Queen and the Princes on either side.'

Richard Bond recites the ditty that locals use to remember the Georgian street plan.

'You're not a Scot yourself?'

'Good Lord, no – I'm Namibian by birth. When things got a bit lively I was packed off to board at Eton – got a place at Imperial – landed a job in the City – worked out in HK for a few years before coming back to Blighty.'

'Where did the army fit in?'

Richard Bond glances sharply at Skelgill.

'I was a territorial.'

Skelgill makes a questioning sound in his throat.

'I didn't realise you could join the SAS as a territorial.'

'Indeed – we are called the Reserve. The emphasis is upon surveillance and reconnaissance.'

Skelgill nods pensively. He notes the man's allusion to continued membership of the regiment – a manner of speaking he has heard from other former military personnel. His silence seems to prompt a question from Richard Bond.

'Are you thinking you should have given it a shot, Inspector?'

Skelgill has acquaintances who have served Queen and Country, including close relatives – but somehow it is a concept that has never engaged him – the prospect of killing people on foreign soil. If there is a sense of duty deeply rooted in his psyche it is to protect his native patch, and its hard-working inhabitants. He would be one of those grim pitchfork-wielding types braced gimlet-eyed that made invading soldiers wish they had never enlisted for war. And yet there is something that rankles – he might be more outdoor-savvy than most, a fellsman, a fisherman, in the mountain rescue and all – but not to have tested himself against the elite of his generation, perhaps leaves a tinge of regret. Then again there is the sheer impossibility of it all.

'I'd have lasted ten minutes, taking orders.'

Richard Bond laughs appreciatively.

'Yet there cannot be room for insubordination in your profession.'

Skelgill makes a disparaging exclamation.

'Try telling that to my superior.'

'He is a bit of a stickler?'

'*She.*'

Skelgill's intonation conveys in the single word all the listener needs to know about the wayward inspector and his rocky relationship with the Chief. However, Richard Bond seems eager to take his side.

'Nothing wrong with initiative, Inspector. Progress depending upon the unreasonable man, and all that. In my estimation you have acted correctly – somebody needed to take charge.'

Skelgill responds with an inarticulate grunt, which may be an acknowledgement, but otherwise they move on in silence. He imagines that Richard Bond would certainly have assumed command had the team of detectives not been on board – and though he proved willing to take orders, even now he has instigated his own black ops. Indeed, Skelgill is still in a heightened state of alert – although he has been striving not to show it. He is disconcerted that he has been stalked and crept up on. Can he seriously believe that Richard Bond did not know it was he? What about that determined look in the man's eyes in

120

the split second between Skelgill's turning around and the swoosh of the club that sent him keeling backwards?

Perhaps Richard Bond detects that some unfavourable thoughts are troubling Skelgill's mind, for he makes a hearty effort to change the subject.

'I gather your good Sergeant Leyton has some high jinx lined up for us tonight.'

'Come again?'

'Postprandial entertainment – I caught a snatch of his conversation with that young waif of a housekeeper – apparently the firm that had booked for their Christmas event had ordered an evening of traditional pub games – so we are to have the benefit of the arrangements.' He guffaws explosively. 'I'm not sure how it will go down with the likes of Wiktoria Adamska – she is more accustomed to *The Savoy* – can't say I've ever seen a cribbage board in that august establishment!'

9. PLAYING GAMES

Thursday, 8pm

'Didn't realise you played arrows right-handed, Guv.'

'I don't.'

'But, Guv – you were chucking with your right – everything else I've ever seen you do, you're a southpaw. I suddenly realised when we were up against *Dire Straits* in the final – the McLeod geezer being a cack-hander an' all.'

'Cuddy wifter, we call it round here, Leyton.'

DS Leyton blinks somewhat vacantly.

'So, what are you saying, Guv – you were giving the rest of this crowd a chance?'

Skelgill looks disgusted at such a suggestion – or maybe he is distracted, for at the bar billiards table now is the striking figure of Wiktoria Adamska, upon whom most of the people in the room have their gaze fixed. She has dressed for dinner in a skimpy silvery see-through outfit and trademark high heels, her unrestrained pale locks and various bangles and pendant earrings apparently not a hindrance when she takes her turn. Even with the very best of intentions it is difficult not to look on; even the females seem entranced by her alluring presence. Skelgill and DS Leyton are fresh from a comfortable victory in the darts contest – a performance perhaps reflective of their social backgrounds – and that Skelgill is an occasional player in his local. Although he was surprised by DS Leyton's skill, the latter claiming not to have stood at the oche for a good decade. They made an effective tag-team, the taller Skelgill piling up the 20s; the shorter DS Leyton from a lower trajectory regularly nailing double 16, or its fall-back double 8. Eventually Skelgill responds, albeit somewhat obliquely.

'Next time you write a cheque, Leyton – turn the book upside down and try to fill in the stub.'

'You what, Guv?' The sergeant sounds entirely bemused.

'You'll see what it's like being left-handed in a right-handed world.'

'Mind you, Guv – how often do you pay by Gregory these days?'

'It's not just cheques, Leyton. I'm surrounded by stuff that doesn't work. That's why I've had to learn to use my right hand. Try cutting with scissors in your left. Try flicking through a magazine left-handed. Even those fancy dessert forks we were given tonight – they had the blade on the wrong side.'

DS Leyton regards his superior suspiciously; the handicap did not prevent him from devouring a second generous helping of sticky toffee pudding. He shifts forward with a grunt that reflects the degree of difficulty of the manoeuvre. His aim is to reach his drink. He has a pint of lager and Skelgill has reluctantly opted for *Guinness*. They sit adjacent upon a low, deep sofa at one side of the room that has been given over to games, a kind of informal lounge in which a couple of areas have been cleared for darts and bar billiards respectively. There is shove ha'penny and a pub quiz to come. A *Wurlitzer* jukebox is rendering dated hits – presently *'Take Me Bak 'ome'* by British glam rock band *Slade*, which has Skelgill rhythmically patting the arm of the settee. It seems the firm from Glasgow were intent upon wearing clothing to match the themed era; the evacuees have settled for pairings named after 1970s pop groups; Skelgill and Leyton perhaps rather unimaginatively *The Police*. DS Leyton meanwhile produces his notebook and lays it on the coffee table before them. He flips it over and acts out a little pantomime of writing.

'Yeah – I reckon I see what you mean, Guv. The spine gets in the road.' He does not sound all that convinced – but brightening he waggles the notebook. 'Want me to give you a quick rundown of the interviews? At this rate I reckon it'll be another twenty minutes before we're back on.'

'Aye, why not.' Skelgill does not appear to share his colleague's enthusiasm.

'I'll do it in order, shall I?'

'Whatever.'

123

'I started with the train driver, Laura Wilson. Obviously, she was in her cab the whole time from Euston until we crashed – but there was one interesting thing, Guv – we stopped.'

'What?'

'She reckons there was a red signal just north of Crewe.'

Not Crewe again, Skelgill is thinking.

'What time?'

'Just before a quarter to three. She checked the time because she was keeping an eye on the schedule.' DS Leyton regards Skelgill rather apprehensively – as if he has made too much of the news. 'Thing is, Guv, it was for less than a minute. And we were in darkness in farmland. There's no way any passenger could have known we were going to stop. And hardly enough time to do anything.'

Skelgill's eyes have glazed over. Judging by his expression he is suffering some inner discontent. But suddenly he realises he has been staring at Wiktoria Adamska, who has risen from bending over to take a shot, and she sees his apparent interest. She returns his gaze – an enigmatic smile and no trace of offence. She nods to him – he gives an awkward wave – just the lifting of one hand – and then he turns ostentatiously to look at DS Leyton. His sergeant realises he is expected to speak.

'Obviously that don't tie in with what Ruairidh McLeod told us.'

'He was probably having a kip.'

'The driver said as much, Guv. He's supposed to stay awake – but it being a night shift it's easy to nod off. She intercommed him when the train hit the snowdrift – but there was no answer – then they crossed paths at the lounge car.'

'Aye – that's where I found them.'

There is another silence, which DS Leyton takes as a signal to continue.

'I spoke with the American geezer next, Guv – Bill Faulkner – being as he was in the first group to board and was travelling alone – I thought if anyone noticed a Mr Harris it would be him. But he claims he was reading *The Grapes of Wrath* on his mobile phone and didn't pay much attention to the people around him in the queue. That said – he couldn't remember anyone else – and to cut a long story short, Guv – they've all said the same thing. Neither hide nor hair of the Harris cove.' Now DS Leyton's heavy jowls crease as he sinks rather dejectedly into his seat. 'They just kept giving me grief about when we're getting them out of here.'

Skelgill mutters an expletive – although he disguises it by casually glancing about the room. Frankly, he was not expecting any progress on the absent Mr Harris – indeed he knows his sergeant would have sought him out immediately upon his return had there been some information in this regard. And he reminds himself again that there are more important matters at stake than the non-passenger. However, had any of the real travellers 'showed their hand' as his sergeant had put it – he would also have known by now. He realises he must steel himself – there may be something DS Leyton has discovered that has not as yet revealed its significance. But such stoicism does not come easily – he is both physically tired and, by the same token, mentally fatigued. And in the jovial atmosphere it is tempting to forget altogether that they may be in the midst of a sinister plot. But he cannot ignore the facts of the death of Mikal Mital, the manuscript, the shake hole incident, the tampering in the cabins – and even in his own bedroom here.

'So, what are they all up to?'

His words might have a deeper meaning – but DS Leyton frames his reply in the context of his notes.

'Well – Bill Faulkner, Guv – he works for an American bank in the City. He's from New Orleans. Says he's due to fly home late on Christmas Eve. He's arranged it so he can fly back to the States from Edinburgh – he's travelling up for a couple of days' sightseeing. There's some German outdoor market that's all the rage – beats me why they wouldn't have a Scotch market – what with whisky and tartan, haggis, shortbread – they've got those Jimmy hats, Loch Ness monster memorabilia –' DS Leyton glances inquiringly at Skelgill, but sees this is not a diversion he wishes to suffer. 'Then, er – Sir Ewart Cameron-Kinloch – he lives up there in Scotland, anyway – but he and his colleague

125

Ivanna Karenina were returning to work – seems that Russian TV company keeps broadcasting right through the holidays – and they're both involved in news and current affairs. Obviously I didn't speak to Richard Bond – '

DS Leyton taps the man's name on an otherwise blank page and looks hopefully at Skelgill, who takes a gulp of his drink and scowls disapprovingly – but then he is more forthcoming, as though the unpalatable liquid at least has some lubricative effect.

'Bond didn't see owt – as far Harris is concerned. As for the trip, him and his oppos were due to see financial clients in Edinburgh. Easy enough to check out.'

DS Leyton looks a little perplexed.

'What about that conference, Guv – that Mikal Mital was supposed to be speaking at?'

Skelgill does not seem particularly troubled.

'It's probably been cancelled – I doubt if anyone's made it. Never mind their keynote speaker's out of the equation.' He swallows another mouthful of his drink, but looks no more like he is getting used to the gassy stout. 'Bond never mentioned it. I didn't see that I should bring it to his attention.'

Now DS Leyton realises that Skelgill has some artfulness when it comes to avoiding leading questions, if only out of bloody mindedness. But, for his part, he has rather given away that he has raised the subject.

'Thing is, Guv – when I spoke to the young French geezer, François, he said him and his workmate Egor wouldn't be going to the conference – that it was above their level – it's for chief executives and other bigwigs. Then I reckoned he was about to say that Richard Bond would go – and he sort of changed his tune and acted like he didn't understand me very well. I never really got a straight answer out of him.'

Skelgill shrugs.

'I'll ask Bond if necessary – he can't deny it – not if he's booked in – he'll be on the delegates' list. But we can probably find out ourselves once we've got some communications.'

DS Leyton nods glumly.

'Thing is, Guv – when I spoke again to Jenny Hackett – I mean, she was quite open about going to the conference – and that Mikal Mital was the main attraction. She's still full of conspiracy theories – that he was about to blow the gaff –'

The sergeant's voice tails off.

'What, Leyton?'

'Well – it's still looking like Jenny Hackett might be right – that someone's headed him off at the pass.'

Skelgill gives an ironic laugh.

'At the cutting, more like. Shake Holes cutting.'

'Well – exactly, Guv – although they couldn't have planned that, could they? I mean, no one knew we were going to smash into a snowdrift and get stranded.'

Skelgill tilts his head to one side.

'It's not like there weren't straws in the wind, Leyton. Look at Wiktoria Adamska.' DS Leyton does so – and at this moment the young woman is poised to take a shot, and revealing a considerable expanse of seamed nylons and steepling thighs. Skelgill follows his sergeant's widening gaze. 'What I'm saying, Leyton, is that she took the train because flights were already being cancelled. So what was the big hurry to get to Edinburgh?'

'Er – that was – er – oh, yeah – she reckoned there's a premiere, a fashion show – at the Edinburgh branch of *Harvey*, er – *Nicks*. Her new collection, er – lingerie – know what I mean?' DS Leyton yields to the fact that he is floundering, and takes temporary refuge in his glass of lager. After a moment his composure is restored. 'Just in time for all the geezers who can't think of what to buy the missus for Christmas, I suppose, Guv.'

'Like what you see, Inspector?'

Skelgill suddenly starts – the voice belongs to Wiktoria Adamska – and he realises she has turned to catch him star gazing for a second time. Colour comes rushing uninvited to his high cheekbones.

'I'm sorry, madam?'

'My billiards – don't you think I am improving?' She wields the cue triumphantly above her head. 'We cannot have *The Police* winning every event.' She smiles, her pale hair and eyes glinting

127

beneath the spotlight that is trained upon the table. She seems amused by Skelgill's discomfiture, and takes a few elegant steps across the room. 'And where is your delightful colleague? I might have been paired with her. Then *Blondie* would have been entirely fitting.' She leans forward, revealing little in the way of underwear beneath her dress; she lowers her voice. 'My partner – this American – he is rather staid, wouldn't you say?'

'Sorry, madam – I can't be held responsible for picking the teams. Or the names.' Skelgill glances rather accusingly at DS Leyton. 'But to answer your question about Sergeant Jones, I'm hoping she'll return soon.'

Wiktoria Adamska smiles again; displaying her perfectly arranged and whitened teeth.

'Is this one for us?'

Her cryptic remark is explained as she turns to move away, for she has recognised that the track now playing on the jukebox is *Denis* and she begins to sing along in a clear soprano.

'Oh embrasse-moi ce soir!'

She swoops upon the table and executes her next shot with a flourish, winning chivalrous hurrahs from opponent Richard Bond, as both red and white are fluked simultaneously. Skelgill and DS Leyton are left sitting rather stiffly. After a while DS Leyton clears his throat; Skelgill thinks he is about to remark upon Wiktoria Adamska – but in fact it is the American to whom he refers.

'Speaking of Bill Faulkner, Guv. I asked the passengers about what happened when they turned in – in case someone saw Harris or any movement around his compartment. Answer no to both. They more or less all went to bed around the one-thirty mark. Sir Ewart Cameron-Kinloch and Ivanna Karenina scooted off first with Wiktoria Adamska, closely followed by Richard Bond and his two young geezers – they were sharing a cabin, anyway. Jenny Hackett and Mikal Mital hung back to finish their drinks and left the lounge car together about ten minutes later.'

'How can you be sure about that?'

'It tallies with what they individually told me, Guv. On top of that – like I say – Bill Faulkner – he was the last to go – he saw it all.'

'So he was more observant this time.'

Skelgill looks at the man. He is quietly watching the game in which he is a participant, standing a little aloof, rather like a sentry, with his cue at his side and the butt resting on the ground. But the larger-than-life Richard Bond would overshadow anyone. And there are the flamboyant Russian females.

DS Leyton continues with his account.

'He mentioned he'd had the buttering up from Jenny Hackett. He seemed amused by that. Said she eventually gave up on him and turned her charms – and the *Glenmorangie* – on Mikal Mital.'

'It's pronounced *morangey*, Leyton.'

Skelgill does a passable impression of Ruairidh McLeod's Scots accent – but then he glances urgently about the room to check he has not been overheard. The guard, however, is nursing a drink – which may or may not be the said malt, but certainly not his first of the evening, and is looking more flushed than ever as he sits in a group that comprises his games partner and colleague Laura Wilson (their team *Dire Straits)*, and their next opponents Sir Ewart Cameron-Kinloch and Jenny Hackett *(The Pretenders)*, who chatter and laugh boisterously and occasionally chime in with the line of a song while they wait their turn at bar billiards.

DS Leyton humours his superior with a forced *ha-hah* – but there is plainly a more serious matter on his mind – and he frowns inwardly, as though it is a point that has just struck him.

'Thing is, Guv – that probably means Jenny Hackett was the last person to see Mikal Mital alive – but for how long?'

Skelgill drains his glass of *Guinness* and turns the visual effects of the disagreeable pasteurised aftertaste upon his colleague.

'What do you mean, for how long?'

'Well, Faulkner reckons that when they left he saw them through the sliding door – and they linked arms.'

Skelgill's features are implacable, verging on grim.

'Leyton – Jenny Hackett was well tanked up when she came to pick our brains. She probably grabbed hold of the old fellow because she could hardly stand.'

DS Leyton is silent for a moment.

'Interesting that Faulkner noticed, though, Guv. He kind of winked at me as he said it. But, surely he wouldn't mean – like – *how's-your-father?*'

'Strange things happen on sleeper trains, Leyton.'

DS Leyton jerks his head sharply to look at his superior. Given everything that has occurred it seems a curiously facetious remark for him to have made. But Skelgill springs to his feet with his empty glass in one hand and holds out his other, demanding his colleague's.

'Drink up, Leyton – there's nowt else for it. The best thing we can do tonight is win this tournament.'

DS Leyton does as bidden, looking slightly surprised that his superior is volunteering to obtain refills. He gulps the last of his beer, in his urgency dribbling down his chin.

'Cheers, Guvnor – same again – pint of Forsythe.'

Skelgill moves swiftly through the lounge and into the adjoining snug, where the servery is located. It is a small cosy beamed room, with a fire burning in the grate and half a dozen low tables with easy chairs grouped around them. It is empty but for Richard Bond's employees, François and Egor, paired together for games *(Simon & Garfunkel)* and presently deep in conversation. They glance up simultaneously and nod respectfully to Skelgill; he greets them with a convivial, "Alreet, lads" but continues to the bar, where the housekeeper, Samanta is emptying a dishwasher of steaming glasses, and only the top of her dark head is presently visible.

'Pint of your best real ale please, landlady.'

She jumps to attention – and seems disconcerted by Skelgill's apparently serious demand. He moves to assuage her alarm.

'Only joking, lass. It was too much to hope that that company had ordered a firkin of *Cocker Hoop* for their Christmas do.'

She looks a little relieved.

'Mr Merlyn says we don't have enough call for it.'

Skelgill rocks his head from side to side.

'Happen there's only one thing worse than no cask ale – and that's cask ale that's gone off.' But he hesitates, and stiffens disapprovingly. 'Make that *two* things – and a landlord that tries to flog it to you.'

The girl simpers, though she must be humouring him; he does not expect her to appreciate that he has excused the innkeeper's stocking policy. It strikes him that Joost Merlyn is probably just the sort of penny-pincher he has denigrated; certainly he does not shy at extracting his pound of flesh from this young staff member. Skelgill's tone softens.

'Looks like we're running you ragged. Waitress, barmaid, chief cook and bottle-washer.'

'Oh – I did not cook – chef had prepared the meal before he was sent home. The food – it was good – there was sufficient?'

'Aye – no complaints on either front.'

Skelgill looks a little red-faced; he had suspected during the meal that she singled him out for seconds. But he tackles the notion head on.

'And the service was top-notch. We need to organise a whip-round – so you get a decent tip, lass. Don't want you missing out when your boss fellow puts in his inflated compensation claim to the railway company.'

The girl seems a touch embarrassed – but she also has something to say.

'Oh – but – I do not think he will need to do that?' Her inflexion is questioning – as though Skelgill ought to know. 'Ms Adamska – she has presented her *Amex Black*. To cover any costs for the entire party while you are here. Everybody can have whatever they wish.'

Skelgill raises an eyebrow – this is news to him. He grins, perhaps a little inanely.

'I might have to reconsider my order of a lager and a *Guinness*.'

'I am at your service.'

131

She regards him unblinkingly, her dark eyes suddenly imploring. He realises that for the first time since his arrival she is wearing make-up, in particular a concoction of mascara and eyeliner that expedites a hitherto unseen worldliness. Her hair is glossy beneath the bar lights, and her sleeveless halterneck black dress reveals a discreet tattoo, a series of runes that must run in a crescent, like a necklace across her breastbone. He becomes conscious that he ought to reply.

'Couple of bags of cheese and onion?'

The girl lowers her gaze and smiles demurely.

'Of course, Inspector.'

When Skelgill returns to his colleague he feels the noise level has been cranked up a notch or two; perhaps it is the freely flowing drink and the *Hawkwind* track emanating from the jukebox like a jet aircraft preparing to take off. DS Leyton has been watching the game still in progress between the pairings of Wiktoria Adamska and Bill Faulkner, and Ivanna Karenina and Richard Bond, *Blondie* versus *Abba*. Skelgill bangs down their drinks in a rather cavalier fashion, spilling some of the liquid from the brimming glasses. In a lowered voice he speaks out of the side of his mouth.

'Leyton, did you know Wiktoria Adamska's footing the bill?'

'What do you mean, Guv?'

Skelgill explains what he has just learned. DS Leyton takes a cautious sip of lager and wipes foam from his lips with the back of his hand.

'Suppose when you're hitched to a billionaire it's a drop in the ocean. No wonder that Merlyn geezer's been hopping around on his stick with a grin like a Cheshire cat. I thought they were pushing the boat out with the fancy wine at dinner. Mind you, Guv – he'll be on tenterhooks – what use is a posh credit card with no internet or phone line?'

Skelgill grins wryly, but his tone is disapproving.

'I reckon we'd better have a word with her. I don't like charity at the best of times – and we can't be seen to be in anyone's pocket.'

DS Leyton's attitude is more phlegmatic.

'She seems quite happy to be the centre of attention, Guv.'

At this moment it appears that the woman in question has played the match-winning shot – for Richard Bond, despite being her opponent, is quick to move in with a congratulatory bear-hug, from which she disentangles herself to enjoin in a more subtle embrace and exchange of air kisses with Ivanna Karenina. Her playing partner Bill Faulkner appears estranged from this extravagant show of affection and, so eclipsed, turns to set up the balls and skittles for the ensuing match. However, with characteristic American candour, he calls out across the room.

'Hey, y'all – who dat?'

That he does not precisely mean who is next on the table but refers to the so-far all-conquering *Blondie* nonetheless serves to summon *The Pretenders* and *Dire Straits*. Skelgill is watching him over the rim of his pint glass, and the man notices his attention just as Richard Bond heartily declares that the departing foursome should make an expedition through to the bar. As he pays lip service to a high-five from the animated financier, he flashes Skelgill a stolid grin. Plainly he is tolerating the events of the evening, but would much rather be undertaking something of his own design. It is a sentiment with which Skelgill can identify, and he returns a sympathetic raising of the eyebrows as if to say one may as well make the best of one's circumstances.

And making the best of it is perhaps a fair description of what follows. Certainly Joost Merlyn adopts such tactics, evidently detailing his young female assistant to circulate in order to ensure that any glass nearing empty is replaced with a fresh drink, while he holds fort at the bar to watch the pound signs ring up on the cash register. The jukebox volume seems to be progressively raised, and rarely can the ancient game of shove ha'penny have been played to so raucous an accompaniment, not least when 1970s tracks *Love Train* and *Hotel California* are belted out by those present, the singers presumably not deaf to the irony implicit in their lyrics. It emerges that Ruairidh McLeod, the guard, belying his somewhat dour demeanour, is responsible for these mischievous selections, his defence that these were big hits of his youth.

133

As for the tournament itself, Skelgill might affect indifference to his opponents, but DS Leyton knows that this is not a state of mind of which he is capable. Indeed, his suggestion that Skelgill was not trying at darts was well wide of the mark, and the latter remains true to his stated intention to win outright. His competitive spirit is not something to rub up against, and thus DS Leyton pulls out all the stops for fear of incurring the wrath of his boss. Having already triumphed in the darts, *The Police* thus claim victory in both the bar billiards and the shove ha'penny contests, leaving themselves the luxury of being able to come last in the pub quiz (which they do, much to Skelgill's chagrin). This final leg is comfortably won by *The Pretenders* – the rest of the party no match for the pairing of the former politician and the journalist, who demonstrate that inebriation need be no impediment to delving into the prodigious knowledge banks that their respective professions have bequeathed them. Skelgill did however take some consolation in being the only person in the room correctly to answer the question, "What is an Allis Shad?" – a rare migratory species he most recently hooked in spring from the Solway.

The winning team's prize turns out to be a jeroboam of champagne, which they have little choice but to bow to public pressure and crack open (Skelgill feigns but then stops short of spraying the audience). By now it seems the unfortunate predicament that the party shares has been forgotten, they have shrugged off their cares and inhibitions, and they crowd together into the snug to continue their celebrations. Under normal circumstances these might have stretched long into the night, but the laws of biology are only so malleable. A late finish on the train, a rude awakening before 5am, an arduous trek through the blizzard, and the stress of the entire experience, complemented now by the soporific warmth from the hearth and the narcotic effect of alcohol; these factors combine to take their toll. Eyelids begin to droop and heads begin to nod and even Richard Bond, he who appears to be possessed of unbounded energy shows signs of flagging. Indeed, it is the former soldier that announces a pragmatic surrender and a last toast to *The Police* – both as worthy winners of the tournament and champions of their hopes for getting the hell out of here tomorrow morning!

No pressure. But Skelgill is rescued from the obligation of making some sort of victory-cum-valedictory speech, by the jukebox and the irresistible *a cappella* opening harmony of *Bohemian Rhapsody*. The group spontaneously launches into one last communal bout of karaoke, and retreats in disorderly fashion up the staircase to the strains of its mournful finale. In due course, Skelgill is still tunelessly rendering poignant snatches as he emerges from his shower *("Caught in a landslide, no escape from reality")* when there is a light tap on his bedroom door. Embarrassed by his falsetto, he waits a moment. Silence. DS Leyton would call out. Finally the knock comes again. He wraps a towel around his waist and cautiously opens the door. In the dim nightlights of the corridor hovers the slight and spectral figure of Samanta. Her long hair trails over her bare shoulders and amidst the dark make-up her eyes are concealed in shadow. She speaks in a hushed voice that makes her Eastern European accent seem more pronounced.

'Mr Merlyn – he has gone to bed.'

Skelgill is a little nonplussed by her words – but he sees immediately that she is carrying a round bar-tray with two bottles of beer upon it. The girl continues quickly.

'He keeps this for himself – hidden in the cellar. It is not cask ale, of course – but it is an award-winning craft bitter.'

Skelgill blinks a couple of times. There is the double incongruity of her presence at this juncture, and her hitherto hidden expertise. More tangibly congruous is that beside the two bottles stand two glasses. He leans out as far as modesty will permit and looks in both directions along the landing. Then he takes a step back.

10. FLYING VISIT

Friday, 6am

As hangovers go, Skelgill's first impression of this morning's is that it is of the heavy metal variety, with head-banging sound effects to match. However, as he rolls over and clamps his pillow tightly around his skull, he receives a shock – for the persistent *dub-dub-dub* diminishes. The pulsation must be emanating from outside his room; indeed, as he experimentally removes the makeshift muffler, he recognises the chopping engine of a helicopter.

He hobbles to the window and parts his curtains. It is still dark but the aircraft's blinding searchlight creates a great white pool out of the parking area. Instantly he notes two facts. Firstly, it has stopped snowing. Secondly, the pilot does not intend to hang about – for a figure is being lowered by winch – and if he is not mistaken he recognises the slight but capable athletic form.

Thus by the time a sockless Skelgill has donned a rudimentary outfit and made his way out of doors via the tack room as the most expedient route, he finds DS Jones striding across the stable yard, presumably having had the same idea. She unslings a small rucksack from her back and presents it to Skelgill as they converge.

'I have to be really quick, Guv – they're waiting for me.'

Skelgill looks momentarily panicked. The beat of the rotors bounces about the courtyard like an insistent summons. But he figures they will have allowed time for her to make her way inside the building. He jerks a thumb over one shoulder.

'Come in – tell us.'

DS Jones's shrewd hazel eyes meet his. She gives a nod. They have equipped her with an olive-green jump suit, and a black helmet and combat boots, and with a full body harness she looks the part of serving flight crew. She follows him inside. He tugs shut the stable-style doors to reduce the noise. She pulls off

136

her helmet and shakes out her fair hair; it seems an extravagant gesture under the circumstances.

'Guv – the demands on the helicopter are unbelievable. There are people trapped left, right and centre – some really urgent cases. I've managed to get us a window. I cleared it with the Chief. I've had two forensic officers brought down from Penrith. We're going to collect Mikal Mital's body from the train – and they'll grab what evidence they can and seal off the sleeping car. We've also got an old lady on board, from Ulphathwaite where I spent last night – she needs urgent dialysis. We'll be at maximum payload.'

Skelgill nods grimly. Despite that he knows all about the significance of payload when it comes to such aircraft, she is being somewhat diplomatic in her rationale. But, he has to admit; they don't call her 'fast-track' back at the station for nothing. There are calculations that balance the requirements of the case (its seriousness as yet unconfirmed) with the obligation to extract the stranded passengers and reinstate them upon their journeys. Notwithstanding, Skelgill is troubled by the prospect that DS Jones is about to be snatched away from him without a proper explanation – but her next words anticipate his concern. She reaches out to pat the bag.

'There's a two-way radio – and a charger. We'll be able to speak in a few minutes. I initiated enquiries via the landline yesterday afternoon and received preliminary feedback before the close of play. When we reach the train I should have a quarter of an hour while the guys are doing their stuff.'

'Then what?'

'I'll go in person to brief the path lab. And once I'm back at my desk I can coordinate any further investigations you want me to make.'

Skelgill's features remain stern. He snaps open the clip of the rucksack and delves inside.

'Okay. This is the same model we use for mountain rescue. Better get you back on board before your pilot starts honking his horn and wakes every one up.'

DS Jones affects a wide-eyed double take – and smiles at his joke. She flicks back her hair and pulls on her helmet. She is wearing gloves and struggles with the chinstrap. Skelgill intervenes. Compliantly she tilts back her head. He hesitates, as though to speak – but then instinctively he glances around – and he realises that Samanta is standing in the doorway to the corridor, a barely illuminated silhouette. She seems to have on the same dress as last night.

DS Jones raises a hand in acknowledgement – but Skelgill fastens the buckle and pulls her away.

'Come on – I'll make sure your harness is properly clipped on to the winch.'

As they begin to exit Samanta's voice follows them.

'Inspector – do you want a coat?'

Skelgill hesitates.

'It's alright, thanks – it's stopped snowing.' He makes a face of artless mea culpa. 'I could do with some paracetamol.'

'Sure.'

The girl bows her head and turns and disappears as silently as she came.

Out front Skelgill and DS Jones duck into the downdraught and Skelgill sees to the suspension strop. He signals to the winchman, and then has to shout to DS Jones.

'You're good to go, lass.'

His colleague leans closer to make herself heard.

'You okay, Guv? You look a bit – dishevelled.'

Skelgill grimaces and mouths back.

'You should see Leyton.'

DS Jones grins – but the crew have no time to spare and she is promptly hoisted aboard and almost immediately the helicopter banks away into the void. Skelgill watches its blinking lights disappear. As he begins to trudge back he looks up at the inn. In the gloom he gets a vague impression of faces at several of the windows. They might almost be pale ghosts of past travellers.

*

138

'Can you hear me okay, Guv? Over.'

'Aye, but it's not great. Over.'

'This cutting is so deep – it's almost like a tunnel. And the pinewoods are between us. I think the signal will be clearer when I'm back at base. Over.'

'What's the score? Over.'

'Everything seems to be going to plan here – they're dusting and taking swabs right now. Just to bring you up to speed. Yesterday we reached the post office with no problems. There was a spare room – they were happy for me to stay. Lucinda Hobhouse returned to her stables complex. I got straight onto HQ. Believe it or not they just assumed we'd arrived and were sleeping off hangovers! Independently Gold Command were aware of the train being stranded – but it was low on the list of emergencies – the scale of the chaos is immense – all of Cumbria and Northumberland, the Scottish Borders, and the central belt from Edinburgh to Glasgow. Everything has been brought to a dead halt. Our helicopter was due out to inspect later today. Network Rail have moved snowploughs to start work at first light, from both north and south, but there's about 100 miles of track affected and there are stretches where they think they'll need excavators – such as here. Obviously, once I was able to inform them that everyone was safe it took the pressure off – but they want to get the line open anyway because there's no means of getting between England and Scotland. Thousands of people are scheduled to travel home for Christmas – and there's a big issue with food getting through. They think they might be able to open one of the carriageways of the M6 by tonight – but there are hundreds of abandoned vehicles, so they can't just plough straight through. The good news is the snow has stopped sooner than expected.'

'Aye – I just listened to the forecast while I was waiting.'

'Any significant developments there, Guv? Before I tell you what I know so far. Over.'

'Not unless you count me and Leyton winning the pub games tournament last night.' He half-yawns-half-groans but offers no explanation for this. 'They're all keeping their cards close to

139

their chest. Jenny Hackett's the only one talking openly about what happened to Mikal Mital – seems she and him ended up drinking together and toddled off to bed at the same time – linking arms according to Bill Faulkner.'

Skelgill is silent for a few moments, but does not use the customary "over" and so DS Jones also waits for a while before she speaks.

'Maybe she was really determined to get a look at that manuscript, Guv. Over.'

'If she were – and if she took it – like I've been saying – it's probably hidden here somewhere.' Distracted by this thought it takes him a few seconds to realise he has finished. 'Over.'

'At least it can't leave for the time being, Guv. I just need to get you some conclusive evidence. Over.'

Skelgill is thinking that his ideal scenario would be summarily to order everyone onto a bus without their possessions and get a team of officers to search the inn. (Albeit that right now, other than the manuscript, he doesn't know what he is looking for.) But this is cloud cuckoo land, given the national emergency. Going by what he heard on the wireless even the hurriedly mobilised British armed forces are stretched right now. Any serious deployment of resources does depend upon DS Jones feeding back something conclusive, as she has put it. But, what if – as is perfectly likely – Mikal Mital died of natural causes? Then he is jolted by the memory that he did see the manuscript with his very own eyes, and now it is gone. Except there is the possibility that the man voluntarily gave it to someone else to read. Perhaps it will be innocently produced in due course. But he is halted in this erratic train of thought. For when he does not answer DS Jones presses on with her debrief.

'Guv – yesterday afternoon I supplied a list of passengers and asked both for their families to be notified and for them to be vetted. Along with the driver and the guard – oh, and Lucinda Hobhouse.'

Skelgill makes a rather scornful exclamation – but his intention is to communicate that his subordinate is becoming as cynical as he is. She seems to understand his sentiment.

140

'You have to admit, Guv – her appearance on the train was hardly run-of-the-mill.' She pauses, although she has not signalled for him to speak, and after a brief hiatus she continues. 'Besides, as it turns out she does have connections with what you might call the world of high finance. Her brother-in-law is a merchant banker in the City of London – for a firm that has been under investigation for its dealings in the British Virgin Islands. She is also related to a titled peer whose cousin is a long-serving mandarin in the Treasury. The riding school at Ulphathwaite appears bona fide – but the postmistress was telling me there has been a colossal investment since Lucinda Hobhouse took it over. That stallion we rode back on – according to the village rumour mill she rejected a multi-million-pound offer for it to be sold to stud.'

'I should be so lucky.'

Skelgill's choked retort is purely rhetorical – but DS Jones waits in the event that he might wish to comment on these findings.

'It's a long shot, Jones.'

DS Jones appreciates that the impossibility of knowing the train would come to a halt rules out the notion of a premeditated conspiracy. But there is the faint possibility that Lucinda Hobhouse had responded to the aftermath out of more than altruism. And when Skelgill remains taciturn DS Jones iterates this argument.

'She did get to a landline first thing yesterday morning, Guv. It is feasible that someone suggested an opportunistic visit to the train. I realise it's unlikely – but the point is I didn't want to ignore her completely. Let's see what comes of the team's investigations. I've briefed them to be alert to anything that may pertain to potential money laundering. For instance we've had it confirmed that the TV news channel that employs Sir Ewart Cameron-Kinloch and Ivanna Karenina is definitely owned by the billionaire Bogblokinov. The idea that he, or the company, operates entirely independently of the Russian government is unthinkable. And as Jenny Hackett pointed out he has significant property holdings in London, and probably elsewhere.

141

Then Wiktoria Adamska's husband is not so far behind in the rich list. For her part, there's no indication that the fashion business is anything other than above board – it's a UK registered private company and its accounts are up to date and are in a healthy state. The same can't be said, however, of Richard Bond's company. It's listed on what's called the AIM – the Alternative Investment Market. It seems they bought into a portfolio of high street retailers – and that whole sector is struggling. Bond's firm recently issued a profits warning and its shares have virtually halved from their peak value. Apparently they've been slogging round with the begging bowl trying to drum up venture capital. No accounts have been filed for the last two years.'

DS Jones seems to hesitate – but then Skelgill hears her voice, more distant. "Sure – I'm nearly done – one minute, okay?" Then she comes back more clearly. 'Sorry, Guv – that's the team leader wanting us out of here. Just to finish. Going back to Sir Ewart Cameron-Kinloch – again, as Jenny Hackett told us – he instigated the Golden Visas scheme to encourage inward investment into the UK. There are no suggestions that he benefited personally – but it places him in the financial orbit, so we're looking into that. His colleague Ivanna Karenina – not much so far on her – but we've put out the appropriate feelers to see if she has any connections other than with her direct employer, if you know what I mean. Then, finally, there's the American, Bill Faulkner.'

'He works for a US bank.' Again Skelgill ignores the radio protocol. 'He told Leyton.'

'That's right. Apparently we received a cool reaction from the firm. They went to some lengths to verify that we were the police. And then they provided only the most basic information – confirmation that he's an employee and his temporary address in London. But at least he seems to be who he claims he is. Obviously, Guv – this is all work in progress. The team will be back onto it once work starts this morning. Over.'

Skelgill seems a little surprised to have the baton passed at this juncture, and all he can manage is, "Aye, over."

142

'Sorry I can't be much more enlightening than Jenny Hackett was.' His colleague sounds apologetic – as though she thinks he might be dissatisfied. It seems that she is about to sign off – but then she obviously remembers a salient point. 'Oh – there is one more thing – about her, Guv. She's been given notice of redundancy. We've spoken to her editor. Evidently he was a bit cagey – the DC got the distinct impression that they're effectively firing her. Of course – the first inclination is to assume she's been underperforming – but when you search online she comes up as winning a hatful of awards for investigative journalism over the past few years. So we've looked into the ownership of *The Inquirer*. It's positioned as campaigning for transparency – but the media group to which the newspaper belongs is owned through a shell company in the Cayman Islands and the family who control it are tax exiles in Monaco. So who's to say she's not been getting uncomfortably close to some home truths? And –'

But DS Jones is unable to proceed with this last sentence – for Skelgill hears an impatient summons, harsh and insistent.

'Oh, Guv – that's it – I need to fly – *literally!* How about if I call you at 12 noon with an update – to save you carrying the radio around? With luck I'll have some news from the lab. Over.'

'Aye – just make sure you put a rocket under Herdwick. Tell him from me –'

But there is an explosive crackle on the line – and now it goes dead. Perhaps her battery has given up – or the signal is disrupted as she retreats towards the waiting helicopter. It is a state of affairs with which he is familiar; the successful use of two-way radios in fell country is something of an arcane craft. He curses that he has not conveyed sufficiently the requirement to browbeat the pathologist – that the experienced but cantankerous doctor must be made to pull out all the stops. However, on reflection, DS Jones has powers of persuasion that are more akin to diplomacy than his own. Pensively, he turns off the volume and slots the handset into the charger on the floor beside his bed. He drifts to the window and takes a deep breath;

143

exhaling slowly he watches the condensation expand before his eyes. It is still dark – and above the horizon he can see stars, the Plough and Polaris – the sky has cleared, and the first signs of dawn will come earlier this morning. He looks forward to his first proper view of the lie of the land. After a few moments he turns and pads through into the bathroom, where he drinks directly from the cold tap – the water is icy and it jars upon his teeth, and he can feel it going down, another little reminder that it is freezing outside. But at least the conditions are now more benign; it appears the forecasters were hedging their bets.

Skelgill sinks down upon his bed, not bothering to straighten the disorganised covers. He slides his hands behind his head; he realises his pulse has risen during the exchange with DS Jones, and the thump of his underlying headache has returned. He should have asked for more pills. But it could have been worse; with an effort he raises his torso, a kind of sit-up – across on the dresser is the tray with the two bottles of precious craft ale; neither is opened.

11. MISSING

Friday, 8.15am

Skelgill is tucking into his second helping of breakfast when a bleary-eyed DS Leyton trudges across the dining room and sinks heavily into the seat opposite his superior at a table set in the most secluded corner.

'Cor blimey, Guvnor – this burning the candle at both ends malarkey. I reckon it's easier being at home with the nippers. Plus I'm out of practice with drinking – two nights on the bounce, an' all.'

'You reckoned you were out of practice with darts, Leyton – but it soon came back to you.'

'So it did, Guv.' DS Leyton brightens. 'I suppose it's muscle memory, ain't it? Like riding a bike.' But now he seems to suffer a little rollercoaster of sensations. He rubs his stomach gingerly. 'Can't say the same for the old Derby.'

'Get yourself a couple of Cumberland sausages before they're gone, Leyton – they'll soon sort you out. Best hangover cure this side of Hadrian's Wall.'

DS Leyton pulls a face as if he begs to differ – but then his eyes begin to rove over hotplates that are laid out upon trestle tables beneath the windows. He scrutinises the various remaining morsels on Skelgill's plate – if his boss is true to his word, then he has consumed his own sausages first (which, in DS Leyton's estimation would make sense, his superior not being a man habitually to save the best until last). Skelgill does not however elaborate upon either his reasoning or his suggestion that the Scots have a more efficacious morning-after remedy. Perhaps he means *Irn-Bru?*

'I might manage a small one, Guv.'

The expression 'small Cumberland sausage' is a contradiction in terms, and Skelgill is quick to recognise this fact as his colleague rises with a groan and pads across to the buffet.

'I'll split it with you, Leyton.'

145

When his deputy returns Skelgill waits for him to divide the coiled sausage and pass half over before he addresses him.

'You missed all the fun and games this morning, Leyton.'

DS Leyton seems preoccupied with the contents of his plate.

'How's that, Guv?'

'Jones was here.'

DS Leyton – now having taken a bite of fried bread – can only respond with a look of consternation.

'You didn't hear the chopper?'

DS Leyton shakes his head and swallows with difficulty.

'I reckon I was dead to the world, Guv.'

Skelgill frowns rather doubtfully. But it is true to say his sergeant's bedchamber is on the opposite side of the quadrangle to his own, and thus would have been most insulated from the clatter of the aircraft's moving parts. However DS Leyton's expression begins to exhibit a spark of recognition. He raises his knife in lieu of an index finger.

'Now you mention it, Guv – I did have a dream with a flippin' great chugging noise in it – it was about how we saved Christmas. We were on board this old steam loco – yeah – I remember, it was the *Flying Scotsman* – it was broken down – but we managed to get it going – over Shap summit – bingo! Only we didn't know how to stop it – and it was like the runaway train, speeding faster and faster down towards Penrith. Course – we'd got sacks of Christmas presents on board for all the kids in the town – and we only just figured out in the nick of time how to chuck 'em off like they did in the old days, into those big rope nets.'

Skelgill is chewing somewhat uninterestedly.

'What happened to us?'

DS Leyton shakes his head despondently.

'I reckon we ended up in the Scottish Highlands – stuck in the snow. Missed Christmas.'

There is a wistful note in his voice – Skelgill wonders if it is a deliberate reminder that he has undertaken to DS Leyton that he would be home by tomorrow, Christmas Eve – and now he feels a pang of guilt that DS Jones has, through chance circumstances, got the break that has repatriated her to relative civilisation; certainly she will be able to get home. Reflecting on this it strikes him that she would willingly have swapped places with her married colleague, had he asked her – but the notion had not occurred to him while the opportunity existed. Moreover, if he is honest, he prefers the status quo – DS Jones is by far the most efficient and inquisitive of them all – she is in the right place for what needs to be done; and DS Leyton is well equipped for the task in hand, stoically sitting out their confinement, a stolid police presence; and frankly a more apt companion, less controversial for him to be trapped in a hotel with, given the propensity for gossip back at the station. Skelgill, nonetheless, shifts a little awkwardly in his seat. He looks about, to check no one is eavesdropping, and lowers his voice.

'Leyton – strictly between you and me – I've got a two-way radio. Jones is calling in at noon.' He adds a belated postscript. 'If you want to get a message to the wife.'

'Struth, Guv – you're making it sound like we're being held hostage.'

DS Leyton's voice rises a little hysterically, and Skelgill's eyes dart about the room to check if they have been overheard. Thus far, only Richard Bond, who sits together with his two young colleagues, and Bill Faulkner and Ruairidh McLeod, who sit apart, have made it down to breakfast; probably the sorts – like himself – that in are the habit of rising early, for whom a lie-in is anathema when there is a day to be dealt with, worms to catch, fish to fry. But they are subdued, and variously preoccupied – the financiers with occasional conversation punctuated by restrained guffaws from Richard Bond; Bill Faulkner with his mobile phone (and *The Grapes of Wrath* presumably, since there is still no signal); and the fiery-browed Ruairidh McLeod with his own thoughts, and black they look.

'That's what I'm worried about Leyton. Some of this crowd were gawping out of their windows at the chopper – I'm surprised no one's asked when it's coming back.'

147

Skelgill attacks the last couple of curving inches of the surrendered Cumberland sausage. DS Leyton clears his throat uneasily.

'What's the score on that front, Guv – er, in case I'm asked?'

Skelgill shrugs.

'Your guess is as good as mine, Leyton. Jones had managed to get dispensation to bring down a couple of SOCOs – extract the body from the train. But they'd also got a sick old lady on board they'd picked up from Ulphathwaite. Sounds like they're up to their necks with casualties for the foreseeable future.' DS Leyton once again looks dejected – that his superior is not exactly letting him down lightly. Skelgill rather unconvincingly tosses in a concession. 'There's talk they might get the M6 moving tonight. If push comes to shove we could yomp across and get you picked up by a patrol.'

DS Leyton appears curiously chastened. He regards Skelgill earnestly.

'I ain't gonna leave you in the lurch, Guv – not while there might be a job to do here.'

Skelgill, true to form, shuns his colleague's demonstration of loyalty.

'Let's see what Jones comes back with. We might the lot of us be able to yomp it tomorrow, get on a bus – if this turns out to be a storm in a teacup.'

At this he examines his own teacup, and lifts the pot but it is also empty – and yet as if by magic Samanta appears at his shoulder and pours from a fresh pot. She is wearing her regulation black staff outfit beneath a navy catering apron.

'Are you feeling better, Inspector?'

Her tone is sympathetic, but her smile slightly knowing; DS Leyton looks on with faint amusement at the special attention his superior is receiving. Skelgill is plainly embarrassed.

'Aye – not bad thanks.' He begins urgently to ladle sugar. 'I'll be right as rain once I've got enough of this down me.'

The girl bows and retreats, looking satisfied.

DS Leyton chuckles.

'She's taken a shine to you, Guv.'

When Skelgill might customarily capitalise upon the opportunity to preen, he scowls disparagingly.

'Happen she knows which side her bread's buttered. I said last night we'd have a whip-round. I wouldn't trust Joost Merlyn to split the spoils of this little windfall.'

DS Leyton looks rather conflicted – but any disagreement would relate to his contrasting reading of the girl's motivation. As to the unprepossessing landlord, he shares his boss's cynicism.

'I reckon he's a sly old fox, Guv. He looks like he's trying to make up his mind whether to cosh you with his stick or pick your pocket – he's like a cross between Bill Sikes and Fagin out of that there *Oliver Twist*.'

Skelgill harrumphs. Or Scrooge, maybe. Certainly the man's countenance displays a permanently self-despising expression that hovers between avarice and anger. Skelgill pities the poor girl Samanta; it does not feel a healthy working environment – although he supposes under normal circumstances there will be other members of staff upon whom she can lean for moral support. Anyway, it appears he has deflected his colleague's assertion and with it the scope for mild innuendo. Now he moves the subject forward more decisively.

'I reckon you could have a quiet word with him, Leyton.'

'What's that, Guvnor?'

DS Leyton tries to conceal his trepidation – patently this is something that Skelgill does not intend to do himself.

'Until I hear from Jones I'm keeping a low profile. I don't want folk mithering me every five minutes about when they're going to get out of here. The fact is I don't know the answer – and subject to what Jones comes up with, we might want to delay their departure. But we'll need to come clean about the chopper – and tell them we've got a team getting in touch with their nearest and dearest.'

'So, where does old Merlyn come in, Guv?'

'Get him to put up a notice at reception. Say we're hoping to hear about evacuation plans by this evening. Otherwise we've been instructed to wait here for our own safety. That'll put a damper on any of Bond's crackpot schemes.'

DS Leyton squints surreptitiously to where the former soldier sits with his colleagues – but it is another person who prompts him to mutter under his breath.

'Looks like we've got company.'

Skelgill glances up to see that Wiktoria Adamska is making a beeline for their table. She is barefooted – bare legged, indeed – and wears only a short flimsy silk salmon-pink dressing gown, tied with a waistband, that she holds together at her throat with one hand. She is naked of her customary white gold jewellery. Her hair is as dishevelled as he has seen it; it has a straw-like quality, and together with her lack of high heels gives her a more voluptuous appearance. Most striking of all, however, is the look in her pale eyes. She fixes Skelgill with a stare that he reads as one of infuriation tinged with distress. Her imposing presence silences what little conversation prevails, and even the clink of cutlery becomes muted – indeed the room might almost be a film scene held in freeze frame with only one actor that moves. And reaching the detectives' table – unfazed by the attention she has garnered – she pulls out a seat and sinks elegantly upon it, sliding one long thigh over the other and causing both males to stare determinedly at her face.

'Inspector – you must come to my room.'

She utters these words in barely above a whisper. In the circumstances it might almost be scripted importuning – but her agitated tone belies any such intentions. Skelgill, conscious of other eyes upon them, has his fork suspended between his plate and his lips, and he rather casually holds this pose. But he too speaks quietly in response.

'What's the problem, Mrs Adamski?'

Perhaps he highlights her marital status as if to eliminate any doubt about his reading of her demand – and it *is* a demand – but what lies behind it remains unclear. The woman casts briefly about the room – she might note that successive pairs of eyes drop away beneath her gaze.

'During the night – I have been violated.'

150

Skelgill just catches DS Leyton's involuntary, *"Whoa"* – though it is barely breathed – before her words begin to crash about inside his head like a band of lunatics hijacking the asylum. In an instant he is reversing his assessment that to be without DS Jones is a satisfactory state of affairs. This is the last thing he needs! But his inner turmoil is superseded as the woman rises and steps back from the chair.

'Come – I implore you.'

Her tone is no less insistent – and she leaves him little choice – for she strides away. Skelgill is striving to appear composed – he remembers the food on his fork – and plunges it into his mouth before dropping his cutlery with a clatter upon his plate. He rises, leans over to swallow a gulp of tea, wipes his lips with his shirt cuff and sets off. But he has taken only three paces when he stops and turns to glare at his colleague. He gives a sharp jerk of his head – his meaning is clear – what does his sergeant think he is doing sitting on his backside?

DS Leyton resignedly abandons his breakfast and sets off in pursuit. Reaching the reception area he sees Skelgill taking the stairs two at a time, and further above, fading into the womblike burgundy gloom, the elegant figure of Wiktoria Adamska.

The staircase meets the first floor landing on the north side of the quadrangle; Wiktoria Adamska has a room facing south. She does not wait for Skelgill, obliging him to follow several yards behind; her gait is elegant and upright, the practised poise of the catwalk, her head held perfectly still like a hunting feline. She moves with deceptive speed, and in keeping pace Skelgill extends his stride. Beneath the ubiquitous maroon carpet the floor has been repaired in places with sheets of spongy plywood that feel close to collapse. In his slipstream the bulky DS Leyton makes correspondingly undulating progress.

The woman's bedroom door is wide open; she enters, but Skelgill holds back for DS Leyton. They file in like miscreant pupils summoned to the principal's office; but it would be a schoolboy's fantasy headmistress that greeted him in a revealing nightgown, perched upon the edge of a king-sized bed. They loiter rather awkwardly – until Skelgill indicates that DS Leyton

151

should shut the door. In response Wiktoria Adamska waves an imperious hand towards a chaise longue beneath the window.

'Please – make yourselves comfortable.'

The detectives do as bidden – they seem to settle unnaturally close to one another – while at the same time Wiktoria Adamska shifts into a side-saddle position in order to face them. It strikes Skelgill that as a former model perhaps she is simply not self-conscious in the normal way – having changed a thousand times backstage where nudity is the norm and prying eyes not considered to be malevolent. Truth be told, she has little to be self-conscious about – but he casts such sentiments from his mind – and falls back upon the tongue-tied policeman's stock question.

'Madam – would you like to tell us what happened?'

'See for yourselves.'

Again there is the regal gesture – now she refers to an alcove, marked out by a blackened beam, that serves as an open wardrobe. Hanging from a rail Skelgill recognises the two-tone outfit of the train, and the shimmering silver slip of a dress of the games night. Beneath lie her matching suitcases, the tiny and the supersized, open like clamshells with their lids resting against the wall. The small valise appears dedicated to an extensive confection of lacy underwear, mainly in black with ribbons of scarlet and purple. The large case is given over almost entirely to two bulky fur coats, one jet black and one pure white, folded neatly and placed side by side. Skelgill stares for a few moments – but despite his best endeavours at deduction, he remains in the dark.

'Madam – just now, you said – that you had been – *violated.*'

He finds himself unable to prevent his voice from rising on the last word. But the reaction it generates is not what he anticipates. The woman pulls herself up onto the bed and in the same movement folds her legs beneath her and sinks back upon a collection of pillows. If it were a scene from an old movie she would now raise a cigarette in an ivory holder and expect one of them to come forward to light it for her. Instead she casually

152

combs her long pale hair away from her face with the fingers of both hands.

'A man entered my room. I was paralysed.' She stares at Skelgill with some belligerence. 'He groped about – for – it seemed an eternity.'

She falls silent – as though she deems it unnecessary to say more. Skelgill realises he must prompt her.

'You wish to report an assault.'

She responds with a narrowing of her eyes.

'It was not an assault – I told you, it was a violation.' She stares at him evenly. 'He stole something of immeasurable value.'

'You mean – you *weren't* physically attacked?'

'What – of course not!' Her perfectly arched brows become momentarily knitted. 'Do you think I would be this calm?'

Skelgill hears a hiss of breath – of relief – from his sergeant. He holds up both hands, palms facing the woman.

'So – you're okay? That's the main thing.'

'It is hardly the main thing.'

Though in control of her outward emotions she is plainly conflicted – not least that she now has to explain herself. Skelgill can see this, and he leans forward and rests his forearms on his knees. It a pose that suggests he will give careful consideration to whatever she has to say.

'Madam, when did this take place?'

'I do not know.' She glances at the nightstand on one side of the bed where there is an old-fashioned wind-up alarm clock. It would show nothing in the dark. 'My phone is out of charge – it is useless at the moment.'

Skelgill is looking puzzled.

'But it was some time in the night – between your turning in and waking just now?'

'In the night.'

'Was your door locked?'

'I did not hear the door. The first I knew was of the presence of a man.'

'Could you see who it was?'

153

'I could see nothing. I doubt if I opened my eyes.'

'Are you certain it was a male?'

'Of course.'

She seems determined, sufficiently so that Skelgill feels it would be pedantic to oblige her to expound upon her reasoning.

'Can you describe further what took place?'

'Simply that he searched among my belongings.' She gives a light shrug of her shoulders; she seems intent upon persisting with her laconic style.

'And then he left the room?'

'I can't remember – I must have passed out.'

Skelgill glances at DS Leyton who responds with a somewhat unguarded frown. The woman notices the exchange and is quick to respond.

'Do not doubt what I say, Inspector.'

Her tone is steely.

'Madam, was something stolen?'

Now she hesitates.

'I cannot tell you what has been taken.'

On the face of it this is an ambiguous statement – but Skelgill understands by now that her pared responses are carefully crafted.

'You mean something is gone but you don't want to say what it is?'

Perhaps to the detectives' surprise, she frowns self-reproachfully.

'I was foolish to have it in my possession.'

'Are we talking about an item of jewellery?'

She compresses her lips broodingly.

'You will know it when you find it. I wish to avoid any publicity. Its potential value would soar and I would never see it again.'

Skelgill regards her rather severely. But he understands that she will have weighed the likely fidelity of any vows of confidentiality they might render.

'That doesn't make it easy for us, madam.'

'I'm sure you will find a way, Inspector – a resourceful man, such as you are.'

She smiles engagingly – almost irresistibly – and Skelgill discovers he is nodding in agreement. He can sense DS Leyton is straining at his side.

'And now if you will excuse me, officers, I shall take a bath.'

She slips off the bed and glides past them into the en suite.

She only part-closes the door and there is the splash of water beginning to cascade abundantly into the cast-iron tub. Skelgill rises and glances about the room – but when he looks back at his still-sitting sergeant he sees the man transfixed – for he has inadvertently glimpsed a reflection from a full-length mirror as Wiktoria Adamska hangs her silk gown on a hook. Skelgill cuffs his colleague on the back of the head.

'Come on, Leyton.'

They exit, and begin to perambulate the first-floor landing. DS Leyton looks a little stunned.

'Cor blimey, what do you make of that, Guv?'

Skelgill might wonder to exactly which aspect his sergeant refers – the theatrical summons, the dramatic account, the abrupt termination – or his accidental *'What the butler saw'* moment. As for the latter, he is thankful that he insisted upon a chaperone. He growls elusively.

'You tell me, Leyton.'

'Well – I mean, Guv – her claiming she's been robbed – no idea of who – and won't tell us what. What are we supposed to do? We can hardly turn out everyone's pockets and pat them down on her say-so. See if some tea leaf's got a priceless diamond tiara stuffed down their underpants.'

Skelgill shrugs somewhat unconcernedly.

'I would have thought a set of papers was more likely, Leyton.'

DS Leyton cocks his head interrogatively to his superior.

'What – are you thinking of Mikal Mital's manuscript, Guv?'

'Why not?'

After a few moments' deliberation DS Leyton inhales to speak – but he realises they have walked full circle (or, more

155

accurately, full *square*) and are lapping Wiktoria Adamska's door. He hesitates until they have turned the next corner.

'Why didn't you ask her, Guv?'

'And let the cat out of the bag?' Skelgill's retort is sharp-tongued. 'That's why I said jewellery. If she'd had the manuscript, Leyton – then she must be in on whatever's been going on. I don't want her or anyone else knowing we're looking for it.'

Now DS Leyton rocks his head from side to side, as though he might be suffering from a stiff neck – but his words reveal it to be an accompaniment to some troubling speculation.

'I imagine if she'd have knocked on the old fella's compartment wearing that pink affair – he might have let her in, Guv.'

'Red affair, Leyton.'

'Come again, Guv?'

'Remember – Ruairidh McLeod told us he saw a woman in a red dressing gown.'

'Maybe she's got a whole troop of colours. There's enough underwear in that little case to last a fortnight.' And then a thought dawns, for the sergeant's voice takes on a note of heightened interest. 'And she was standing right next to Jenny Hackett when she got shoved into that snake pit, Guv.'

At this juncture they reach the head of the main staircase. Below in the lobby Skelgill sees that Samanta is standing to attention before the reception desk; from out of their line of sight he hears the gruff voice of Joost Merlyn – indeed he catches the words, harshly spoken: "And that is how it will remain. No matter what that –"

Samanta suddenly glances anxiously in their direction. Whether by accident or design it must betray their presence to her employer for he breaks off his sentence – and must dismiss her with some signal, for she bows her head obediently and turns and quickly walks away. By the time the two detectives have descended, the area behind the counter is deserted.

But Joost Merlyn may be lurking in the back office, and Skelgill points towards the front door. It is unlocked and they

156

emerge beneath the part-recessed portico onto the raised step. Here the snow is just a few inches deep, beyond lies a good foot and a half. Its surface is pristine, the only tracks some fifteen yards away being those of DS Jones's arrival and then her departure assisted by Skelgill, leading to and from the archway further along the front of the building. The inundated parking area is level, reflecting the old inn's location at the confluence of Ulpha Beck and Shake Holes Beck, effectively a little floodplain of alluvial deposits. Encircling them, bare oaks striped with driven snow rise up against a steep fellside; the deciduous wood has a dense ground layer of rhododendrons; these add some colour, albeit a deep winter green, and the bushes are heavily laden with snow. There appears to be a ride, tunnel-like – perhaps a footpath – that disappears into the bank of shrubs, and Skelgill can just a make out a sign fixed on the trunk of a tree, peeling lettering that might read "Bath House". The surrounding fells crowd in upon the scene, and although there is a clear blue sky, cerulean in its intensity, the low winter sun has not yet risen sufficiently to illuminate the inn and its environs, and so the more immediate snowscape lacks definition. Earlier, beneath the turbulence of the helicopter, Skelgill had not appreciated quite how comprehensively the wind has dropped. Neither flora nor fauna move – yet from the woodland fringe emanate the purring contact calls of a party of invisible long-tailed titmice; a sign that not all life has been stifled.

'It's flippin' Baltic, Guv.'

Skelgill nods appreciatively. He watches the warm plumes of their breath drift up and slowly dissipate.

'Baltic without the Blast.' Skelgill sniffs, as if the cold air is causing his nose to run. 'It's going to be a sight easier to get about. The visibility's perfect.'

DS Leyton makes an ambiguous quavering sound.

'I wouldn't fancy falling into one of those holes, Guv.'

Skelgill raises an eyebrow – is it a hint that his sergeant would rather sit tight than risk a trek across country to rendezvous with a rescue vehicle? However, he reverts to their paused conversation, now that they have privacy.

157

'She weren't too fussed about locking her doors, Leyton.'

'Nor even shutting 'em, Guv.'

'Aye.' Skelgill senses that his partner has not quite recovered from their interview. 'Invitation to trouble, wouldn't you say?'

DS Leyton is frowning, gathering his thoughts.

'She's not shy, is she, Guv? I mean – calling you up to her room – wearing next to nothing.' Now he punctuates his sentence with a deliberate "ahem". 'And what Jenny Hackett told us on the train – that she's got a bit of a reputation.'

'What are you saying, Leyton?'

'Well – what if she'd left her door unlocked on purpose? That she was expecting a visitor. But she nodded off. Then she was too shocked to do anything when things didn't go to plan. Meanwhile, whoever it was – maybe even a different geezer – took advantage of the situation.'

Skelgill is making pained faces during this rather disjointed description. Clearly he is unhappy with the whole scenario.

'What she described there, Leyton – sounded to me exactly like a bad dream.'

'A dream?'

'The feeling of paralysis – the invisible intruder – the way it blacks out with no conclusion. All that's missing is being in the Chief's Monday morning meeting, naked from the waist down.'

DS Leyton chuckles. He tucks his hands beneath his armpits and blows out a stream of mist.

'Trouble is, Guv – something's been half-inched.'

But Skelgill seems to be shaking his head minutely.

'*Trouble is,* Leyton – we can't be sure who's telling us the truth and who isn't.'

Despite that DS Leyton groans in frustration Skelgill suspects it is a sound effect engineered to disguise an involuntary shudder.

'Come on, Leyton – let's get a hot cuppa – find somewhere quiet where we can work out a plan of action.'

Skelgill spins around easily on the snow and opens the large oak door sufficiently for them to slip inside without allowing too much heat to escape. As he enters he realises that Samanta is close by, arranging brochures in a slotted tourist-information display unit. Her response is to check about the lobby and then to fix him beseechingly with her large dark eyes, crescent shadows prominent beneath. Skelgill mutters something to DS Leyton and then casually saunters over to the girl, leaving his colleague to head in the direction of the breakfast room.

'Got any decent suggestions for how a dozen folk might spend the day? Mostly city types.'

His words seem to catch her by surprise – and she begins to take him literally, raising a hand to indicate that there are indeed many attractions in the vicinity – no matter that such a notion is entirely impractical in the circumstances. Skelgill gives a wry grin. He pulls out a leaflet at random and appears to peruse it. It is a somewhat amateur production, entitled 'Shake Holes Historic Trail'. He lowers his voice and speaks without looking at her.

'What was that all about – when you were just told to make yourself scarce?'

Again Samanta glances across at the reception desk – but it is still unmanned. Nonetheless she too responds in hushed tones.

'Ah – he noticed I had taken the beers – the craft ale?'

'What?' Skelgill's tone is indignant.

'He says he has locked the cellar permanently – and I must ask him for the key each time I have to fetch stock.'

Now Skelgill swears an oath under his breath. He bridles that the girl has landed in trouble for his sake. He looks as if he would like to punch the man.

'Where is he? I'll put him straight.'

The girl is alarmed – she reaches to place a palm on Skelgill's arm.

'No, no – it is best that you do not. It is not a problem – I can handle it.' She regards him earnestly, as if to be sure of his cooperation. She takes a step closer, now gripping the sleeve of his shirt. 'But there is something –'

But the sudden explosion of the one-man hullabaloo that is Richard Bond truncates her sentence. The burly fellow strides into the lobby, apparently calling out orders to himself – and then exclaims loudly when he spies Skelgill. In one hand he

159

grasps a bundle of material, red in colour. In his wake a somewhat alarmed looking DS Leyton paddles to keep up, and the disturbance lures a limping Joost Merlyn from his lair beyond reception. Skelgill folds the leaflet out of sight into his back pocket and steps protectively in front of the girl.

Richard Bond marches up to Skelgill. He gives the kind of nod that might be appropriate to informally acknowledge a more senior officer.

'Jenny Hackett has left the building.' He raises the red material, which unfurls in the shape of a dressing gown. 'She abandoned this in the tack room. It has her cigarettes in the pocket.' The ex-military man's staccato sentences are delivered like little bursts of gunfire.

They crowd rather vacantly around the gown, as though something might reveal itself – it is a silk kimono, with a subtle oriental pattern in different shades of crimson and scarlet that is only evident on close examination. But Skelgill is thinking he is unaware that she smokes, and wondering that Richard Bond knows better – and DS Leyton now voices a concern along similar lines.

'How can you be sure it's hers?'

However, it is not Richard Bond that answers, but Samanta.

'I have seen it – while I serviced her room – hanging in the bathroom.'

Skelgill raises his hands. They are getting ahead of themselves.

'Hold your horses.' He gestures that Richard Bond should lower the article, and the man drapes it across his forearm. 'What makes you think she's missing?'

Richard Bond regales Skelgill with the self-reproachful simper that he has employed each time there might be a question of insubordination on his part.

'I went along to the tack room – in my role as, er – *ahem* – unofficial quartermaster. I reasoned we might be making a break for it today – so I decided to identify the most suitable kit – get everything shipshape, and all that.' Now he leans towards Skelgill, and adopts a tone of expert-to-expert, as if his words are

160

not intended for the others. 'I thought alpine-style roping, in view of the risk of shake holes – in threes with each female between two males?' (Skelgill nods encouragingly – but he just wants the man to get on with it.) 'I realised immediately that one of the smaller outfits was gone, and boots – and there are fresh disturbances in the snow leading across the stable yard. I made a mental list of those I have seen this morning at breakfast – narrowed it down to Jenny Hackett. I tried her door – there was no answer – but it was unlocked and the room empty.'

DS Leyton seems rather peeved; perhaps that Richard Bond is intruding upon his territory.

'She could be with someone else – or in one of the public rooms – the library.'

In turn Richard Bond looks irked – as though he considers DS Leyton to be of a lower rank than he and that he finds the sergeant's contention impertinent. He turns to face Skelgill.

'I've had a preliminary scout around. I think you'll find she is definitely gone, Inspector.'

Skelgill nods curtly.

'Let's make doubly sure, eh – protocol, and all that?'

'Absolutely.'

Skelgill places a hand on DS Leyton's upper arm.

'Leyton – you check upstairs – with Samanta.' He regards the girl in a businesslike manner. 'You've got a master key, aye?' She nods, and her hand moves to cover the pocket of her apron. Skelgill continues to address her. 'See if you can tell if anything else is gone from her room.'

Now he turns to Richard Bond. He knows he must act decisively before the man sets his own agenda. But there are not enough police officers for what he needs to do. If he asks Richard Bond to conduct an unsupervised search and later it proves that something was overlooked he, Skelgill, will take the rap. But there is a more disquieting aspect: the stalking incident in the woods is still raw in his memory, his confidence shaken – but if he excludes Richard Bond now it will give the game away.

'Richard – can you take the ground floor yourself? Public rooms *and* staff quarters.' Skelgill does not pause to gauge the

161

reaction of Joost Merlyn. 'Check everywhere methodically, including all the store cupboards. And the freezers and suchlike.'

Richard Bond is nodding enthusiastically. Skelgill holds out his hand for the garment – its exchange frees the man into action. He clicks his heels and sets off for the corridor that leads eventually to the tack room. 'I shall work clockwise.'

Skelgill hands the red gown to DS Leyton. 'See if anyone else recognises this. Then you may as well put it back in her room.' He gives a tip of his head to indicate that his sergeant and Samanta should embark on their task.

Skelgill is left standing with the sour-faced Joost Merlyn, the latter leaning heavily upon his stick; he looks like he may be calculating whether these events will have any impact on his takings. As such, and still irked by Samanta's little revelation, Skelgill cannot resist a small impertinence.

'At least it's not Ms Adamska that's done a runner, eh, sir?'

The man mumbles something unintelligible – perhaps it is a curse in his native tongue, but Skelgill does not have Richard Bond to translate. He issues a rejoinder that he considers will carry commensurate weight.

'Perhaps you and I can check the more unexpected places, sir – places the average daft country copper wouldn't think of looking. How about we begin with the cellar?'

The man glances sharply at Skelgill, and looks like he might object, his scowl fiercer than ever – but then he shuffles around the fulcrum of his walking stick and begins to hobble away. If Skelgill were meeting him for the first time he would judge him singularly uncooperative, but in fact this surly behaviour is just par for the course. He follows into the back office, which to his surprise is barely more than an unlit butler's pantry into which has been squeezed a worn leather armchair and an electric fire. On a shelf sit a kettle, a mug and spoon, and a jar of instant coffee. It is like a nightwatchman's den – and appears to rely on ambient light from the reception area. The back wall is taken up by a planked door that could do with a fresh coat of varnish. Without a word Joost Merlyn rests his stick against the armchair and delves into the pocket of his baggy cardigan and pulls out a blackened hand-forged key and fits it into the body of an equally ancient mortise lock. It seems both lock and hinges are well oiled, for there are no melodramatic sound effects that would befit the gloom and the hunched gaoler-like character. He reaches to throw a switch that casts the scene beyond into adequately if not brightly lit contrast. Leaning to look past the man Skelgill sees an unguarded ladder-style staircase descending steeply beside several courses of exposed foundations.

He might expect Joost Merlyn already to have stated that Jenny Hackett cannot possibly be in the cellar because it is locked – but there is the matter of timings conveyed by Samanta. The door would presumably have been open last evening for the transfer of miscellaneous beverages, and perhaps even the requirement to change a barrel. But the man's taciturnity in this respect nevertheless strikes him. He decides the natural reaction is for him to raise this question.

'When was this door last unlocked, sir?'

Joost Merlyn does not make eye contact.

'I locked it last night – around midnight.'

'You wouldn't want folk helping themselves.' Skelgill's tone acquires a note of sarcasm. 'Then again – maybe you would. I understand there's a special arrangement in place to cover your costs. The more the merrier.'

There is a snarl that may be a sign of assent.

'That'll save you all the red tape involved in submitting a compensation claim to the railway company – won't it sir?'

Skelgill's expression of concern is plainly disingenuous. He means he is onto him if he is thinking of double claiming. Joost Merlyn declines to be drawn.

'You going down, or what, Inspector?'

'Are you not going to show me?'

The man shifts a hand and places it upon his raised hip, and grimaces ever more hideously.

'Not unless you want to carry me back up.'

Given what he knows, Skelgill is unconvinced by this little charade – but he opts to take the retort at face value. Joost Merlyn is a large man – if he were not stooped by his affliction

163

he would reach Skelgill's own height and is both bulky and overweight. Not to mention his disagreeable features and questionable personal hygiene. Manhandling him is not an appealing prospect. Skelgill shrugs indifferently – the man moves aside to allow him to pass. As he does so he has to hand over the sprung door – and as Skelgill takes control he jerks the key from the lock and steps over the threshold. He responds to the man's strangled protest with an insouciant grin.

'Wouldn't want the lock to jam. Happen that'd give you all another problem, breaking me out, eh?'

He does not wait for a reply, and descends confidently, facing out and no-handed, when actually the stair is steep enough to merit facing in. The door swings to above him. His first impression is that the air is fresh, when he has anticipated a stuffy cobweb-festooned staleness. There is a hint of beeriness, although not a patch on the uplifting yeasty aroma of real ale venting from its casks.

Skelgill is not expecting to find Jenny Hackett hiding down here. That he personally opted to search the cellar is a decision driven as much out of devilment as professional curiosity. But suddenly alone he is able to reflect upon the practicalities of the situation. The prima facie evidence is that Jenny Hackett has, as Richard Bond put it, "left the building". He considers this is likely to prove a reliable assessment. And they shall in due course set out in pursuit – because surely she will not make it far, and will encounter danger despite the more benign climatic conditions. But no police officer worth their salt would embark without checking thoroughly her last known whereabouts. He inhales through gritted teeth – for the corollary of a search that includes cupboards, freezers and suchlike is that foul play is suspected. He trusts that those civilians enlisted can be relied upon to refrain from subsequent scaremongering.

For his part, this first stage of the task is not going to be onerous. Illuminated by a chain of bulkhead lights at head height, the cellar is less extensive than he has anticipated. It is basically a vaulted cavity that must run along the front section of *Shake Holes Inn* – probably the footprint of the original building, a more rudimentary edifice than exists today (the upper floor, and the wings that enclose the stable yard appended at a later date). The arching sidewalls and ceiling are of roughhewn limestone, the end walls of brick construction. To Skelgill's left – the east, he concludes – beneath what must be the snug bar stands a cluster of stainless steel beer kegs. Several of these are connected by clear tubes to electric wall-mounted pumps, the tubes in turn snaking into the darkness above – presumably through a duct directly into the bar itself. The long rear wall is lined with galvanised steel racking, on its lower shelf crates of mixers, pops and sodas, canned beers, ciders and wines. Its upper shelf is reserved for spirits – vodka, gin, and rum. Skelgill is about to pass these by, when something about them strikes him. Up in the bar, the bottles on the optics and on display behind are all those of the leading international brands. *Smirnoff, Gordon's, Bacardi.* But none of those names are to be seen here – these are all cheap supermarket own-labels, imitations that retail at half the price. Skelgill nods grimly. Joost Merlyn is engaging in what is known in the trade as 'decanting' – passing off cheap liquor as top quality in order to turn a fatter margin of profit. An inverted plastic funnel confirms his deduction. Skelgill scoffs disparagingly – but he cannot say he is surprised. This is the man that keeps fine bottled ale for personal consumption. And Skelgill wonders where it might be.

At the opposite end of the cellar is a wooden chute and, at its foot, a traditional 'pig', a cork-filled jute sack to absorb the impact of the kegs dropped by the drayman. Skelgill reasons that there will be a trapdoor that opens at the front of the inn. He ducks beneath the ladder to inspect. He is right – at the top of the chute there is a hinged wooden hatch held fast by an iron stay. Ordinarily he would expect to see chinks of light, but there are none because of the thick blanket of snow above. And yet he feels a faint draught – and at the same moment gets a hint of some floral bouquet – it is a fragrance he recognises without being able to place it. He looks to his left; against the end wall is a tall oak bookcase that has been pressed into use for storage purposes. Scrawled in black ink on the edge of the top shelf are

165

the words 'cocktail ingredients'. It is actually an impressive collection – and he notes that these are genuine brands, variants of vermouth, triple sec, blue curaçao and the like. On lower shelves are mixers, syrups and small bottles that contain bitters.

He takes a step closer – but feels the sudden crunch of glass beneath his foot. As he recoils he realises he is standing in a pool of tacky liquid. There is a broken bottle, more or less flattened, but its fragmented label is just sufficiently intact for him to be able to read the words 'Crème de Violette'. He grimaces at the prospect – but he supposes it explains the flowery scent. And now he recalls last night a sub-committee making the case for mixology – in particular the two Russian females and their compatriot Egor, and Sir Ewart Cameron-Kinloch – egged on by an inebriated Jenny Hackett, who nonetheless seemed to know her *Moscow Mules* from her *Molotovs*.

On reflection they must have had Samanta up and down the cellar ladder like a jack-in-the-box, in their quest for ever more exotic concoctions. And he remembers Joost Merlyn's self-satisfied smirk as the tab escalated. Cocktails? *Ka-ching!* Poor Samanta, perhaps, run off her feet, arms overloaded, she dropped this bottle – and if Joost Merlyn has inspected, then no wonder he has castigated the hard-working girl.

Skelgill's distaste for the man is renewed. Once more he feels impelled to confront the miserly landlord. Not least that his treatment of Samanta is despicable. But – hold on – he inhales deeply, his face a picture of discontent. It is not like him to get sidetracked by personal enmity – nor to resort to jibes or harbour grudges. Either punch his lights out – or forget it – for the time being. There is feedback from the others, and a search party to be organised. Better to focus. He decides this is a moment to let water pass under the bridge. There will be more bridges.

He returns to the ladder in the centre of the cellar and ascends. Joost Merlyn has been keeping watch. He prises himself from his armchair. Skelgill hands back the key. He does not comment on his findings.

'Where else is there, sir?'

'There's nowhere else – your soldier man is checking the stables and the stores.'

'What about this Bath House place?'

Skelgill's tone is neutral. He seems to have caught the man off guard.

'What?' There is a moment's hesitation. 'It is nothing.'

'Well – it's not *nothing*, is it? I saw the sign across the car park – and it's mentioned in your guided walk pamphlet.'

'Ach.' Joost Merlyn almost expectorates. 'That is an exaggeration – the bath house is a ruin, a pile of stones. Some former owners produced that leaflet – there's no call for history these days. You'd be wasting your time. It is bricked up. '

'All the same, sir – we still need to look. I wouldn't be doing my job.'

167

12. BATHOLOGY

Friday, 10.30am

The bath house is the last structure a casual rambler would expect to stumble upon in this rugged rural corner of Cumbria. Even a hotel guest, following the marked trail and therefore in expectation of 'something', would find it incongruous. While the inn has a workmanlike perpendicular Georgian facade, austere and unornamented, here there is the sudden illusion of a time-travelling spacecraft having crash-landed in the forest. Set in a small round clearing, the bath house is a construction in the neoclassical style. From a circular stone base arises a chiselled Doric temple with its snow-capped domed roof supported by ten fluted columns. In the centre beneath the dome and otherwise exposed to the elements stands a sculpted statue; the brochure in Skelgill's back pocket would tell him this is *Hygeia*, the Greek goddess of good health. She bears a chalice, and the fingers of her left hand caress the head of an asp that winds its way up a pedestal at her side.

For some this lofty vision might evoke feelings of enchantment – but Skelgill, ever practical, has his mind set on the more prosaic foundation. It resembles the lower storey of a medieval watchtower, a round turret of undressed rocks of local origin. Ostensibly its role is as a plinth to elevate the temple – but, in fact, reaching a height of perhaps seven feet, this must be the actual bath house itself, possibly a much older edifice. He guesses it was built over the sulphurous mineral spring that he can smell even now. It has no windows and – as Joost Merlyn had presaged – in effect no door, for the narrow portal beneath a stone lintel is indeed blocked – the single aspect that is displeasing to the eye, a slapdash score of courses of blue engineering bricks of a similar vintage to those forming the end walls of the cellar.

On his approach through the dark tunnel of rhododendrons, a steeply rising path that has received only a sprinkling of snow,

Skelgill has followed no human tracks, and the snow in the clearing and around the bath house is virgin but for the spoor of a roe deer that has passed this way. Nonetheless, he satisfies himself that there is no other means of entry, and that none has been attempted, and circles the building. Back before the blocked doorway he faces outwards, his breath coming more steadily as his pulse rate eases. Even for a fellsman of his experience, the scene is uncannily silent; no sough of the wind, no mew of a buzzard, no bleating of sheep, no tractor chug of a farmer on the move; and not even the distant drone of traffic.

After a while, however, Skelgill fancies he can hear running water – it intrigues him what might be inside the tower base – a spout filling a stone bath of sorts, he supposes, where those Victorian diehards immersed themselves in hope. It would be cold, year round – although ironically in these sub-arctic conditions the ground water would provide protection against frost. He is reminded of Joost Merlyn's belittling of history; neither is the subject his own bag – but to allow this hidden treasure to fall into ruin seems a travesty. But what chance the man would put his hand in his pocket to restore it – when a few paintball pistols will do the trick for the gung-ho urban clientele he aims to attract?

Skelgill ponders his next move. A wren momentarily appears on a protruding twig and gives its too-big-for-its-boots alarm call. 'Jenny Wren', indeed. Where has Jenny Hackett gone? As he had anticipated – and to the patent satisfaction of Richard Bond – the search of the inn had drawn a blank. That is to say, as far as she in person was concerned. Her luggage and toiletries remained, but of the most salient item in the detectives' minds – the late Mikal Mital's manuscript – there was no trace; nor could DS Leyton find her mobile telephone or wallet. Moreover, his sergeant's questioning of her fellow passengers had proved unproductive. All retired collectively – shortly before midnight – and none admits to having arisen before breakfast, or having heard a disturbance in the night. Wiktoria Adamska's earlier testimony is of course the exception to this rule, and had prompted DS Leyton to confide in his boss a revised hypothesis.

"What if it were Jenny Hackett in her room, Guv? Say she suspected that Wiktoria Adamska had the manuscript – sneaked in – nicked it – scarpered. Next thing it'll be splashed all over the front pages."

As Skelgill replays this notion his eyes narrow. Would Jenny Hackett seriously have considered making a dash for freedom? How desperate was she – *is* she – to impress her editor? It was still snowing heavily when they went to bed – and by his estimation had continued to do so until shortly before the visit of the helicopter. She could of course have waited for dawn – but that would have risked being seen by one of the patrons or staff. Besides, in spite of Richard Bond's excitement about tracks leading from the tack room and across the courtyard, on closer inspection these proved to belong to the two detectives. No footprints extended beyond the winch point above which the chopper had hovered. Indeed, no new tracks could be discovered leading from the inn. This entailed falling back on the theory that, if Jenny Hackett had departed, she did so in the dark, while it was still snowing – and her footprints were subsequently buried.

Or, like 'Mr Harris', she is possessed of supernatural qualities!

Skelgill gives a frustrated gasp, his breath forming a confused cloud before him. There was one snippet of interest. When quizzed by DS Leyton as to whether Jenny Hackett had given any indication of her intentions, Ruairidh McLeod had asserted that, when the two teams *(Dire Straits* and *The Pretenders)* were seated together before their bar billiards contest, Jenny Hackett had declined a refill of wine, proclaiming that she "needed to keep a clear head" and had tapped the side of her nose. At the time the guard took this to mean so that she would perform well in the pub games – but with hindsight, who knows? However, Skelgill had dismissed the significance of this account. His recall is of Jenny Hackett filling her boots from the free bar – not to mention the potent cocktails later. He had expressed this doubt to his subordinate, but DS Leyton had offered a rejoinder.

"What if she were just getting everyone else smashed, Guv – especially Wiktoria Adamska – if she planned to creep into her room? We just assumed she was knocking it back because of the night before – but for all we know she might hardly have touched a drop."

Skelgill remains unconvinced by this argument. It would seem more likely to him – knowing what he does of Jenny Hackett's personality and penchant for a tipple – that if she did concoct a plan to steal and make away with the manuscript, she did it under the influence of alcohol, a spur-of-the-moment whim that has likely led her into trouble.

The guard had also been questioned about the red kimono. His response had been that, yes, it was the identical colour, and, yes, it could have been Jenny Hackett whom he glimpsed slipping from view – but that he had no way of being one hundred per cent certain on either count. Corroboration, however, comes in the testimony of the remaining females – none of who lay claim to the said garment. So here is some small evidence to suggest that Jenny Hackett was prone to nocturnal wanderings. But did she finish at the inn what she started on the Midnight Express? Or has she gone back to the train?

Skelgill checks his watch. He has not shared his thoughts about Jenny Hackett's motivation – nor indeed his reasons for setting out alone, among which the missing journalist is only secondary. His primary purpose is concealed in his backpack – the walkie-talkie and the conversation that is scheduled with DS Jones. His explanation to the others was that the train has been sealed off by order of the Coroner – standard protocol in the event of an unexplained death – and that only the police may cross the tapes. He had convened a meeting that comprised himself and DS Leyton, Richard Bond and his two associates, and Bill Faulkner. These he considered to be the most able bodied. On interrogating the latter three on their outdoor proficiency (Richard Bond's skills he took as read), it emerged that, while the two younger men were athletic but not country types, Bill Faulkner confessed to being a fully paid-up duck hunter, indeed part-owner in a syndicate of two thousand acres of prime Louisiana coastal marshes, a shooting cabin that sleeps twelve, a brace of Labrador retrievers, and – by the sound of it –

a different gun for every species he bags. It seems there is more than meets the eye to the quiet American, and that he is perfectly capable of covert operations, creeping about the countryside and interpreting the signs. Skelgill had noticed Richard Bond looking on with affected admiration, a glazed stare and a fixed smile that he suspected to be a cover for competitive envy. But Skelgill was convinced. And thus, for the purposes of avoiding a further calamity, he paired Messrs Bond and Faulkner respectively with each of the younger men. Richard Bond would take Egor and Bill Faulkner, François – this a relatively arbitrary choice, although Faulkner had joked that he also speaks French, albeit the New Orleans version. DS Leyton – to his poorly concealed relief – was once more delegated to man the fort. Clearly, under the circumstances, a police presence was required – both to reassure those remaining, and in the event of further unexpected developments.

The triumvirate of Skelgill, Bond and Faulkner had then pored over a map to agree upon a plan of action. Ulpha Beck cascades from north to south along the margin of the woodland. The pairs would split up and head in opposite directions, sticking to the bank of the stream. When they reached the respective polar limits of the plantation, they would each strike west across the open fell country, and swing around in a wide pincer movement, until they met up. In effect they would draw a circle around the inn. If tracks were found, the more experienced man was to follow and the second to report back. They had bemoaned the lack of a mobile signal. Of course, Skelgill had to keep mum about his radio. But giving it to one of them would be pointless – and it would defeat his own main objective. Besides, in his bones he held out no great hopes for their locating the missing journalist. But they will do their best, and Richard Bond's cabin fever is circumvented for the time being. Meanwhile Skelgill may inspect the train, which is a mite more promising.

*

From the bath house it takes Skelgill about twenty minutes through the woods to reach the West Coast Main Line, and five more to find his way to the footbridge that carries the bridleway. Rather than descend immediately he walks to the centre of the bridge. It is the first time he has been able to survey the area in clear, bright conditions. At this distance the scene looks almost picturesque, it could be a still photograph of a snow-covered train deep in the steeply banked cutting, just about to turn the distant bend. But the astute observer would spot the clues: the front of the locomotive seems to merge into a bank of whiteness; and, at the rear, surely a moving train would clear a path, but no rails are visible. And one other point, of more interest to Skelgill – just beyond where the track begins to curve out of sight the top of a pylon protrudes from the snowdrift, and belatedly displays a red signal. Perhaps some form of power has been restored to the network?

On approach Skelgill finds signs that were less obvious from afar. The snow alongside the train is more heavily trodden than on his last visit, and white tape with familiar blue lettering ("police line do not cross") has been strung from the rear carriage to a trackside post. With a practised dip he passes the barrier and enters the train by the door he knows to be the back of the sleeping car. It seems like an age since they boarded at Euston station – he reminds himself it was only thirty-six hours ago. On board he stands; all is quiet. He has seen no obvious fresh tracks coming down the embankment near the footbridge – although in the light of day it is not the exclusive means of approach. After a few moments, he calls out.

'Jenny. Jenny – are you here?'

His exhortation is met with silence. He is not expecting a reply – although if she were aboard, surprised, a movement would more likely betray her presence. But he can see no logic for her to have remained, had she come here at all. He wonders – how well prepared would she have been – assuming she was in full possession of her wits? Richard Bond had postulated that she could wade into Ulpha Beck to conceal her tracks, and use the stream itself to guide her to Ulphathwaite – where there is of course access to a landline (although its significance would not have been apparent to him). But Skelgill had dismissed this as 'SAS thinking', beyond her metropolitan guile and physical limits. A more practical alternative would be to continue east to the M6 motorway. Vehicles will be abandoned with their keys left by order of the authorities, to facilitate clearance later. A car with a full tank of fuel would be a perfectly warm and comfortable haven, with a radio for company until the tow trucks arrived. An *Asda* lorry loaded with provisions – in his book – even better.

Certainly, if she did come to the train it would make sense to keep going in the same easterly direction. But why *would* she come to the train? There could only be one reason. Skelgill begins to make his way along the corridor of the sleeping car. In his mind's eye he pictures Ruairidh McLeod; he imagines himself in the guard's shoes, in the early hours of Thursday – and there goes the scarlet kimono! He does not trouble himself with any of the berths, but instead makes his way to the next vestibule and yanks open the normally power-assisted door of the lavatory.

On-board WCs have their own special position in the pantheon of public toilets, and are far from the most salubrious of their species; indeed they are places where the majority of travellers would rather not go, ahem. But the first-class nature of the Midnight Express, and – credit where it is due – thanks to what must have been the diligence of the guard-cum-steward-cum-orderly – the loo that Skelgill now enters is clean and pine-scented.

Skelgill, however, has no wish to dwell and he homes in on a maintenance panel above the toilet itself, attached to the bulkhead by four large plastic screws. It is apparent that the screw heads are damaged by the use of the wrong tool – a two pence coin, at a guess, going by the scarring around the drive slots. He has in his backpack a modest assortment scavenged from a tool chest in the tack room. He selects a wood chisel as an appropriately oversized screwdriver, and easily removes three of the fixings, two at the top and one at the bottom. He allows them to fall directly upon the floor. When he loosens the final screw the panel swings free, but remains held in place, inverted.

He locates his railway-issue torch and shines it into the cavity now exposed. There are pipes and wires but, as far as he can establish, there is nothing else. He examines the interior and its various surfaces. Surely the dust and the debris in places are freshly disturbed? He ponders for a moment, his expression somewhat pained. He doubts that the forensics team had either time or, frankly, the notion to take samples from the washroom – but he suspects that if someone has recently tampered with the screws or the panel, or poked inside, they may have left traces, depending upon their degree of professional acumen. But this thought must now be put on hold, for his backpack crackles and DS Jones's static-altered voice emanates from within.

'Hi, Guv – it's me here. Over.'

Skelgill delves for the handset.

'Jones – it's a bad time. Over.'

'Guv – it's noon. Over.'

'I mean I'm in a toilet. Over.'

'Oh.'

Skelgill grins wryly.

'Listen – the signal's crap. I'm on the train. Give me five minutes to get up on the footbridge. Over.'

'Sure, Guv. Over and out.'

*

'How's that, Guv? Over.'

'Aye – much better.' Skelgill rests his elbows upon the snow-encrusted steel parapet of the footbridge. He is facing north, to the train, and the midwinter sun has reached its meagre zenith and slants across the cutting beneath, leaving the western embankment in deep shadow, but reflecting with startling brightness off the drifts on the east side. It is a contrast challenging on the eye, and as his gaze wanders from one side to the other he makes facial contortions accordingly. 'Jones – before you start – in case this battery packs up – you need to know that Jenny Hackett's disappeared. There's no sign of her at the inn. Some outdoor gear's gone. There's no manuscript or

175

mobile or wallet amongst her belongings. She possibly left during the night – during which Wiktoria Adamska reported an intruder in her room and the theft of an item she won't identify. We can't find any tracks. We've got three teams including me out looking for her now. If there's a chopper passing this way, I wouldn't mind if they could do a five-minute scout around.' Skelgill hesitates but it is plain he has more to say. 'Obviously if Mikal Mital's big story suddenly breaks – we'll know she's smuggled it out. Over.'

DS Jones gives a light whistle – an acknowledgement of the gravity of his news.

'I can confirm there's nothing so far – I was online a couple of minutes ago – and obviously we've established a channel of contact with her employer. I'll get it double-checked as soon as we're done. Do you want me to mention her disappearance to them? Over.'

'Happen we should let sleeping dogs lie. Over.'

'Are you worried, Guv? Over.'

There is a strained note in DS Jones's voice that conditions his response.

'What do you mean? Over.'

'That something sinister has happened to her. You see – the initial pathology report has come back – the Coroner wants to classify Mikal Mital's death as suspicious.' She hesitates, as though she might momentarily have suffered a small wave of emotion. 'Over.'

'Well – tell us, lass. Over.'

Skelgill hears DS Jones clear her throat, although she has obviously moved the microphone away from her mouth. Then she speaks with renewed composure.

'The cause of death was cardiac arrest. Obviously – in an elderly man that might not be unexpected – but I've contacted his doctor and he'd given him a clean bill of health three months ago – and he had no history of heart problems. But the precursor, Guv – is indicated by the preliminary toxicology. Mikal Mital had ingested a compound called flunitrazepam – it's a benzodiazepine – a tranquiliser. You know the trade name –

176

Rohypnol?' (At this Skelgill makes a choked ejaculation, for the compound is notorious as a date rape drug – but he does not interrupt, and DS Jones continues.) 'Its effects are magnified by alcohol – the patient can slip into a coma and their vital functions shut down. It's usually prescribed on a very short-term basis for chronic insomnia. Except it wasn't prescribed – at least, not by his regular GP.' Again she pauses before passing the baton rather uncertainly. 'Over?'

It takes Skelgill a moment to respond.

'How easy is it to get hold of? Over.'

'I've talked to the drugs squad – there's a thriving black market in all these tranquilisers – or he could have obtained it under the counter from an accommodating pharmacist. Over.'

Now Skelgill's tone becomes self-reproachful.

'I was joking when I said Jenny Hackett must have slipped him a Mickey Finn. Over.'

'The thing is, Guv – the empty blister pack was in his toiletries bag. There are no prints on it – it's being despatched for analysis for contact DNA. Obviously – it's possible he obtained the drug privately and self-administered – took an overdose by mistake – especially if he was intoxicated. The amount in his blood was about three times the prescribed dose. The toxicology showed he'd drunk whisky – and possibly other spirits – I guess the guard might recall how much exactly. Over.'

'Aye – I'll ask him.' Skelgill hesitates, as though a little scenario is running through his mind. Then he picks up DS Jones's main thrust. 'What if he were intentionally poisoned – are there any other forensics? Over.'

Now it is his sergeant's turn to produce a sigh of sorts.

'Sod's law, Guv. I briefed the team on the possibility of him having been drugged – so they were going to bag any drinks receptacles they could find. Unfortunately, the guard was too efficient. All the glasses served in the lounge car were neatly stacked in a dishwasher in the galley – and the wash cycle had finished before the train's power was switched off.' There comes another hiss of vexation from Skelgill, and DS Jones now sounds a little downcast. 'Also, there was no contamination in the water

177

bottle – remember, the one at the foot of his bed that I thought had been moved? Over.'

'Aye – but that was after you'd found him dead. Over.'

A moment's silence ensues – it seems DS Jones is formulating her thoughts.

'For the record, there are some prints – but pretty much as we'd expect. Mikal Mital's on the label – and on the screw top Ruairidh McLeod's thumbprint – he's on the biometric database – I'll explain that in a minute. But inside a cupboard in the guard's van there was a bottle-carrier – like a sports team uses. It had been filled up with ten individual bottles from a shrink-wrapped outer – and they all had similar prints. So it looks like that's how he distributed the water to the compartments from his central stock. Over.'

'Aye. That's more or less what he told me and Leyton.' Skelgill's pause hangs heavy with frustration. 'What else have we got? Over.'

'From a scientific perspective, Guv – there are unidentified prints from several individuals in and around compartments one and two. But it's a public space – so it's only what we would expect to find. Bear in mind there would have been a different set of passengers every day of the week. I mean – we *may* have swabbed traces of DNA that will prove significant – but only if we can identify someone who shouldn't have been in either of those cabins. The best we can hope for is alien DNA on the blister pack.'

'When do we expect the results? Over.'

'I've been quoted twenty-four hours from receipt, Guv – but we're still working on a way to get the samples to the lab. They're going to have to travel by helicopter somehow – and the availability is obviously really limited right now. Over.'

Skelgill registers the vexation in his sergeant's voice. She has within her grasp the tantalising prospect that Mikal Mital may have been poisoned, but cannot deliver the forensic coup de grace. Perhaps inadvertently he makes what is a consolatory remark.

'Happen we're not going anywhere in a hurry. Over.'

'Apart from Jenny Hackett? Over.'

'Aye – I don't know what to think there.' Skelgill seems wrong-footed by his sergeant's quick rejoinder. His is vaguely aware that he ought to commend her efforts – frankly she has worked wonders in galvanising pathology and forensics departments, when there is a regional crisis underway and many staff will not even have reached their places of employment. But she has not even hinted that a word of praise would be appreciated. And there is limited airtime before he must return to recharge his battery. 'Anything new on the other folk? Over.'

'Guv – I've been concentrating on liaising with Dr Herdwick – but the team have come up with a smattering of information.' It sounds like she is sifting through some notes. 'I'll be brief – I'm afraid there's no smoking gun –' She breaks off for a moment's mirth. '*Hah* – although, on that note, Bill Faulkner – we have nothing more from a professional perspective as far as his London job is concerned – but there are some personal details. After college he served with distinction in the US military – and subsequently as a civilian he won prizes for shooting in Louisiana state competitions. A pretty impressive achievement, by all accounts – looks like he could have made the American Olympic skeet team, but didn't take it further.'

'He weren't so hot at darts.' There might be a small element of envy in Skelgill's impulsive reaction. DS Jones opts to proceed without comment.

'Richard Bond. The MOD have confirmed he served as he claims, and his record was exemplary, too – they won't release any details, given the nature of the regiment. It appears, however, that for two years after discharge he worked in the Middle East as a private security expert. That can be a euphemism for mercenary. And it's just possible there's some link between the bankrolling of his business and contacts he made out there – and clearly petrochemicals has been a major source of laundered funds.'

Skelgill seems to have settled into listening mode, so DS Jones continues.

179

'This is in no particular order, Guv – I don't want to give the idea there's some theory developing here, or connections between either these new findings or what we know already. Concerning Mikal Mital, then. His early background behind the Iron Curtain seems fairly anonymous – it appears he was an academic, an economist, until after the fall of the Berlin Wall – then the first official notice is as a visiting professor at Harvard Business School. It seems from there he moved into professional consultancy and stayed under the radar until relatively recently – when the anti money laundering movement gathered pace after the 2008 financial crisis. He acted as an advisor to a consortium of European governments about property dealings around the Mediterranean – on the face of it that looks like suspected dirty money coming out of Russia and the former Soviet republics. I guess he would have had access to networks he built up during his time on the communist side of the fence. It corresponds with what Jenny Hackett suggested.

'Staying on the Russian theme – one small point of interest is that *VoxNews* hasn't reported that two of its key staff are trapped in the snow. Obviously we let them know around this time yesterday. You would think given Sir Ewart Cameron-Kinloch's profile they would have made a feature of it. Last night they played out a repeat of his current affairs show. Neither is there any reference on the *VoxNews* website.

'We've been in touch with City of London Police's money laundering investigation unit. They have passed on all the names of the non-British citizens on the train to Europol and Interpol – that includes Ivanna Karenina, Egor Volkov, François Mouton, Wiktoria Adamska and Bill Faulkner – so we're waiting for feedback – but we did get an immediate notification that Wiktoria Adamska's husband, Artur Adamski has companies on a watch-list for cross-border financial transactions.

'Then – Mr Harris, Guv.' DS Jones makes a curious cough, as though she is reminded of the improbability of his existence. 'I still think we're some way off from identifying him. We've contacted the ticketing operators – they've been able to tell us that the booking was made online – as they generally are – and the payment transacted in US dollars with a foreign charge card from a business account. The company name doesn't seem to mean anything – we're trying to establish where it's incorporated – but the bank appears to be domiciled in the Virgin Islands.'

Skelgill utters what must sound like an expletive to DS Jones – for she gives a nervous laugh.

'I know, Guv – it does rather stir the pot. If he'd been plain Mr Harris from Hampstead it would be easier to put him to one side. As it is, I checked the latest status and the American Virgin Islands – if that's where the account proves to be based – are still on the EU blacklist of tax havens. My concern is that when we approach the card operator they'll simply hide behind the defence of client confidentiality.'

Skelgill scoffs contemptuously.

'So what do we do, send a gunboat?'

DS Jones treats his question as rhetorical.

'We have some limited information on the railway employees.' She gives a little chuckle. 'I thought I'd better make sure they're who they claim to be! Laura Wilson the driver is from Penrith – I realised I know her younger sister, Jackie, she works in the probation service – so there's no question there. Laura left school to become a firefighter, but just over four years ago she received a serious spinal injury attending a blaze in the Whinlatter, and after she recovered she retrained as a train driver. The guard, Ruairidh McLeod – his employment on the railways dates back to the nationalised days of *British Rail*. Prior to that he was a steel worker at the Ravenscraig plant in Motherwell. He gained a reputation as a trades union firebrand – and a criminal record – that's why we have his prints on file. During the 1980 steelworkers' strike he served four weeks on remand for secondary picketing at Sheffield – an incident that culminated in some considerable violence. Ironically he and his union comrades were cleared of the picketing charge but were given fines and suspended sentences for affray. Then for a period at *British Rail* he held a position as a convenor and was considered to be on the militant side – but after privatisation in 1997 and the break up into franchises he relinquished his union role and seems

181

to have kept his head down – maybe with an eye to his pension. He's currently rated as a reliable employee with a good disciplinary and attendance record. Over.'

Skelgill mutters something unintelligible. But it seems there is a hint of sympathy in his tone.

'Happen he'd make a half-decent union rep – bolshie type like him. Probably drives him crackers seeing all these rich folk lording it in first class. Over.'

DS Jones does not respond directly to her superior's observation, and instead presses on with her account.

'The financial conference in Edinburgh, Guv – it's actually still taking place – the majority of attendees flew in ahead of the storm and are lodging within walking distance of the convention centre. Although it must be scaled down – and obviously they've lost the likes of Mikal Mital's slot. We got hold of the delegates' list – Richard Bond is on it,' (Skelgill makes a grunt of acknowledgement – it was as he expected) '*VoxNews* are sending a reporter, although no mention of Sir Ewart Cameron-Kinloch or Ivanna Karenina. But the one delegate that did stand out, Guv, is described as "Representative, *Adamski Corporation*" – it doesn't say who by name – so it could be anyone right up to the top man – in other words, Wiktoria Adamska's husband. Which might explain why she was so determined to get to Edinburgh. Over.'

Skelgill makes a disdainful grunt. He is thinking that 'husband' may be jumping to conclusions. But he offers an alternative justification.

'She told Leyton she's showing off her latest undies at some fancy shop. Her luggage is packed with fur coats and frilly knickers. Over.'

DS Jones gives an appreciative laugh.

'All a girl needs, Guv. Especially in this weather. But, seriously – on the conference – we've looked back at the pre-publicity – the general tenor seemed above board and quite altruistic. I've got the headline here – I'll read it: *'Wealth of Nations* – an executive-level symposium to promote international money flows, and the benefits of relaxing exchange controls for

182

world trade and global prosperity." I know what Jenny Hackett said about Mikal Mital – that he was supposedly going to drop a bombshell – but assuming that was true, then I don't think the conference organisers knew it was coming. Over.'

'Except Jenny Hackett had wind of it. And others, maybe –'

Skelgill is evidently sidetracked by some thought, for he does not formally hand back. After a short while DS Jones again takes the initiative.

'Guv, the national grid are predicting tomorrow evening for power and communications to begin to be restored. I briefed the Chief first thing this morning and she wanted me to review any findings before I updated you. I've just come off a *Skype* call. Now we've got evidence that points to a potentially suspicious death, I asked about extracting everyone from the hotel and interviewing them under caution. What do you think? Over?'

Skelgill is not expecting to be put on the spot like this. His sergeant's account implies that the decision is in his hands – that he has only to say the word and they will all be whisked off to a mixture of Christmas and captivity – despite there being many more deserving calls upon the rescue services. On the face of it the idea is appealing, but he is reminded that this is a high-ranking group of wealthy individuals – there is no way they would tolerate voluntary detention, when expensive lawyers will tell them they can simply walk away unless charged (and *whom* would they charge?). As things stand, he has them in a somewhat less contestable confinement, trapped by an act of God. Here the only downsides are an outbreak of cabin fever and the risk of some precipitate action – witness the latest Jenny Hackett episode. So whatever logical arguments play out in his mind, his gut feel is less equivocal.

'As you just put it – I reckon we need a smoking gun. Over.'

There is a pause while DS Jones reads between the lines of her superior's reply.

'Ah – that's interesting, Guv. I mean – to be honest, I wouldn't say the Chief was enthusiastic about the idea of an

183

evacuation – I think she could be swayed if you were vehement. But if you're happy to sit tight –'

'Jones – when am I happy to sit tight – unless it's me day off on Bass Lake?' Skelgill makes a scathing *"tcha"* – as though this sudden notion is so far away from the present reality as to be a pipe dream. However, his words gainsay his cynicism. 'But something tells me I should – and if you need twenty-four hours to get those results. What day is it tomorrow? Over.'

'Christmas Eve, Guv. Obviously it would be good to get you all out then.' DS Jones sounds apologetic, a sentimental note creeping into her voice. Then she brightens, although in a somewhat conspiratorial manner. 'To be frank – you know how when you ask the Chief something that must have ramifications, she's got this way of not blinking –?'

'Jones – I've *never* seen her blink.'

DS Jones chuckles at his intervention.

'Guv – I feel she knows something – not so much the fine detail of this case – but the bigger picture – something that she's not inclined to reveal. Over.'

Skelgill does not sound fazed.

'Happen we shouldn't be surprised. We know all about her and the corridors of power. And we know first hand the national press are sniffing about. Over.'

'Guv – if you can live with it – I think she'd consider that a good outcome. While we wait for Forensics I'll marshal any resources that I can in relation to Jenny Hackett. Obviously if we can pick her up it might provide us with some answers. Over.'

'Aye – well, you've got about three hours' daylight – you'll need to get your skates on. Over.'

'What do you think is the most likely explanation? Over.'

Skelgill proceeds to outline the various tactical options that lay before Jenny Hackett – his favourite being that she has fled fearing for her own safety – and that a friendly farmhouse or an anonymous vehicle would be her most likely refuge. But there is the caveat that she left no tracks. Of course – he may learn otherwise when he returns to the inn – and he agrees to contact

DS Jones accordingly. Failing that, they commit to a radio rendezvous at 10am tomorrow. Skelgill's battery begins to protest its limitations. They sign off with an exchange in which he complains they have run out of ideas for pub games, and DS Jones suggests that she saw a book of *Daily Telegraph* crosswords in the library, and that he might enjoy the cryptic challenge.

A rueful Skelgill checks his watch; the time is 12.30pm. He casts about. Ordinarily the scene with which he is presented would lift his spirits: beneath a clear blue sky a silent snowscape beckons, and there is a sense of heavenly elevation up here in the Shap Fells, a tilting tableland stretching to distant horizons. He wanders to the end of the footbridge, noting that the only footprints are those he makes himself. To the east of Shap Cutting unfurls a great white carpet of moorland, rising gently to an undulating ridge some three or four miles hence. Somewhere in between, the snowbound M6 motorway lies hidden. In the more immediate foreground Skelgill's focus adjusts to a fascinating spectacle. The snowfield is cratered by scores of crescent-shaped shadows – these are shake holes, filled by snow but their rims sufficiently prominent to be picked out by the angled sunlight. Perhaps this is what it is like on the surface of the moon? He wonders if there can be any better way to locate these mysterious depressions – though how many more are concealed, smoothed beneath drifts? He knows the old trackway runs roughly to the north-east; after about a mile it picks up an unfenced B-road that in turn links the A6 and the M6. But he doubts the merits of trying to navigate safe passage in these conditions – it is a game of snakes and ladders, mainly snakes – and he grins wryly, thinking DS Leyton would probably have coined such a metaphor.

185

13. GAINED IN TRANSLATION

Friday, 1pm

Trudging back through the forest, descending steadily, Skelgill recognises the approach to *Jenny's Hole*. He is reminded of his resolution to return in spring – and he renews this vow – after all, this is a pretty decent neck of the woods, worth exploring, there might be secretive red squirrels and elusive redstarts, and lively trout to tempt out of one or other of the becks; he could bring the dog, leave his car at the inn, have a pint afterwards – well, maybe not the pint – there'll be real ale up the road at Shap. It is a curious, almost vicarious daydream that he allows himself – and he realises that he is in fact fantasising about the burden of this case being lifted – because, by spring (by *next week,* he hopes – but unquestionably by spring) the snow will be gone and with it the shroud it has cast over certainty.

If he were subliminally to draw an idiom from his present surroundings he would be excused for thinking he cannot see the wood for the trees – for that is an accurate description of the dense plantation that hems in the bridleway. Despite the brighter overhead conditions, the line of sight rarely extends beyond three or four drills. And thus it strikes him that not a great deal has become clearer, despite DS Jones's best efforts, and events at *Shake Holes Inn.* Their early assessment of what fate might have befallen Mikal Mital (and his manuscript) still holds good as a hypothesis, and that Jenny Hackett played some role is, if anything, reinforced by her disappearance. But while DS Jones might yet find some clinching forensic clue – or evidence that points to some overwhelming motive – he feels the solution already lies within his ken. He knows what he has seen, heard – smelt, even – and though these fragments of experience do not as yet form any coherent image in his consciousness – merely they swill about in the unruly maelstrom that lies just below its surface – he suspects it is just a matter of taking them by surprise, to come upon the flotsam as it fleetingly coalesces to reveal a collective meaning.

This sentiment, not even wittingly expressed, nonetheless cheers him – though it is a frisson quickly superseded by a more prescient awareness that time is not on his side. They *will* have to get everyone out of here soon – before more folk start taking matters into their own hands. If the cell phone network comes back up, no doubt all hell will break loose. Pensively, he re-enters the inn via the courtyard, and takes a moment to check on the Fell pony. He feeds an apple from his backpack into its soft bristly mouth. It seems content enough, although surely an animal like this must experience its own version of cabin fever. By association the notion leads him to think sympathetically of Richard Bond, whose antics seem to stem from an innate hyperactivity, that possesses him at all times, ever ready to burst out like a greyhound in its trap. Bill Faulkner, by contrast, exists at the opposite end of the spectrum, and contains both thoughts and urges without effort or outward signs of inner tension; yet by all accounts the American is no less competent a man of action.

These things considered it is no surprise that Skelgill, having discarded his outdoor gear in the tack room, first hears the booming voice of Richard Bond as he pads along the stone-flagged passage towards the lobby.

'I said to Egor – we should have brought the *Lee Enfield* that the Merlyn chap has in his quarters – it would have been roast venison for dinner!' And the statement is followed by a voluminous belly laugh.

'That's a British rifle – point 303, right?' These are the American's more measured tones. 'I thought you Limeys weren't allowed proper guns.'

And now a braying retort from Richard Bond.

'*Hah* – it's probably a decommissioned heirloom. The Boers captured thousands of them. We used to keep a fully loaded pair on our stoep – they might have been antiques but they would take down a buffalo at a quarter of a mile. Or whatever else you cared to pot!' Again there is the insistent guffaw, ratifying the wit of his remark.

187

Skelgill emerges from the shadows of the corridor to find the two men standing beside the reception counter still clad in their overalls. There are little piles of melting snow around their boots and an incomplete trail leading from the front door – evidence of their means of entry. They each have a steaming mug – and Skelgill notices Egor and François sitting at a low table in the waiting area next to the leaflet display unit; their faces are flushed and their hair damp and tousled in the aftermath of exertion; they look bushed. Before them is a cafetière, and a milk jug, although no spare mug that he can see.

He realises that Richard Bond is regaling him with ingenuous optimism, and his peculiar, slightly insane forced smile. Skelgill quickly makes a thumbs-down sign.

'She's not been to the train. At least no trace that I could see. And no one has crossed the footbridge heading east. It's the obvious way over the railway – else there's a mile detour north or south.'

Richard Bond seems to Skelgill to be relieved; his forced mask relaxes into an expression of affected concern. Could it be that he was anticipating the 'worst' – that he may have 'lost' the competition to locate Jenny Hackett?

'We too have drawn a blank, Inspector.' The man does not look at Bill Faulkner for corroboration; clearly he considers that he speaks for them both in his assumed role as the senior ranking among them. Skelgill glances at the American and notices just the faintest compression of his neat mouth. Richard Bond continues. 'The occasional muntjac – which we were just discussing – but otherwise neither journalist nor sasquatch, eh what?' He chortles and nudges Bill Faulkner with an elbow; the man stands his ground and grins stoically.

For his part, and rather uncharacteristically, Skelgill, steps closer and claps a hand on each man's shoulder.

'Happen if you saw deer they'd be roe – muntjac's barely the size of an average dog – besides, they stick to the woods. I spotted some roe deer tracks myself – they'll be foraging for food – they'll dig in the snow for bilberry shoots. The beasts look delicate, but they've got a thick winter coat this time of year – it can make them seem almost black.'

Skelgill is wondering why he is expounding upon wild game – but it vaguely occurs to him that it might prevent some ill-considered thought gaining precedence and making itself known. Richard Bond does not seem to be absorbing the information, but Bill Faulkner watches him shrewdly. However, the latter reveals his interest to lie with their human quarry.

'What's your prognosis for Jenny Hackett, Inspector?'

The question catches Skelgill off guard, and he cannot prevent an involuntary hardening of his features. The American's use of the medical term conjures in his mind's eye the image of a casualty, such as he has had the misfortune to discover more than once in his years as a mountain rescuer, a curled figure in a rudimentary snow hole, seemingly slumbering in peace, but literally frozen to death. He steps away from the two men.

'I'll get back to you on that. I need to have a confab with my sergeant. Thanks for your efforts.'

*

'Jones is trying to organise a chopper to get us all out of here.'

DS Leyton's ears prick up.

'When, Guv?'

'Probably close of play tomorrow. I'm speaking to her at ten in the morning. Sounds like the Chief was willing to do it today – pull a few strings – but Jones wants to wait to give Forensics the best chance. We might regret it if we let this lot scatter to the four winds.'

DS Leyton cannot know that his superior is being more than a little disingenuous by shifting blame to his fellow sergeant. His jowls droop in a rather hangdog fashion. Rather too late, Skelgill realises he should have reconfigured the story to place the responsibility entirely at the feet of their commander.

'Ah, well – if it's for the best, Guv. I expect she'll be keeping the nearest and dearest up to speed. I only hope Her Indoors doesn't lose her rag and shoot the messenger.'

'Cheer up, Leyton – if we get the timing right we'll dress you as Santa and drop you on your roof. That'll surprise the lot of them.'

'Thankfully we ain't got no chimney – else that's where I'd be spending Christmas!' He slaps his ample midriff. 'Let's hope this works out and we nick the Russians.'

Skelgill's brow becomes furrowed.

'What makes you so sure it's the Russians?'

'Stands to reason, Guv – it's the Russians' MO, ain't it – a spot of poisoning?'

'Leyton – the Russians' MO is weapons of mass destruction – not knock-off date-rape pills you can pick up from some donnat on the street corner.'

'Maybe they've learned their lesson, Guv – all that business with nerve agents – and radioactive gear – it leaves a glowing trail right back to its point of origin. Your common or garden benzos – like you say, any Tom, Dick or Harry could get their mitts on them. Far easier to blag your way out of the bad publicity. No need to memorise the height of the Scott monument. Besides – law of averages. Wiktoria Adamska's Russian. Ivanna Karenina's Russian. Bond's young geezer, Egor Volkov – he's Russian. And Sir Ewart Cameron-Kinloch works for the Russians. That's four out of nine passengers – even if we count Harris and Jenny Hackett.'

Skelgill gasps with exasperation and slumps back in the winged chair. The fire is beginning to crackle, having benefited from his attention. A hopeful-looking Samanta has delivered tea and crockery for several people – although a reticent Skelgill seemed to disappoint her with his lack of engagement. His mind has been continually distracted by the same warp of time and information he endured on his return through the woods. Having briefed his colleague on DS Jones's latest report, he finds him apparently all too willing to leap to revised conclusions.

'Thing is, Leyton – it's all very well thinking some malign government or fat-cat oligarch wanted to silence Mikal Mital – but look at the plain facts. Jenny Hackett had the motive – she even told us. She had the opportunity – she was seen toddling off to bed with him, unsteady on his legs. Even the sleeping pills are the sort of thing she'd keep in her handbag. And now she's done a runner. Of all the permutations it's the neatest by a country mile.'

DS Leyton, however, is looking at his boss with an expression of considerable distrust.

'Except you ain't convinced, Guv – I've known you long enough to see that.' He cocks his head to one side, as if the altered perspective might reveal otherwise. 'For a start – it don't fit with Jenny Hackett being shoved in the snake hole – *shake* hole – nor the intruder in Wiktoria Adamska's room. For me, these things rank Jenny Hackett further down the pecking order – feeding on scraps.'

Skelgill is forced to admit to himself that DS Leyton is right; he is not convinced by the basic logic – and moreover his sergeant's intuition chimes with his own. But they have been hamstrung by the need to remain covert. They can only ask certain questions without revealing their hand; indeed, without revealing that they are investigating at all, and in effect consider everyone to be under suspicion. While Skelgill mulls over their dilemma DS Leyton reprises his theory.

'See, Guv – as you know – I reckon that was probably Jenny Hackett looking for the manuscript – getting in on the act after the fact.'

'Maybe it's time to find out.'

'You mean ask Wiktoria Adamska, Guv?'

'Aye.'

'I'll fetch her, shall I?'

Skelgill does not reply – he seems to take his sergeant's response as a statement of intent – and instead he rises and stalks across to the old map of the district on the wall. He sways a little to and fro, straining his focus to gain a purchase in the fading afternoon light. He recognises now the tiny circle quite close to the outline of the inn that must be the bath house. Beyond, higher up the fell a monument is marked – he recalls the leaflet, still in his back pocket, there was something about an obelisk erected to commemorate the accession of Queen Victoria in 1837 – another little of piece of history that Joost Merlyn has chosen to reject; yet his predecessors felt it worthy of incorporating into their visitor trail. He saw no trace – although of course conifers will surround it – something else to look out for in spring. But the entrance of the extant Victoria, Wiktoria Adamska, curtails any such thoughts. No less regal in her manner, she does not wait to be questioned.

'Inspector – you have some news for me?'

She holds a blue concoction in a cocktail glass – which perhaps explains her speedy expediting from what is the nearby bar. Skelgill returns to the cluster of chairs before the fire. He gestures that she should take a seat, but she regards the antique furniture with a look of vague horror; certainly her outfit of the short leopard-pattern dress and matching platform shoes in which she appeared at Euston Station is more suited to a barstool three times the height. She faces Skelgill defiantly and simply raises her glass to drink. Skelgill and DS Leyton have no option but to remain standing. Skelgill digs his hands into his trouser pockets and affects an uncompromising air.

'Madam – about the item you reported stolen.' She regards him unblinkingly; it is a countenance that tells him that she remains disinclined to reveal what it is. 'Obviously, when we spoke with you earlier, that was before we realised that Ms Hackett had gone missing. As part of the process of looking for her, we've conducted a search of the premises. Nothing – how can I put it – *outstanding* was found – and certainly not Ms Hackett. Which leads me to ask – you stated it was a man in your room in the middle of the night. Could it have been a woman – in fact could it have been Ms Hackett?'

She has listened implacably – and without hostility – if anything she displays a mien of mild amusement.

'Inspector – it was a man.'

192

She takes another sip of her drink; plainly she considers no further elaboration is needed. Skelgill is obliged to persist.

'Madam, you said you were awakened – it was dark – and you nodded off again. We'd all been in the bar – it would be understandable that you were drowsy, and not fully cognisant.'

'Inspector – would you know the difference between a man and a woman?'

Skelgill is caught on his heels. He inhales – but before he can formulate his thoughts she has a rejoinder.

'I know the presence of a man. I know the presence of a woman. It was a man.'

There is a purring animal quality in her tone that is both authoritative and overwhelming. Skelgill knows he cannot tender the question for a third time.

'That's fine, madam. It might just have provided the explanation for Ms Hackett's unannounced departure. Her being a journalist – with a nose for a story.'

The implication of his rather thinly disguised hint being that such a motive might apply if what is stolen is newsworthy in some way – but she simply ignores any such inference.

'And when may we expect our own departure?'

Once more Skelgill is unprepared for her question. He glances at DS Leyton, who avoids eye contact in anticipation of being pressed into the firing line. Thus forsaken, Skelgill has to resort to bluster.

'You'll be aware that DS Jones has been airlifted to police headquarters. She was in no position to call the shots this morning – but her stated aim was to organise a slot for us. You understand the demands with sick and elderly and very young people stranded. We're hoping to be evacuated by this time tomorrow.'

She regards him with what now may be a hint of impatience. 'If we had communications –' she snaps her fingers, producing a sharp click that is seemingly unconstrained by her considerable nails, 'I should organise it like that.' She compresses her lips, but they are too voluminous to produce anything other than an alluring pout. 'It is highly inconvenient – for us – and for those who do not know our circumstances.'

Skelgill holds up a palm in protest.

'DS Jones will have ensured that her team contacted everyone that ought to be informed.'

Wiktoria Adamska narrows her eyes, as if to say he can't possibly know that. Peremptorily she turns and strides elegantly towards the door. DS Leyton shuffles ahead of her to open it. As she departs she drains her glass and tilts it from side to side as if to suggest a refill calls. And without a backward glance she has the final word.

'I don't believe you are just sitting on your hands, Inspector.'

Skelgill looks a little sheepishly at DS Leyton. It would appear he feels they have come off worse in the exchange. He sets his jaw.

'May as well haul in the guard, Leyton. Let's see if we can think up a way of asking him what we want to know without setting alarm bells ringing amongst the lot of them.'

'Mind you, Guv – we can probably trust him to keep his trap shut. He's not exactly talkative at the best of times. Besides – him and the driver – I know it's a private company – but they're public officials really, aren't they?'

'Aye, if you say so.'

When DS Leyton returns with his quarry Skelgill is pouring himself another tea. He points the spout at the rather surly looking guard.

'A cuppa, Mr McLeod?'

'Ne'er say nae.'

Also way of not saying thank you, Skelgill notes; he uses the tactic himself when he senses someone is trying to butter him up.

There is, however, no battle of wills over sitting or standing – the guard painfully lowers himself into a chair, as if to emphasise his unfitness for any antics they might be about to put him up to. Skelgill does not recall such incapacities when it came to performing his duties on the train. With a grunt the guard helps himself to milk and sugar. Skelgill sees him eyeing the biscuits. Since only two survive, it is perhaps to his subordinate's surprise

194

that he offers the plate. The guard takes a shortbread finger and without ceremony dunks it in his mug, holding it for a few seconds. Skelgill is watching closely – perhaps it is the tension of whether he has submerged it for too long – but he successfully slots it into his mouth. Conscious of Skelgill's attention he scowls rather belligerently – but Skelgill grins and more or less copies the procedure. He gives a wink to signify their social equivalence.

'Mr McLeod – you'll have gathered that we haven't found Jenny Hackett.' (The man's expression remains truculent.) 'Obviously, when communications are restored, or when we're out of here – whichever comes first – I hope we find she's made it to some place of safety.' Skelgill looks at DS Leyton, who nods encouragingly. 'But in the meantime we wouldn't be doing our job if we just sit twiddling our thumbs. I want to get to the bottom of why she decided to take matters into her own hands, and risked setting out alone. It might give us a clue for where to look for her.'

He pauses deliberately. After a few moments the guard inclines his head.

'Aye.'

His taciturnity permits only the monosyllable. Skelgill, however, is ready to elaborate.

'She's a colourful character – a bit of a live wire. She was getting into the spirit of things last night. On the walk here she had a self-inflicted brush with danger. In the early hours on the train you caught a glimpse of what was probably her. And prior to that she'd been getting familiar with all and sundry in the lounge car – including us, the police.'

'Aye – Ah mind that.'

'She was brass-necking it for a story – you know, a scoop they call it?'

The guard nods, though it is plain he remains suspicious of Skelgill's direction of travel. His bushy ginger eyebrows have converged like jousting caterpillars.

195

'And then you told DS Leyton that she hinted at having some plan up her sleeve. What we're wondering is – had someone divulged information that she considered to be hot property?'

Ruairidh McLeod shrugs defiantly.

'Ah wouldnae ken.'

Skelgill is undeterred.

'Your travelling clientele – present company excepted – whichever way you look at them, they're a VIP crowd.'

The guard grimaces.

'At those ticket prices, what dae ye expect?'

Teeth bared, Skelgill draws an apologetic breath.

'Happen the taxpayer was footing our bill. Saved the cost of a night in Mayfair – and put us back on the beat a day early.' But now he makes a frustrated exclamation. 'Well – it would have done.'

Unexpectedly, the guard leaps to their defence. His small beady eyes are suddenly alight with a previously unseen vehemence.

'The high heid yins cannae blame youse fae that. We should all be claiming overtime.'

It seems the union man in him is alive and kicking, workers' solidarity an ingrained reflex. Skelgill is encouraged.

'If she got some titbit of gossip – nugget of news – we think it were most likely on the train. Like I say, we saw her doing the rounds – plying folk with drinks – you'll remember you had a little ding-dong with her over the *Glenmorangie*.' (Skelgill pronounces it to meet with Ruairidh McLeod's satisfaction.) 'From interviews with the other passengers, we've established that she went to bed at the same time as Mr Mital – and maybe some words were exchanged, possibly in either his or her compartment.'

The guard is nodding. His demeanour is lightening. Perhaps he was anticipating that, being singled out and hauled before this inquisition, some accusations were coming his way. Now he sees this is not the case.

'Aye, right enough.'

Skelgill glances around. So they are in unison on this point.

196

'What about Mr Mital? Other passengers saw Jenny Hackett drinking with him. We know she'd had her fair share – but I'm wondering, what about him?'

Skelgill pauses and Ruairidh McLeod suddenly realises he is expected to answer. But now he shakes his head determinedly. It is difficult to discern if he is pleased to be able to inform them, or disappointed because the answer will not be what they want to hear.

'He wasnae drinking.'

'Are you certain?'

'It's mah job tae *sell* alcohol. He said he'd work tae dae. And he came on board sober. That's not tae say yer lady journalist didnae have a bottle in her luggage, ken?'

Skelgill's expression is attentive. But his head is spinning from the concentration of effort – rarely has he ever had to beat so elaborately about the bush to flush out a single response. But now he can relax; and his next question is succinct.

'When you saw the lady in the red nightgown – could she have come out of Mr Mital's compartment? It was the last but one at the far end, as you were looking.'

The guard frowns. But perhaps he is just trying to replay the scene in his mind.

'Aye – she could. But Ah didnae see that – Ah just caught a glimpse of her going round the corner. Ah didnae think much of it – guests use the toilets – smoke when they shouldnae, ken?'

'You didn't hear the click of the door closing – I mean with too short an interval for her to have got to the end of the corridor from her own cabin – she was in number seven, right?'

The guard shrugs. He seems not to remember this.

'Ah didnae hear a button. Not above the noise of the train.'

Skelgill nods. He asks the guard several relatively innocuous questions, such as Jenny Hackett's manner on arrival at the platform, and with whom she first sat in the lounge car; their purpose further to distract from the central point of interest. And when they conclude, in response to Ruairidh McLeod's parting query about their tenure at *Shake Holes Inn*, Skelgill duplicates the answer supplied to Wiktoria Adamska. The detectives left alone once more, DS Leyton is eager to ratify his take-out from the interview.

'What do you reckon, Guv? If he's right, the only person that gave Mikal Mital a whisky was Jenny Hackett.'

Skelgill is looking pensive.

'Jones reckons the toxicology indicates he may have consumed other alcohol.'

'Maybe he necked a couple of cheeky vodkas in the waiting room, Guv. If I recall, booze is buckshee in the first-class lounge at Euston. Or, like the guard says, she might have had a bottle stashed away.' DS Leyton runs the fingers of one hand through his mane of dark hair. 'They work quickly, don't they – these date-rape drugs? It would be his last couple of drinks that we're bothered about, yeah?'

Skelgill is nodding grimly. Then a wave of hopelessness seems to crash over him. But he heaves himself up and aims a kick at a recalcitrant log in the grate.

'Leyton – let's have a word with the driver. I'm not quite sure why – but I wouldn't mind a chat with her.'

'She's kept her head down since we've been here, Guv.'

'She's probably still mithering herself about being at fault.'

DS Leyton makes a face of protest.

'I don't see what else she could have done. Besides, we took charge pretty much from the off. They were lucky to have us on board, Guv – else that Bond geezer would have had 'em kipping in igloos!'

Skelgill grins wryly. Evidently his sergeant is still irked that the former soldier has muscled in on his territory.

'Aye – he's a loose cannon, right enough.'

DS Leyton appears satisfied with this assessment.

'I'll go and find her, Guv.'

But as he rises to make for the door there comes a sharp knock and it opens sufficiently for a head to be inserted in the gap. It is the man in question, Richard Bond. DS Leyton glances at Skelgill and fleetingly pulls a face of panic – that they have narrowly escaped being overheard (or perhaps not). But Richard Bond seems unperturbed; his expression conveys that he wishes to make a polite enquiry. Seeing that they do not have company, he steps into the room. He has changed into a casual outfit of a tailored Tattersall shirt that emphasizes his muscular build, shocking maroon corduroy trousers, and heavy brown brogues.

'May I have a quick word, Inspector? I gathered you were holding court in here.'

DS Leyton looks questioningly at his superior, but Skelgill indicates he should carry on with his mission and he leaves, carefully closing the door behind him. Skelgill rises; he does not intend for Richard Bond to make himself comfortable. But standing seems to suit the ex-military man, and true to form he comes directly to his point.

'Inspector. About this American, Bill Faulkner. François privately informs me that his behaviour during the search gave cause for suspicion.'

Skelgill inwardly bemoans this news; the last thing he needs is another fly flailing about in the already crowded ointment.

'In what way?'

'He paid no heed to several promising sets of tracks that crossed their path. He dismissed them out of hand as animal prints. If he were a man of Montana I should bow to his superior knowledge – but this fellow hails from Louisiana; more snow falls in Hades.'

'And what was your lad's opinion of these tracks?'

Skelgill can see that this question rather takes the wind out of Richard Bond's sails. Interviewed earlier, the young Frenchman had confessed to spending almost his entire life in urban Paris and London. His experience of following tracks in snow is probably limited to those made by skis. Richard Bond takes another tack.

'I suggest that I go out again – to retrace the southern loop while there's still enough daylight.'

Skelgill instinctively glances at the window; outside dusk is already falling.

'Richard – you'd be cutting it fine. I can't afford to go another man down.'

199

Richard Bond diplomatically scoffs at Skelgill's suggestion that he might not make it back – for they both know that is unlikely – but Skelgill senses in his body language a reaction of relief. Perhaps he does not actually want to venture forth at all – but simply feels he needs to make the proposal – for his training will be always to offer a solution, not just a criticism (and hats off to that attitude) – and that his sole purpose is to bring attention to his deeper-felt concern over Bill Faulkner. But at this moment DS Leyton returns with the train driver in tow, and he enters without knocking.

'Oh, sorry, Guv – didn't realise you hadn't finished. We'll come back, shall we?'

Richard Bond intervenes before Skelgill can answer.

'No – please enter – I shall leave you in private.' He addresses Skelgill. 'By the way – I have browbeaten that miserly Boer Merlyn into putting on afternoon tea at three-thirty – so those of us that missed lunch may refuel in good time for dinner.'

Skelgill signs his approval. With a meaningful nod, Richard Bond slips away. DS Leyton settles the train driver beside the hearth. She is a slight figure, and like many of the party in possession of a limited wardrobe, and today she is wearing her navy railway-issue cotton trousers and sky-blue shirt, which in tandem with her tied-back blonde hair gives the impression of an anxious schoolgirl. Skelgill moves to calm her nerves.

'Seems our colleague, DS Jones, knows your kid sister.'

'Oh.'

She is not sure how to react, perhaps anticipating that she is under investigation.

'Aye – happen they've crossed paths before now.'

'Jackie? Has she spoken to her, like?'

Her question is tentative, as if she feels it is not her place to ask. Skelgill, becoming fatigued by oblique conversation, decides it is simpler to take the bull by the horns.

'Listen – Laura – between these four walls –' He glances about and sees that DS Leyton is regarding him with trepidation. 'We're in contact with police HQ – we've got limited two-way radio service. I've kept it under my hat to avoid being inundated with daft requests.' He waves a hand in the direction of the door. 'Also – we're investigating what could be a murder – in the case of Mikal Mital.'

The woman is nodding, concentrating hard on what Skelgill has to say – but her eyes widen with alarm when he mentions the possible crime.

'There's a good chance we'll be airlifted out of here by tomorrow evening. In the meantime we're waiting for some test results from the lab. It might just suit us to keep everyone together a touch longer. Once they're back at Penrith – there'll be nothing to stop them getting road transport – the M6 could be open tonight.'

'I understand.'

'You still look worried to me, lass.'

'The train crashed while I was driving. There's folk missing. And now there's been a *killing.*' Her voice rises with a note of hysteria.

Skelgill is scowling fiercely. His prediction has proved accurate.

'Aye – maybe driving the train was your responsibility. But not the signalling network that didn't warn you of an obstacle. Not the storm that's brought half the country to a standstill. And definitely not what some shady passengers might have got up to. Listen – you acted impeccably – you kept everyone safe while they were on the train. And you've got three coppers as witnesses – at least two that'll be taken seriously.'

She doesn't get his self-deprecating joke – but DS Leyton only half suppresses a snigger, and with a delayed reaction she grins reluctantly.

'There'll be an investigation.'

'Aye – and we'll back you up. Don't you fret, lass.'

The woman nods. She is silent for a few moments.

'What you just said – that you've not told any of the others – not even Ruairidh – or Mr Bond?'

Skelgill leans forward, resting his forearms on his thighs.

'In our job, you get a sense of who can keep something to themselves and who can't. Besides, we're all in the same boat – you'd have been dealing with this if we weren't on board.' He grins, perhaps a little ghoulishly. 'Just your bad luck, *hah!*'

But the woman regards Skelgill earnestly.

'What you've done is marvellous – to get us here – to safety. I dread to think what it would have been like trapped on the train with no power, no light or heating.'

A little uncharacteristically Skelgill seems to feel the need to deflect the compliment.

'It's hardly been plain sailing, Laura. If you knew half of what's spinning around inside our heads.'

He glances at DS Leyton, who nods supportively, but whose blank expression seems not to concur entirely with his superior's assertion.

'There's no news on the missing lady – Jenny?'

Skelgill shakes his head.

'As a matter of fact your oppo reckoned she hinted at some escapade – while you were waiting your turn at billiards.'

Laura Wilson frowns.

'I don't recall that.'

'Did anything strike you – about her behaviour – that might explain her leaving?'

Her features become more troubled, but it seems she feels she ought to be able to contribute something of consequence.

'Only that she was – well, a bit eccentric – and then she fell in that pit on the way here. I suppose if you were to nominate anyone that might do something strange, happen you'd pick her. But –'

The woman hesitates – it seems to Skelgill she is formulating her thoughts, rather than holding something back. He delays for a moment before offering a prompt.

'But, what?'

'Oh – I was just thinking that I quite liked her.'

Laura Wilson looks at Skelgill as though he may disapprove, given the nature of their discussion. But Skelgill makes a face that conveys "fair enough". He relaxes back into his chair, as though he considers the matter complete.

'How were you originally getting home?'

'My shift was due to finish at Edinburgh. I would have hitched a lift on the next train down that stopped at Penrith.'

'What about your guard?'

'He lives in Edinburgh – he would have clocked off at Waverley when we changed crew. He would have been home.'

Skelgill now rises and offers some rather stilted praise for her cooperation. He accompanies her to the door and holds it open. She pauses beside him – and places a hand on his upper arm.

'You can trust me to keep quiet. Thanks.'

And with that she stretches up and pecks him on the cheek. When Skelgill turns from closing the door he sees DS Leyton is silently chortling.

'You've got admirers flocking at you from all angles, Guv.'

'Leyton – when a woman shows interest in me, the first thing I ask myself is who have they mistaken me for? Failing that, what do they want?'

DS Leyton grins ironically. He wonders if Skelgill is fishing for a compliment – or to be reassured that he is not a soft touch when it comes to the fairer sex. But he decides to stick to the safer ground of mickey taking.

'Maybe it's that *Brut* aftershave you use, Guv?'

Skelgill growls disparagingly – but by the same token he begins to finger the two days' growth that adorns his face. Then he grins, boyishly, and mimes a sniff of one armpit.

'*Ee, Ars reet foily, marra.*' And in case DS Leyton does not exactly get the drift, he adds a postscript in plainer English. 'I reckon I'll get a shower before they lay on that spread.'

*

'This is becoming a habit, lass.'

'It is your tea, Inspector.'

There is something about Samanta's insistence and her urgent glance back towards the top of the staircase that causes Skelgill

203

not to question her presence and instead to step back to admit her to his room. His reference to habit is that for a second time she has interrupted his ablutions. He is lacking a shirt, and is in the process of towelling his damp hair.

'I thought there's tea downstairs at half-past?'

'That is correct – I invented your order.' She narrows her eyes rather mysteriously. 'I have been trying to speak with you. I feel Mr Merlyn is – as you say – on my case. Even just now I heard him looking for me.'

'Aye?'

Skelgill frowns. He has no doubts that the man likes to keep her on a short leash – but he suspects it is not solely an economic motive that underlies his possessive behaviour. And it plainly troubles him that the girl – if only because of her extra mobility – ends up knowing more about what is going on around the place than he does. Skelgill closes the door, pressing it carefully to and slowly releasing the handle to avoid a telltale click. Samanta brushes past him and carries the tray she bears to the dresser by the window. Skelgill stands his ground beside the bathroom. He drapes the towel around his neck, like a boxer in the gym. The girl turns and approaches, she comes close – her voice is unnaturally low.

'Last night – or, in the early hours of the morning – you know it was?' (Skelgill looks perplexed.) 'After I left your room? I went downstairs – the lobby was in darkness, and I noticed a small light along the corridor that leads to the tack room. It was the linen cupboard – perhaps I had left it on – I went along to switch it off. Then, just as I was returning past reception to go to the staff quarters, from the balcony above I heard voices – whispers. I did not think so much at the time – but since Ms Hackett has disappeared and you are investigating – I think more now –'

She hesitates but Skelgill nods for her to continue.

'It was a man's voice. And then a woman's. The man said, "It might not succeed." And the woman replied, *"We will live – we will see."*'

'Come again?'

204

'It is a Russian proverb. It means what is achieved now will only become clear later. You see – the voices – they spoke in Russian.'

'How do you know?'

'I am a translator. I worked for two years in Kaliningrad Oblast.' She sees he is none the wiser. 'It is a Russian enclave – it borders my country Lithuania, and Poland.'

Now Skelgill lowers his voice.

'Who was it?'

'I could not tell – I could barely hear. I think they had gone up and did not realise I was there – but they moved away. Like I say – I did not think much of it – and then I heard Mr Merlyn – he was in the back office – also in darkness, asleep in his chair – he began to snore and then awaken. I tiptoed to my room.'

Skelgill is unsure of the import of this news – indeed if it is of any significance at all. The girl's manner is imploring – but to what extent is it a ruse to visit? Since their very first conversation he has sensed she has something more profound to impart. Yet there is a contradiction implicit in her account.

'A Russian proverb. That would take a native Russian to say that, wouldn't it?'

'That is possible, yes.'

Skelgill appears conflicted.

'The woman's voice – could it have been Jenny Hackett?'

'But she is English?'

'Actually, I think she might be Australian – but maybe I've got that wrong – as well.'

Samanta shakes her head. Her long hair is unrestrained, and the movement causes a lock to fall across her pale face. Skelgill has to resist reaching out to brush it aside. After a moment she speaks.

'The voices – they were so faint.'

Skelgill nods. He inhales to respond when a voice, not so faint – indeed, angry – calls out on the other side of the door, just feet from where they stand.

'Samanta!'

205

There now comes a rap on the door – with a stick by sound of it.

Skelgill reacts quickly – he pulls the girl into bathroom behind him, leans in, grabs a toilet roll and positions himself in the part-closed door. He lowers his jeans to half mast (his boxer shorts preserving his modesty). Now he reaches to open the main bedroom door.

Before him looms an agitated but immediately shocked Joost Merlyn.

'Ach – I'm looking for Samanta.' He tries to see past Skelgill into the bedroom. 'She has taken room service – she is needed downstairs.'

Skelgill grins inanely.

'Want to check in here?' He cocks a thumb over his shoulder, indicating the bathroom. The man scowls more fiercely and makes a retching noise that Skelgill takes as a rejection. 'You want to watch it, Mr Merlyn – you work her too hard. She's a little gem. Lose a looker like her, you can wave goodbye to half your regulars.'

The man staggers back on his stick. He is evidently not willing to engage in the debate.

'I will try another room.'

Skelgill gives a friendly wave of the loo roll. He pushes shut the door to the corridor and restores his jeans to their regular position. He beckons Samanta from her hiding place. They stand and listen. They can hear Joost Merlyn working his way along the landing.

'You'd better scarper. We'll wait until he's gone round the corner. What will you say?'

'That I had to go to the bathroom!'

The man's voice diminishes. Skelgill opens the door and peers out. He gives a nod and stands aside. Samanta performs a little curtsey as she slips past him.

'Thank you for the compliment. If true.'

Skelgill grimaces.

'In my job you have to be able to lie and tell the truth in the same breath.'

She turns and smiles.

'I only tell the truth.' She glides away, but he catches her mischievous whisper, which may or may not refer to the imminent tea party. 'Nice buns, Inspector.'

14. ON THE CASE

Friday, 4pm

'Another Chelsea bun, Guv?'

'What?'

'Ain't that what you're eating?'

'I thought it was an Eccles cake.'

'I'll get a selection, shall I, Guv?'

Skelgill appears distracted – and even his appetite seems to lack its regular zeal; it is usually something that can be relied upon, while his moods may be more capricious, and subject to the vagaries of self-absorption – a phenomenon that DS Leyton has long given up trying to fathom. Indeed, his sergeant slips away without further comment, and Skelgill finds himself gazing somewhat vacantly about the lounge in which the 'spread' has been laid. Without actually counting off on his fingers, he has the impression that everyone is present – or at least they were when he arrived – in their default groups, each at a cluster of chairs around a coffee table. One, the financiers, Richard Bond and his 'boys', Egor Volkov and François Mouton (now recovered and groomed); two, the remaining 'Russians' as DS Leyton would have it, Wiktoria Adamska, with Ivanna Karenina and her honorary compatriot Sir Ewart Cameron-Kinloch; three, the railway tag-team, *Dire Straits* as they were for the pub games (and Skelgill for a moment wonders which wag came up with the names); and, four, solitary – no surprise there – Bill Faulkner with his head in his electronic novel. It also strikes him that there might have been a fifth grouping: maybe 'missing in action' – Mikal Mital, Jenny Hackett and the evanescent Mr Harris. Certainly, there is an empty table fit for the purpose – perhaps he just cannot see the phantoms.

By some obscure association an image of DS Jones springs to mind – his last sight of her as she blithely ascended the winch to helicopter heaven, confidently kicking at sky and windblown snow to adjust her position. Of course – he might think of her now because she is also absent from their complement – or perhaps because he experiences some subliminal panic over the writing of the report of what has taken place – or perhaps for other reasons, less tangible. But his thoughts – or, rather, his feelings – are interrupted by the return of his sergeant, who unwittingly keeps something of the prevailing sentiment alive.

'You were right, Guv – Eccles cakes, there's a little printed menu. I should have remembered – the missus swears by 'em. Personally, I can't stand all those flippin' currants – remind me of dead flies.' Skelgill might be listening, if absently – but DS Leyton continues. 'I was thinking, Guv – about the missus – seeing as I've lumbered her with all the palaver of Christmas presents and decorations – maybe I could bring her for a relaxing weekend.'

His final words penetrate Skelgill's daydream.

'What – *here?*'

Skelgill sounds incredulous – and for a moment DS Leyton looks a little crestfallen. But he mounts a defence.

'This gaff is alright, Guv – I mean, I know it ain't the *Ritz* – but it's handy if we had to shoot back in case the nippers were giving the babysitter grief.'

Skelgill pulls a face; perish the thought. What would be the point of that? But with surprising diplomacy he holds his tongue. DS Leyton gestures at the plate of assorted cakes.

'The food's decent – the rooms are tidy – and the staff are friendly.'

Skelgill scoffs at this assertion.

'Aye – so long as you don't have owt to do with Merlyn.'

DS Leyton appears phlegmatic.

'Seeing as he knows us, Guv – might get a discount.'

'Keep trying, you might get blood out of a stone, Leyton.'

But DS Leyton shrugs off his boss's pessimism.

'Besides, in spring we'd be mainly outdoors. It's lovely and peaceful down here in the sticks – I bet there's nice walks. I could take her up and show her where the train crashed – and that flamin' snake hole that Jenny Hackett fell in.' He observes Skelgill's scowl, and grins amiably. '*Shake* hole, Guv – ain't it?

Funny how once you get an idea into your bonce it's hard to change track.'

'Tell me about it, Leyton.'

There seems to be a more profound sentiment underlying Skelgill's platitude, but his sergeant is determined to expound upon his plans for a mini-break.

'I mean, Guv – this old place – it's actually historic. I was reading the hotel services folder in my room – there's been a coaching inn on the site for over five hundred years – you're talking Henry VIII.'

Skelgill gives a sigh of resignation and he yields to his subordinate's persistence. He rocks forward and to one side, and pulls something from the back pocket of his jeans. It is the visitor leaflet, featuring the local heritage trail. It is somewhat creased, but he hands it to his colleague.

'There's supposed to be a monument up in the woods – to Queen Victoria. And an old bath house where they took the mineral waters. I checked it out when I were looking for signs of Jenny Hackett. It's bricked up, mind. It's got some Greek goddess statue on top.'

DS Leyton unfolds the leaflet and with a trombone player's action finds his optimum focal length.

'Well – there you go, Guv – all the more reason to come. The missus loves her historical dramas.'

Skelgill's attention, however, has reverted to comestibles, and he selects an Eccles cake, rotating it to identify the most promising angle of attack. But now he pauses, and cocks his head in a birdlike fashion.

'Did you hear something, Leyton?'

'Hear something? Er, no, Guv – I don't reckon so – just that new track that's started.'

The sound system has been plying its audience with a discreet genre of easy-listening chamber music. DS Leyton refers to the abrupt opening of a more voluminous orchestral affair, and its familiar motif. *Da da da duuum!* Beethoven's Symphony No.5 in C minor.

210

Skelgill looks unconvinced by his sergeant's response. He checks his watch – the time is 4.15pm – and a glance at the nearest window provides corroboration – a late dusk for this time of year, thanks to the day's clear skies.

'Huh – looks like something ain't to their taste, Guv.'

'Come again?'

DS Leyton indicates with a jerk of his head – that from their table the little grouping of Wiktoria Adamska, Ivanna Karenina and Sir Ewart Cameron-Kinloch have risen and are unobtrusively making their way out of the lounge.

'Maybe the music – or Samanta's baking.'

'All the more for us.'

Skelgill finally takes a bite of his own cake. Chewing pensively, he sinks back into the brown study that seems to be dogging him. DS Leyton selects a plain buttered scone. He spreads open the leaflet to display its rudimentary map and sketches of the trail's highlights. He munches contentedly as he peruses its detail, murmuring from time to time. Perhaps a couple of minutes pass without any conversation. Indeed DS Leyton only vaguely becomes aware of his superior rising to gaze towards the partly closed door, beyond which a corridor leads through to the lobby on the other side of the building. However, he has his own point of interest to convey.

'Here you go, Guv – this is up your street. Geology. Listen: *"The ancient coaching inn has its foundations set deep in the bedrock of a limestone escarpment, and the surrounding area is renowned for its hundreds of collapsed shafts known as shake holes. Some of these develop into sink holes, down which water flows, and the subterranean stream may form a cave system. Such a natural passage links the mineral spring in the adjacent bath house (original structure built circa 1720) to a larger chamber which has been adapted as the cellar of the inn."* Amazing, eh, Guv?'

Skelgill does not answer and DS Leyton glances up to find his boss staring at him in a most peculiar manner.

'Leyton.'

Skelgill has many ways of enunciating his name – but DS Leyton recognises this as one of urgency. It means, "come now". Thus as Skelgill strides away, DS Leyton rises so quickly

211

that he topples his chair and does not delay to reinstate it – attracting attention from all those remaining in the lounge.

Skelgill is almost breaking into a run by the time he reaches the lobby – and when he sees the main door is open to the elements he accelerates. But wearing flimsy hotel slippers he skids to a halt on the broad snow-encrusted step. Beyond, where the scene ought to be that of a still and silent fell country dusk, is a maelstrom of sound and light befitting of an action movie set.

A helicopter has landed in the car park.

DS Leyton reaches Skelgill's shoulder.

'Is it our lot, Guv? It ain't very big.'

'You're joking, Leyton – look at it.'

DS Leyton shades his eyes from the spotlight that is strobing the area, intermittently illuminating the woodland backdrop. The aircraft is a neat 4-seater, brand new by the look of it, ostentatiously liveried in glittering gold with – on its side – a black logo incorporating the words *Adamskaya Korporatsiya*.

'Cor blimey – it must belong to Wiktoria Adamska's husband! Imagine having that for your company car.'

'Aye – and she's aboard – and look who else.'

Within the cockpit a light is on. Wiktoria Adamska is nearest, port side front; she has her head turned, but there is no mistaking her blonde tresses. Behind, just visible on the starboard side, is the balding Sir Ewart Cameron-Kinloch, and next to him Ivanna Karenina. Her pale face is implacable, and she meets Skelgill's gaze with a curious detachment – when perhaps a certain smugness might be expected – the VIP about to be whisked in executive comfort from snowbound confinement.

'What do we do, Guv?'

Skelgill does not answer; he is asking himself the same question. He feels a hand on his arm and glances to see Samanta at his side – and he becomes conscious that others have joined them on the step. It is a star-struck audience, perhaps drawn by the detectives' abrupt exit, or by hearing more clearly the engine as successive doors were left open. And Skelgill realises too that, along the frontage of the inn to his right, there is some shadowy

212

movement. He sees that the cellar trap is open, propped against the wall; from within emanates the soft glow of lamplight – and that Joost Merlyn is clambering out of the hatch, with difficulty – and that he accepts a hand up from none other than the train guard, Ruairidh McLeod – and that lying flat in the snow is Wiktoria Adamska's distinctive leopard-pattern luggage – the diminutive case and its king-size facsimile. As Joost Merlyn lurches to his feet he notices Skelgill and the others beneath the porch light, and – bereft of his stick – he begins to limp awkwardly, dragging one leg through the snow, apparently to greet them. But Skelgill is first to speak.

'What's going on?'

Beneath a hideous grimace, the innkeeper appears to laugh.

'Some of my guests have made their own arrangements, Inspector.'

It is an oddly proprietorial use of the word 'guests' – that suddenly they are his to superintend. And his tone is triumphant, as though he detects Skelgill's discomfiture. Indeed, Skelgill is dumbfounded. He feels stranded on the little island of the step, as though the tide of snow has flooded in to isolate him, to render him impotent – and that the flashing of the lights and the clatter of the rotors are symbolic of the cerebral chaos that has paralysed his thoughts.

He sees that what must be the pilot – an athletic-looking man in his thirties with close-cropped fair hair clad in a black flying suit – is waiting beside the chopper – presumably to receive the suitcases – for he has open a hatch inside which there are already bags. Joost Merlyn must notice Skelgill's interest.

'We are just organising the last of the luggage. About time that idle station porter lifted a finger – *hah!*'

Skelgill observes as Ruairidh McLeod labours with the large suitcase, its casters useless in the snow, the man himself further hampered by the small hand-held valise. He is bent over and the effort on his reddened face suggests he has a ton weight in tow. When he reaches the helicopter there ensues some remonstration with the pilot – who gesticulates in frustration and puts his head in the door as if to consult with the passengers. Then he takes

213

out two smaller cases from the hold and places them in the snow.

Skelgill finds himself thinking there will be an issue over the payload. It is a subject he knows something about – indeed it arose with DS Jones's visit by similar means. A small machine like this, four average persons and maybe a hundred and fifty pounds of cargo. And that oversized case – it looks heavy. In fact the two men are struggling to raise it – never mind that they will have to hoist it to shoulder height to slide it into the snug compartment. As he watches, a more profound unease possesses Skelgill. This is the suitcase that he saw DS Jones lift singlehandedly onto the train. And he witnessed something of its contents in its owner's bedroom. Ruairidh McLeod changes position to get what must be his stronger left arm under the bottom of the case. And in recognising such sinistrality Skelgill's troubled mind experiences a flash of clarity hitherto absent. It is as though a conductor's baton has suddenly brought an orchestra of disparate instruments into fleeting unison.

'Left handed.'

'Come again, Guv?'

Skelgill does not take his eyes off the scene of imminent departure.

'Leyton – what did you just say?'

'You mean about the chopper?'

'No – in the tea room – the bath house.'

'Oh – you mean – that there's a tunnel connecting it to the cellar?'

There is a short pause before Skelgill responds.

'Leyton!'

If Skelgill's earlier exhortation was insistent, this one is do or die – and DS Leyton *does* – despite not understanding (but trusting), and he takes off after Skelgill, the pair of them slip-sliding across the icy snow towards the helicopter, where the pilot and the guard have the suitcase on the lip of the compartment and are about to heave it in.

'Stop! What's in that case?'

214

They probably do not hear Skelgill exactly. But though they sense him coming they are trapped in their strained stances and are powerless to react when he launches himself arms outstretched to pull the suitcase crashing down, whereupon it bursts open like a great clamshell. And DS Leyton's concomitant Anglo-Saxon outpouring proclaims the magnitude of the secret within – for, inside the case, curled into the deeper compartment, clad in a paintball overall, is the body of a female. Its hair covers the face, but there is no mistaking the distinctive honey blonde shade. *Jenny Hackett!*

Skelgill is on his knees in the snow. He has lost his slippers. And he seems frozen as he stares at the unmoving figure. But it is the flotsam – the fragments that began to coalesce when he subliminally heard the helicopter and then his deputy mentioned the underground passage; they have taken shape. He does not see the whole picture – but he grasps its essence.

DS Leyton suffers no such mental gymnastics, and where Skelgill's impulse was to go on the offensive, his is to minister to the victim. He pulls away the hair and slides a hand onto the neck.

'Guv! She's alive! She's warm – she's got a pulse!'

And, indeed, it is apparent that she is breathing – slowly and shallowly, as if she is consumed by the slumber of winter hibernation.

'Get her inside, Leyton.'

DS Leyton is not a tall man, but he could give a good account of himself against a charging bull, and with a grunt he has the limp form in his arms and is on his feet and stomping steadily back towards the inn. Subsumed in the snow and the dusk and the flashing lights and the rattling throb of the rotors, neither he nor Skelgill has paid attention for half a minute to their surroundings – but now Skelgill sees Samanta come down off the step and run to DS Leyton to offer him assistance. Amidst the blur-cum-whirr-cum-clatter he becomes vaguely aware now of the movements of others around him – and his senses sharpen to how they ought or might react in these extraordinary circumstances. But what happens next is less predictable – for

215

suddenly the passenger door flies open and Wiktoria Adamska tumbles from her seat and pushes past him to get at the suitcase.

'My papers!'

Although clad in her travelling outfit of striped fur coat and platform shoes she drops undaunted to her knees and snatches up from the base of the case a translucent plastic folder that contains a bound document.

Skelgill is about to restrain her, and they rise together – but at this moment the rear passenger window slides open and there is the face of Ivanna Karenina. Her narrowed gimlet eyes glitter as black as her hair, as black as hell; her thick mascara seems to drip with menace.

'Wiktoria! *Voyti v tebya durak!'*

Skelgill will later learn from Samanta that these words translate as "Get in, you fool!" – but he does not need the rendition to understand the sentiment. This is not some species of benevolent evacuation. It is an audacious escape.

And instantaneously the idling engine erupts into full throttle. The noise becomes deafening and loose snow begins to swirl and fill the air like the visitation of a mini tornado. Skelgill realises that the pilot has abandoned the residual luggage, ducked under the tail and scrambled into his seat. And he sees that Wiktoria Adamska is rooted to the spot, staring uncomprehendingly at Ivanna Karenina. The latter fixes her with an unblinking stare for perhaps five more seconds, before she barks an unintelligible command and simultaneously slams shut the window. In response the pilot reaches to close the passenger door and takes up the cyclic. With a judder, the helicopter pries itself from the icy ground and begins to rise.

For the second time in two minutes Skelgill's instincts gain ascendancy. He leaps at the chopper, obtaining a tenuous grip against the smooth fuselage and a precarious foothold upon the skid.

Whether he hears Wiktoria Adamska's despairing protest, or feels her trying to get a hold on his jeans, there is only a fleeting moment in which he might consider that she is trying to save him from certain death – a fleeting moment because some alternative fate intervenes.

'*Boom – boom – boom – boom – boom.*'

The bangs that emanate in rapid succession from the direction of the inn are accompanied by a simultaneous sequence of cracks – the latter so very close at hand it seems to Skelgill as to be outrageously adventurous – and a neat ring of holes is punched into the aluminium bulkhead beside him – and instantaneously powerful jets of pressurised fuel spurt out.

Skelgill hears a warning alert inside the cockpit – the engine dies and the helicopter drops back to earth with a jolt that throws him out into the deep snow. As he flounders about and gains all fours he looks up at the old building. There, in the strobing light, framed in an open first-floor window, calmly assessing the scene and holding an old-style military rifle at the ready, is the steely-eyed American, Bill Faulkner.

He looses one more shot into the forest beyond; its echo reverberates around the clearing. But if it is intended as a deterrent to malevolent action it is not entirely successful. Skelgill, winded, now kneeling and spitting snow – sees the pilot leap out of the cockpit and hook an arm around the neck of the unsuspecting Wiktoria Adamska. She screams in horror – a vicious Bowie knife is pressed to her throat and the man – who has all the alacrity and muscle of a special forces operative, is using her as a human shield against the rifle. He grunts some order in what must again be Russian and begins to thrust her before him through the snow as though he intends to take her into the hotel.

Skelgill rises, preparing to intercept.

The man snarls at him in English.

'Keep back – or she dies!' Then he calls out to Bill Faulkner. 'Surrender the gun!'

Skelgill is coiled – but he sees the risk before him. And sown in his mind there are seeds of confusion. Could the woman be acting? Is she in cahoots? *It is her husband's helicopter.* But if she acts she excels. And his instincts tell him he must make a move before the man gains complete control of the situation. And

217

then – and then his eyes tell him he is witnessing something that defies logic.

From a snowdrift just behind the pilot and his hostage rises a ghostly apparition that assumes the abominable limbed form of the sasquatch. But as it rises to its full height it is revealed to be a sasquatch that wears shocking maroon corduroys, and when the white bed sheet is silently cast aside not a sasquatch at all – but the imposing, indeed deadly figure of Richard Bond. In a flash he is upon the unsuspecting hostage-taker to snap back his head with an audible crack. The knife falls free into the snow. The body follows.

Freed, Wiktoria Adamska flings herself at Skelgill. She wraps one arm around his neck and kisses him forcefully upon the lips. Pressed between them, hard, he can feel the document file that she has held onto so desperately throughout her ordeal.

15. SHAKE HOLES

Friday, 11.30am – four months later

'Flippin' shame we never found Mikal Mital's manuscript, Guv.'

Skelgill nods pensively. He has a stalk of common rush gripped between his lips; it is plucked from their surroundings, more abundantly herbaceous than on their last visit to the vicinity of Shap Fell. DS Leyton elaborates.

'I feel like we've caught the monkeys but the organ grinders are still plying their trade.'

'I thought we'd got it, Leyton – though I couldn't understand why, when Wiktoria Adamska wouldn't get in the chopper, they didn't try to snatch the folder. I never imagined for a second that it were designs for a bunch of see-through kegs.'

DS Jones appears mildly amused by Skelgill's turn of phrase.

'Her new collection has been a big hit on the catwalks. London. Milan. Paris. New York. She's on the covers of all the glossy magazines. She would have lost a small fortune – not to mention months of original work.'

Skelgill does not answer – he is wondering whether he can contrive a joke about the woman getting her knickers in a twist – but coincidentally DS Leyton wags a reproving finger.

'That'll teach her to make duplicates in future. Belt and braces – my old Granddad used to say. I always photocopy my notebook, the minute I get back to the office.'

'Pity Mikal Mital didn't employ the same philosophy.' Skelgill's tone is distinctly rueful.

'Or that Jenny Hackett can't remember anything he told her, eh, Guv?'

Skelgill turns to DS Jones.

'Is that still the latest?'

DS Jones nods. Being author of their report she has the most comprehensive and up-to-date knowledge of the case.

'As of her most recent medical, about a fortnight ago – I think we would have heard otherwise. She was lucky to survive – the amount of *Rohypnol* they gave her. And fortunate not to have suffered brain damage. She has no recall from the morning of the day she boarded the train until she came out of the coma in hospital a week later. The specialist believes the memories could be wiped permanently.'

'Still – silver lining, Guv.' It seems DS Leyton will put a positive spin on the news. 'Remember she was threatening to write that article about us – *Skelly's Heroes?* Hah! Least we avoided that.'

Skelgill does not appear entirely relieved. Perhaps the images that come hustling back bring with them the frustration that DS Leyton has voiced – indeed, as he graphically put it, of caged monkeys and fugitive organ grinders. And so he does not exactly appreciate what ought to be a few moments of gentle contemplation, as a skylark regales them from on high, turning little cartwheels in the balmy April breeze. Indeed, more reflective of his unease, another sound, unearthly, begins to reach their ears – at first barely tangible, a queer resonance in the air, it seems to emanate from Shake Holes cutting, the chiselled canyon below their vantage point. It becomes a whirring, whining sibilance, growing in intensity until, with a sudden whoosh and the reverberating bass throb of diesel engines the blur of a northbound express train materialises beneath them. In just a few short seconds it slips away and around the bend, passing the spot where they had become stranded. And amidst the returning silence the sweet silver song of the lark regains ascendancy.

'Cor blimey, that was shifting, Guv.' DS Leyton puffs out his cheeks. 'If we'd been doing the ton like that we might have burst through the drift and made it home.'

Skelgill clicks his tongue disapprovingly and tosses away the chewed stem like it is a dart.

'Aye – and then they'd *all* of them got away scot-free. We'd have hopped off at Carlisle. The rest at Edinburgh. They'd have found Mikal Mital later and put it down to an accident. No one would have thought twice about his manuscript being missing. Their plans would have worked out nicely.'

Skelgill lifts an oversized thermos flask from the cast-iron parapet of the bridge and offers to top up the tin mugs he has supplied for his subordinates on this little jaunt down memory lane. A lull in other operations has provided a small window of opportunity, and news of guilty pleas from the Crown Prosecution Service a timely reminder of all things Shake Holes. So he has cajoled his colleagues to join him for their lunch break, to fulfil his pledge to revisit the area when it is not cloaked in snow – to see it, warts and all, and to find out just how deeply he and Jenny Hackett might have sunk. So he has rallied his team and driven them the twenty minutes from Penrith to the point where the bridleway that passes *Shake Holes Inn* eventually intersects with the B-road, and they have come south on foot across the stretch of moorland pocked by actual shake holes – his explanation of such eliciting some reasonable degree of interest from his colleagues. "Time for a cuppa", he had announced as their footsteps clanged onto the iron bridge. Now his sergeants acquiesce, perhaps largely out of politeness. They stand and stare and occasionally sip, as if mesmerised by the empty railway track, with its optical illusion of parallel rails that patently converge. It is DS Leyton who eventually breaks the silence by resurrecting his complaint.

'Okay – we've got Ruairidh McLeod bang to rights. And that's in order – the death of Mikal Mital was by his hand – if not by his intention. But whoever ordered it – they're sitting pretty. Mikal Mital's silenced. And his manuscript that might have pointed the finger – you know, Guv – I reckon it might even have gone up in smoke at the hotel.'

'Didn't you notice I kept checking the fires, Leyton?'

DS Leyton looks at his boss with a rather anguished grimace – that he may share the view that the irreplaceable document met such a fate.

'Why do you reckon they took Wiktoria Adamska's designs?'

Skelgill gives a shrug of his shoulders.

221

'To make it look like Jenny Hackett had some reason to do a runner from the inn. Once they'd concluded that she knew something about Mikal Mital's manuscript – maybe had read it and destroyed it – she *became* the manuscript. They had to take her. They wanted Mikal Mital silenced and they wanted to know what he'd written. When Ruairidh McLeod searched his compartment and found nothing – he suspected her – obviously he'd seen her coming out – although he denied that to us. So she was prime suspect. From then on they were thinking on the hoof. And they nearly succeeded.'

'Except, as it turns out, Jenny Hackett wouldn't have been much use to them, Guv.'

'Aye – but they didn't know that, Leyton.'

DS Jones taps her mug experimentally on the dome of a protruding rivet.

'What do you think they were going to do with her, Guv?'

'Your guess is as good as mine, lass. Spirit her out of the country. Then something with Siberia in the title, I reckon.'

DS Leyton makes a fearful intake of breath, but DS Jones is nodding.

'When I was reviewing the background evidence for the trial of Ruairidh McLeod I came across a classified file. That suggested in the early 1980s he was recruited by communist Czechoslovakia – there's a widespread view that they successfully infiltrated the British trades unions. And despite that his official union activities came to an end – reading between the lines – he has been supplying information ever since. After the fall of the Berlin Wall, the Czechoslovak intelligence networks were inherited by Moscow. With Ruairidh McLeod's job on the sleeper – when you think about it – he was mingling every night with politicians and VIPs, serving their cosy little drinking clubs and eavesdropping on their conversations. The Crown submissions include an analysis of his bank account that showed he was receiving a regular monthly income from an anonymous offshore source. Naturally he has declined to explain that.'

'He's declined to say anything, ain't that right, girl?'

DS Jones turns and nods to DS Leyton.

'It seems he decided that pleading guilty and otherwise holding his tongue is most expedient. Likewise Joost Merlyn for his role in the abduction and kidnapping.'

Now Skelgill interjects, his tone cynical.

'Think about it, Leyton. If McLeod serves – what – eight years for the manslaughter? He's maybe got a light at the end of the tunnel. If he'd blabbed – assuming it's who we think it is behind it all – it would be an express train coming the other way.'

DS Leyton begins to laugh at his superior's apposite metaphor – but it may be unintentional, and he curtails his merriment.

'Suppose so, Guv – they could get at him inside, an' all. He probably ain't got no choice but to keep his trap shut about his handlers.' DS Leyton scrambles a curse in frustration. 'But surely that was Ivanna Karenina calling the shots – on the train – at the hotel? And remember you said there was some female speaking Russian that night?'

Skelgill nods broodingly.

'She was smart. Kept her head down. Manipulated those around her.' He inhales and folds his arms and gazes out into the middle distance, undistracted by a splendid red admiral that purposefully crosses his line of sight. 'Wiktoria Adamska must have known that it was just a matter of time before her husband sent his private helicopter. Naturally, she'd confide in her 'best pal' Ivanna. They'd discuss how the pair of them could hop it – and Ivanna Karenina would suggest taking her stooge Sir Ewart Cameron-Kinloch – make it look completely above board. Just the three of them, VIPs making a casual exit – lording it while the minions loaded their luggage. What could be more normal?'

DS Leyton is evidently reminded of the moment that Skelgill took off through the snow wearing his unsuitable slippers.

'Guv – what made you think there was something wrong with the suitcase? If they'd got that on board – and lifted off – we'd have been none the wiser. And we'd have Jenny Hackett listed as a missing person. End of.'

Skelgill is shaking his head.

223

'Hard to say, Leyton. They didn't foresee that a theft from Wiktoria Adamska meant we'd clock her belongings. And they didn't bank on us rubber-necking their unannounced departure. McLeod and the pilot started arguing about the payload. Why would there be a weight problem if that case contained a couple of fur coats? It just triggered a whole avalanche of ideas. Remember you'd just mentioned the tunnel – I suppose subconsciously I'd considered there being a secret hiding place. And I'd been in the cellar – you know, I realised later I thought I smelt her perfume – they'd smashed a bottle of violet liqueur. I don't know if that were to mask her scent in case a search dog were brought in at a later date – or if it were just an accident when they heaved the shelving unit back in front of the concealed hatch.'

This aspect of Skelgill's account raises a question in DS Jones's mind.

'Obviously I wasn't there for long, Guv. At what point do you think they enlisted Joost Merlyn? There can't have been any premeditation about his involvement.'

Skelgill contemplates his answer for a few moments.

'Let's assume one of the few truths Ruairidh McLeod told us was Jenny Hackett's suggestion that she was up to something. It might have just been the drink talking – but it spooked them. If they thought she had the manuscript, or knew of its contents, and that she were about to do a bunk – they had to stop her, and quick. So they used her 'plan' as a cover story to hoodwink us. She accepted one cocktail too many and got no further than falling unconscious in her own bed. At that point they were going to struggle without Merlyn's cooperation. You saw his reaction to Wiktoria Adamska's generosity – so when Ruairidh McLeod palmed him a couple of grand in unmarked banknotes he'd be putty in their hands. I reckon what Samanta overheard in the early hours was Ruairidh McLeod reporting back to Ivanna Karenina. McLeod and Merlyn had staged the getaway and moved Jenny Hackett to the cellar. Merlyn kept guard overnight – then at some time in the early morning they transferred her up through the tunnel to the bath house.'

DS Jones is nodding.

'Do you believe Joost Merlyn's claim that he acted solely on Ruairidh McLeod's instructions – and was unaware of anyone else giving the orders?'

'That may have happened in practice – but he must have guessed there was more to it – when he saw that the suitcase was going in the chopper and Ruairidh McLeod was being left behind.'

'Until you kyboshed that, Guv. For a minute, I thought you'd gone mad. Instead you saved the day!'

Skelgill makes a self-deprecating growl in his throat.

'Leyton, you seem to be forgetting our secret service chums.'

'Well – fair enough, Guv – they were on their guard, and all credit to 'em – but I don't reckon they were any the wiser when that chopper turned up. I had a chinwag with Bond afterwards, he'd downed a couple of large Scotches to calm his nerves – and he admitted he had no clue that Faulkner was a US agent. And I reckon that was mutual. Then Bond started getting all competitive, saying as how if he hadn't camouflaged himself in the snow we'd all be six feet under. Faulkner was biting his lip – until Bond called his efforts with that old gun of Merlyn's something like "lucky hillbilly pot-shots" – and he got a bit uppity about that. Only time I saw him lose his rag. Can't say as I blame him. They're alright, really, ain't they, the Yanks?'

DS Leyton has become absorbed in his little monologue – and now he glances about to see a perplexed Skelgill, and DS Jones smiling rather more patiently. Thus he addresses her.

'Imagine that, eh, girl – there's us quietly heading home for Christmas – little did we know we'd got a bunch of bandits out to get poor old Mikal Mital – and MI5 and the CIA riding shotgun!'

DS Jones nods encouragingly.

'I don't suppose we'll find out exactly what the intelligence agencies were doing – covertly shadowing him or intending to intervene at some point. I guess it's possible they were hoping to glean information before Mikal Mital made it public – something that would have enabled an arrest or a sanction against a target

225

before they took evasive action.' She gives a shake of her hair with its glinting golden highlights and lifts her face to the sun, momentarily closing her large hazel eyes. 'Notice how they've disappeared into the ether. I suspect that's why the CPS are content with the guilty pleas. If they'd had to call Richard Bond and Bill Faulkner as witnesses – that would be their cover blown and details of their operations laid bare.' She glances at Skelgill. 'Guv – remember I thought the Chief was keeping her cards close to her chest – about the bigger picture? In the final analysis, Ivanna Karenina is probably at best a middle-sized cog in the machine. If the Russian government were ultimately behind the plan, our security services would need totally compelling evidence before they could act.'

Skelgill screws up his features; it is a face of pessimism.

'Even when you catch the Russians red-handed they've got a dozen excuses up their sleeve.'

DS Leyton nods dejectedly – but he offers a small crumb of comfort.

'I thought the chopper pilot had history in the GRU? That's Russian military intelligence, Guv.'

'You may have noticed, Leyton, that Bond didn't give us the opportunity to interview him. It would have been nice to know if he were prepared to exonerate Adamski Corporation. As things stand it's too easy for the Russians to claim it's the work of rogue oligarchs. Pound to a penny you're right, Leyton – that the goon was a plant and Adamski knew nowt about it. If you were going to infiltrate a billionaire's empire, a good place to start would be his private helicopter pilot.'

DS Leyton exhales forcefully, his rubbery lips vibrating.

'No wonder we couldn't get our heads round what was going on – when half the people weren't what they seemed. I mean – take the 'Mr Harris' malarkey. What are you supposed to think when a railway employee tells you he's checked someone in – shows you the manifest – and in fact he's lying through his teeth?'

Skelgill is nodding, his features grim.

'We should have trusted the observable facts. There was no independent evidence that a Mr Harris got on the train – and none that he left it. Even McLeod couldn't describe him! He was never there.'

DS Jones has something to add on this topic.

'Our IT guys believe the booking system was hacked and places reallocated so that the compartment interconnecting with Mikal Mital's was left empty – but reserved for a 'Mr Harris'. It was a clever ploy. It meant Ruairidh McLeod could pass to and fro with impunity. Again – it supports the theory of a state actor, with the technical resources to do something like that.'

DS Leyton is listening to his colleague with renewed fascination.

'So – what do you reckon happened, exactly – to Mikal Mital?'

DS Jones glances at Skelgill – but he seems content for her to continue with her explanation.

'Well – what he has admitted to – in effect, by pleading guilty – is that he poisoned Mikal Mital with *Rohypnol*. He might have wiped his fingerprints from the blister pack, but he left traces of DNA. On that basis he probably dissolved the tablets in a malt whisky – presumably when Jenny Hackett procured nightcaps for her and Mikal Mital. His plan was to enter the cabin at some point before the train was due in at Edinburgh, take the manuscript and pass it on to Ivanna Karenina. But instead there was the storm and the snowdrift – and we discovered Mikal Mital – too soon. I imagine while we were organising the evacuation he went back into the compartment and realised the manuscript was gone. It might also have been a shock to find Mikal Mital dead. Analysis of chemical residue left on the packaging indicates that the tablets were much stronger than the standard dose – in other words, intended to kill. But Ruairidh McLeod didn't need to know that – as has been proven, he is considered dispensable. He tried to make it look like Mikal Mital took the pills of his own volition. He wiped the empty blister pack, and maybe wrapped a tissue around the water bottle to open it, and poured half away and left it with its top off.' DS

227

Jones glances rather mischievously at Skelgill. 'Except you noticed it had been done left-handed, Guv!'

'Aye – too late to make much difference. That was just something that was bugging me but not registering. I only really spotted it when I looked at your photographs when we were reviewing the evidence. He made ticks left-handed – he played darts left-handed – he even dunked his biscuits left-handed.'

DS Leyton, who has been least involved with the process to which Skelgill refers, sniffs the cool air rather like an inquisitive rabbit.

'When do you reckon they hatched the plot? I mean – in the first place – to eliminate Mikal Mital.'

Again Skelgill looks to DS Jones to supply a rejoinder.

'You've been dealing with the spooks, lass.'

DS Jones places her mug carefully on the parapet and leans her elbows on the flaking iron surface, and then rests her chin on her intertwined fingers. She gazes out over the cutting.

'Well – this is their theory. You'll recall Mikal Mital was originally from Prague? There's the possibility that he came to the West as an agent in the first instance – I mean working for the communists. Then maybe the Americans turned him. That would have made him a target for Moscow. To add insult to injury he began to investigate the money laundering activities of the Russian billionaires' cartel. Perhaps they'd been on his tracks for some time – years even. But when it looked like he was preparing to expose them to the world's media – ready to publish everything he'd got – they decided to move. The financial conference in Edinburgh was widely advertised, and as Jenny Hackett pointed out the jungle drums were thick with rumours. So they would have had time to make preparations. It's quite probable that to intercept him on the sleeper was just one of several plans that were activated. But there was the chink in their armour: while they had a longstanding agent perfectly placed, when it came to playing assassin he was an amateur. The plan depended upon the train getting smoothly to Edinburgh. But we crashed.'

'Wait!'

Simultaneously the two sergeants start, such is Skelgill's sudden cry. Raising a finger as though he might be testing the wind, his features are contorted with the anticipation of an impending thunderbolt.

'What is it, Guv?'

It is DS Leyton who poses the question, but Skelgill addresses his response to his female colleague.

'Jones – when you went into Mikal Mital's cabin with the guard – to wake him, to evacuate him – the body was in bed, aye?'

'Aha.'

'So how come when the train hit the snowdrift we all ended up on the floor?' Now Skelgill does look at DS Leyton. 'Leastways – folk like you who were in the bottom bunk without the safety strap.'

Now his associates share his expression of puzzlement. After a few moments DS Jones interrupts the collective silence.

'Can I make a suggestion?'

'Aye.'

'Someone else went into his compartment – looking for the manuscript. To search under the bunk they would need to move the body. The obvious thing to do is to lift him back onto the bed. And then maybe straighten the covers as though everything were untouched.'

Both Skelgill and DS Leyton seem to be nodding in agreement, but it is the former that speaks.

'When I left our compartment to speak with the driver – I came upon Richard Bond – he was half naked and hanging out of the door – like he was looking under the train. He made up some story about assessing the conditions.'

Now DS Jones has a further suggestion.

'Given that MI5 were on Mikal Mital's trail – it's quite likely that he went to check on him. But once he was dead – there was nothing to be done. Richard Bond would have assumed foul play and wouldn't have wanted to show his hand. If he was aware of the manuscript, perhaps he was hoping to recover it – but he was too late. It fits the theory that it was stolen in the period between Mikal Mital retiring and the collision with the snowdrift.'

Now DS Leyton chips in.

'Which brings us back to Jenny Hackett. And it's obviously what someone else believed – since they shoved her in that there pit of yours, Guv.'

Skelgill groans and rather desperately swigs the last of his tea and drops the mug into his rucksack, along with the flask – and he proffers the mouth of the bag for his colleagues to do likewise.

'Speaking of the pit, Leyton – let's get this done.'

'Whoa – I didn't realise you were serious about going all the way, Guv.'

'Leyton, we'll have no couch potato talk. Besides, didn't you come up here with your better half?'

Now DS Leyton looks somewhat dismayed.

'Stone the crows, Guv – that weekend break! I told the missus I'd book it – but you know how these things slip your mind?'

DS Jones responds supportively to her colleague's predicament.

'Actually, I was looking at their website. It says the inn is under new management. I think it has been closed, and only reopened at the end of March.'

DS Leyton appears relieved, but Skelgill exhales rather scornfully.

'It'll take a few bob to put that place right. That miserly old git was milking it for all it was worth.'

DS Jones is more optimistic.

'It has fantastic potential – you can't buy that kind of history.'

And DS Leyton is ready with a quip.

'Or snake holes, eh, Guv?'

'Very funny, Leyton.' Skelgill grins somewhat grudgingly as he swings his rucksack onto his shoulder. 'Come on, let's roll.'

'Get to the bottom of it, you might say, Guv?'

'Aye – have a deek – something like that.'

For Skelgill, who made the trek between the inn and the train several times, and other diversions through the forest, the lie of the land feels familiar, if strangely luxuriant with fresh green spring growth dripping from myriad branch tips and patches of celandine and dog violets adorning the woodland path; the pine-infused air is resonant with bird calls and the drone of insects. His colleagues, lulled into a pleasant state of abstraction, are both surprised when Skelgill veers off the bridleway and announces the location – *Jenny's Hole.*

'It seemed much further than this, Guv. You sure it's the same one?'

'Leyton, you were towing a sledge in a blizzard in pitch darkness.'

'That's true enough – it did feel like it were going on for ever.'

Skelgill's colleagues join him at the rim of the shake hole. It is similar to several they have already inspected. Vegetation, a mixture of heather, bilberry, rush and moorland grasses and mosses spills over its rim and covers its sides and floor. It is probably eight feet at its deepest; there is something of a collapse on one side, and several large moraine boulders lie in the base, they may have been rolled there long ago, cleared from the track. Skelgill is grimacing. He looks like he might be disappointed, that there was not a thirty-foot shaft above which he was suspended only by the friction of the snow during his daring rescue.

'What's up, Guv?'

Skelgill gives a downward jerk of his head.

'Look at that – some donnat's dumped some rubbish. Disgraceful.'

His tone is indignant – and before his colleagues can dissuade him he drops his rucksack, steps over the edge and scrambles down the side of the shake hole, gripping fistfuls of wiry heather to control his descent.

'Cor blimey, Guv – take it easy! What if we can't get you out?'

'Phone MI5 and ask for Bond.'

Skelgill has reached the bottom, and he drops to one knee and delves into a crevice between two of the rocks. With a grunt he extracts something roughly rectangular, about six inches by nine, made of off-white plastic, and considerably stained. As he holds it out at arm's length to inspect it he realises that the stains are in fact a printed pattern of faded pink lipstick kisses, and simultaneously DS Jones identifies the item.

'I think it's a woman's toiletries bag, Guv.'

But Skelgill does not appear to be listening. His face is curiously deadpan. The item – the bag – is heavy and bulging – and the closure not surprisingly rusted. Skelgill – to the consternation of his colleagues – bites at the zipper and gives a jerk of his head – subsequently spitting to one side but thankfully not at the expense of any teeth. On his haunches and with the bag wedged against one boot he prises out its contents. It is a thick sheaf of papers that have been bent over into half their size.

Skelgill presses open the ream on his thigh and stares at the uppermost page. For some moments he does not blink – nor move – nor even seem to be breathing. DS Leyton can hold his tongue no longer.

'Guv, what is it?'

Even now Skelgill does not immediately respond. It is several more seconds before he looks up at his colleagues. He squints, sunbeams illuminating his awed expression.

'Clever woman.'

'Come again, Guv?'

'Never underestimate a journalist – isn't that what I always say, Leyton?'

'Beats me, Guv – I'm confused.'

Skelgill rises to his feet and brandishes the bundle of papers like a town crier about to deliver a proclamation. And indeed he reads aloud.

'"*Revealed: The World's Top 100 Kleptocrats – by Professor M. Mital.*"'

Skelgill's subordinates both squat at the rim of the shake hole to get a better look. Skelgill turns to address them.

232

'When he fell asleep she must have 'borrowed' it. The guard was on the prowl so she hid it in the train toilet. I reckon she was just planning to read it. Then we crashed. There was no opportunity to return it. Then she hears he's dead – she must have suspected he was poisoned. She should have given it to us – but she needed the scoop. Before we evacuated the train she went to the loo – took her wash-bag, slipped it inside her suit. Then it begins to dawn on her that it's seriously hot property. So she jettisoned it – beneath the snow out of everyone's sight – a perfect hiding place. Who would think she'd jump in here deliberately?'

'You did, Guv.'

Skelgill stares for a few seconds at his sergeant, but is unable to come up with a rejoinder that either claims some credit or refutes the accuracy of the statement. The fact is they have the manuscript.

'Here.'

Skelgill passes the document and the wash-bag up to DS Jones, and then switches his reach to DS Leyton, who gets a fireman's grip on his boss, digs in his heels and hauls him with some imprecation on both their parts up the steep-sided bank. They each spend a few moments brushing themselves down, before turning their attention to DS Jones, who is resting on one knee and studiously examining their prize – and making small gasps of amazement.

'Steady on, girl – you'll be hyperventilating!'

DS Jones shakes her head and looks up at her colleagues.

'This is dynamite. You should see the names in the index – pretty much everybody the CPS might be interested in.'

'A for Adamski?'

But DS Jones shakes her head. 'No mention of Adamski – or Adamska, come to that.' She flashes a grin. 'But there is B for Bogblokinov. And a sub-section dedicated to a list of his lieutenants.'

DS Leyton exchanges a high-five with his colleague – but Skelgill is looking on more severely. He retrieves his rucksack from the heather and unfastens the flap.

'Stick it in here – let's not lose it for a second time. Knowing our luck there'll be a tornado any minute. We need a secure collection and copies put into safe keeping.'

While DS Jones carefully packs away the precious cargo, Skelgill takes out his mobile from his back pocket. But now he curses with frustration.

'I've got no signal.'

A frowning DS Leyton is interrogating his own phone. 'Same here, Guv.'

They both look expectantly at DS Jones – who is now checking hers. But she shakes her head.

DS Leyton splutters.

'Fat lot of good that would have done us when we were stranded here – even if the network had come back on.'

'Aye – but they'll have the landline working down at the inn. It's the nearest point by road, anyhow.' Skelgill consults the time on his screen and compares it to his wristwatch. 'Besides – they're open. This calls for a celebration. Even if it is a keg palace.'

There are nods of agreement and the trio automatically begin to move away downhill. They leave one another to their own thoughts for a few minutes, until DS Leyton suddenly chimes in with an observation.

'You were never comfortable with Jenny Hackett being the bad apple, Guv.'

Skelgill shakes his head contemplatively.

'I reckon she boxed herself into a corner – probably sensed the danger she was in – simply by having appeared to have read the manuscript. We maybe convinced ourselves she was kicking up dust – but actually she was pretty honest with us. I'm sure she would have told us soon enough – but they didn't give her chance. Then it didn't stack up – that she'd done a runner. I mean, just like with Harris – where was the evidence? Not one single footprint in the snow. She left behind her cigarettes – *and* her cosmetics.' Skelgill glances at DS Jones, as if for confirmation that the latter of these classes of item would be as essential as the former. 'But there was something else –

234

remember what the train driver, Laura Wilson said? She said she liked her.'

Skelgill's exposition – particularly his closing phrase and its unspoken corollary – seems to strike a chord with his colleagues, and they nod in earnest agreement. But now they emerge from the woodland fringe and *Shake Holes Inn* heaves into view – and its recent makeover wins their appreciation. The formerly cracked and peeling façade has been repaired and repainted and what were garish black window surrounds are picked out in a more tasteful Lakeland pastel teal. The sign has been restored – now there can be no doubt that it is *Shake* and not *Snake Holes Inn* as DS Leyton had first opined. Beneath the portico stand potted lollipop bay trees, and the main door is open in a welcoming fashion. They enter to brighter lighting, scented gardenias in vases and a fresh oatmeal colour scheme that has driven out the oppressive burgundy, contrasting pleasantly with the old beams and on the walls the traditional prints, maps and paintings. It is the time of day between departures and arrivals – so perhaps not surprisingly the reception desk is temporarily unattended. Undaunted, Skelgill leads them towards the snug bar and the pleasing strains of a current pop hit – but on the threshold he stops dead in his tracks. DS Leyton almost collides with him.

'What is it, Guv?'

Skelgill is staring at a *Jennings* handpump.

'First the manuscript – now real ale.'

And, like London buses, there follows a third revelation. Evidently hearing their voices, a young woman appears from the back bar area. The unfamiliar suddenly becomes familiar – it is Samanta. Superficially she looks different, with much shorter, perhaps expensively styled hair and a chic tailored barista's outfit in grey and black. On her breast a badge bears her name and the title, 'Client Services Director'. She seems remarkably unfazed by their unheralded appearance.

'Inspector. Sergeants. Welcome. So nice to see you – please, be comfortable – I shall take your orders. Perhaps I can guess yours, Inspector?'

235

Skelgill grins rather self-consciously as they install themselves at a table beside the window. Samanta attends patiently.

'There's been a few changes.' Skelgill casts about, and then indicates her badge. 'Looks like congratulations are in order.'

'Thank you. You know Mrs Hobhouse – from Ulphathwaite? She helped you, of course.' She flashes a friendly glance at DS Jones. 'She bought the entire property – Mr Merlyn was just the leaseholder. She is making a big investment – to expand the equestrian side – since this was a coaching inn? And we have plans being drawn up to reopen the mineral spring and develop a spa. Mrs Hobhouse is very enthusiastic about the project.'

Skelgill seems to feel he ought to make a further observation – but with characteristic inelegance his words do not entirely come out as he might intend.

'You've fallen on your feet, lass. But so has she, mind.'

Samanta does not seem troubled by his rustic language, though her cheeks seem to gain a hint of colour. She reacts quickly to deflect attention.

'There is another surprise.'

And she turns towards the bar counter and calls out in a foreign language. There comes an answering shout – a male voice. And who should appear but the instantly recognisable big-boned crew-cut blond Egor Volkov – formerly of Richard Bond's employ (although that firm was surely an artifice of doubtful existence). He wears smart black denims and a white polo shirt embroidered with a logo of a prancing horse and the words, *Shake Holes Inn*. He strides across and bows his head dutifully to acknowledge the three detectives in turn. DS Leyton is unabashed in raising a question that has sprung to mind.

'So – have you pair settled down – you're a couple?'

They exchange amused glances – and simultaneously burst out laughing. But before Samanta can provide an answer, there is a further interruption. From behind them arrives Egor's erstwhile colleague – François – wearing the same casual corporate uniform. He slides between the standing pair and links arms with each of them, smiling in his easy Mediterranean manner.

236

'You might say it is a *ménage à trois* — Samanta keeps us straight.'

His words elicit a ripple of polite laughter — but Samanta now evidently pulls rank and makes as if to usher the two men back to their duties.

'Inspector — we shall leave you in peace to get settled. We can catch up later? Will you be eating lunch?' She indicates with a wave of one hand. 'The blackboard — above the bar. We have a blend of local and European dishes. It is on the house, of course!'

She shepherds away the two men, and turns to look back over her shoulder.

'I shall serve your drinks. Inspector — a pint of *Jennings* while your colleagues decide?'

Skelgill gives a discreet nod of approval. DS Leyton leans to his superior and mutters under his breath.

'I didn't quite get the gist of that, Guv.'

'Live and let live, Leyton.'

'Cor blimey — I was just trying to work out if romance was in the air, Guv.'

DS Jones suddenly chuckles.

'Now's your chance — see?' And she reaches to pluck a leaflet from a dispenser on the adjacent windowsill. She displays it and reads aloud. '"Inquire about our Romantic Spring Breaks."'

DS Leyton looks rather uncomfortable. But DS Jones begins to rise from her seat.

'I'll ask for you — besides, I'd better make that phone call.'

She glances at Skelgill, who nods in agreement, his expression more sober. At the counter Samanta is carefully dispensing his cask ale, taking great pains to fill the glass to its brim. DS Jones explains about the landline, and Samanta offers to accompany her to reception in a few moments. While she is waiting, DS Jones produces the leaflet.

'And we have another request.'

Samanta beams.

'Of course! We can arrange our best room – the four-poster.' She leans over conspiratorially. 'The Inspector – he is an attractive man, yes? A little crazy, no?'

'Er – well, actually –'

***

Next in the series...

'A KILLER IN OUR MIDST?' cried a newspaper headline to commemorate the disappearance of Mary Wilson. It is two decades since Britain's first mass DNA sweep failed to incriminate a single local male. Mary was listed merely as a missing person.

Now archaeologists have unearthed human remains in Cummacatta Wood. The forensics match – age, sex, fragments of clothing ... and dental records. But the murder hunt has only just begun when an outsider, a convicted serial offender confesses to the crime.

DI Skelgill is unconvinced. Into the fabric of the tightly knit community are woven ancient alliances, intrigues and enmities. Where his predecessors failed, he is compelled to unravel the prophetic headline – for he believes the killer is still at large.

'Murder at the Meet' by Bruce Beckham is available from Amazon

Printed in Great Britain
by Amazon